SCARLET'S
STORY

MARGOT BENTHAM

Matador
Unit E2 Airfield Business Park,
Harrison Road, Market Harborough,
Leicestershire. LE16 7UL
Tel: 0116 2792299
Email: books@troubador.co.uk
Web: www.troubador.co.uk/matador
Twitter: @matadorbooks

ISBN 978 1803131 030

British Library Cataloguing in Publication Data.
A catalogue record for this book is available from the British Library.

Printed and bound in Great Britain by 4edge Limited
Typeset in 11pt Minion Pro by Troubador Publishing Ltd, Leicester, UK

Matador is an imprint of Troubador Publishing Ltd

SCARLET'S
STORY

ONE

As soon as the noisy group of young women started talking about leaving, the man at a table at the back of the café got up and went to pay his bill. He had been sitting where he could see them, talking on his phone but taking pictures as well, sending them to his colleague outside. The voice in his ear said, "Good body on her but that's one of the things they insist on, isn't it?"

"Enjoying themselves, aren't they?" he commented to the woman behind the counter as he left. "They always do, they're regulars, see you again soon." "I don't think so," he muttered to himself as he left. He settled himself in the spot he and his colleague had decided on to wait. "She is coming" came through as a text message. The sooner this was over, and the target had been delivered and accepted, the better. It had been a long day; they had been following her from early morning, trying to find an opening to pick her up, and it was likely to be a lot longer yet, as there was a way to go after the pickup to deliver her to the clients. She was on her own as she came around the corner, looking at her phone. "Could you tell me where this address is, please?" he asked, putting on a phoney accent. She looked at the paper, and as she did his colleague, who had followed, came up close behind her and emptied the hypodermic, full of a drug to knock her out, into her. Her legs started to buckle, and her eyes flickered shut, and as she collapsed into his arms a woman came past and stopped.

"Is she okay?" she asked.

Just what we do not want, he thought, irritated, *a nosy parker.* "I keep telling her not to drink so much, it's becoming a problem." He put on the phoney accent again and breathed a sigh of relief as she accepted this explanation and went on her way, shaking her head. He put his arm round the girl, pulling her close to make it look as if she was walking, albeit in a very unsteady fashion, while his colleague followed on, carrying her handbag and shopping. They had been careful to check where the cameras were situated before they picked her up, and by the time they reached their van, which had been parked behind her car, she was well under the influence of the drug. There were no other people around, so they got her into the back of the van without any further problems. They both got in, closed the doors and settled her on a mattress in the back, making sure she couldn't move about with the movement of the van. Before they left the car park the driver sent a text message to the clients telling them that they were on the way, and approximately the time of delivery. The driver's colleague sat in the back with her, and for quite a bit of the journey managed to contain his impatience; he kept looking longingly at her.

"I wouldn't mind a piece of this," he said, and, giving in to his curiosity, pulled her bra and blouse up, afterwards unzipping her jeans and pushing them and her underwear down round her hips, making a sound of obvious

2

appreciation when she was fully revealed. Swearing loudly, the driver realised what his colleague intended.

"How many times have I got to tell you, keep your fucking hands off. You will get your chance if they reject her, but if there is anything wrong, we won't get paid. You won't get paid!" By this time, the driver had pulled to the side of the road. He got out and dragged his colleague unceremoniously out of the van. He landed hard with a yelp of pain, hastily zipping his pants up in frustration. "I can't trust you with her so get in the front where I can keep an eye on you." He got into the back and took a good look. Yes, she certainly was good to look at, not the most beautiful woman he had ever seen, that had to be his wife, but beautiful all the same; she had a stunning body, very tempting. The girls were talking weddings, he remembered, one of their friends but also this girl as well. He had heard them enthusing about the wedding dress she had tried on while they were out, how beautiful it was, how gorgeous she would look. He looked at her finger and saw the engagement ring. Some poor guy was going to be mourning the loss of his future wife tonight, when she didn't arrive home, and he thought back to when they were watching her, and one man was a frequent visitor; it looked as if he had been moving in. He thought how he would feel if this had happened to his wife; he would be devastated. Was he feeling guilty and going soft? He pulled himself together. This was no time to be feeling queasy about the job he did, he kept what he did for a living from his wife. She would be very angry with him if she did know; as far as she was concerned, he was a delivery driver, who was away quite a lot. He could not afford to lose the money; their first baby was due soon, making more expense, he needed the money now more than ever. He had to finish the job; he was getting too involved as it was. He told himself to pull himself together and get her delivered. He made sure her clothes were back where they should be and got back in the driving seat. The rest of the journey was carried out in sulky silence.

After a long drive they stopped at a pair of impressive electric gates, a sign outside saying 'The Newford Priory Club'. The driver pressed a button on the unit at the gate, and when it was answered said, "Delivery for the club." The gates opened, and they drove through. When the van reached the large building at the end of a long drive they drove past, round to the back, and pulled up where a group of people stood waiting for them. They gently took her out and onto the stretcher they had ready.

Before she was taken into the building a man came out and said, "Wait a minute, I want to have a look at her." He looked at a photo, to check it was the right girl. "Very nice. Take her inside and take these gentlemen to where they can spend the night." At that he turned and returned inside, followed by everybody else.

TWO

Awakening groggily from a drugged sleep, I found that I was lying on a bed in a room that was bright; and the light was dazzling. Trying to raise my hand to block the light I found I was tied down, and there was a tape over my mouth. I started to shake with fright. Just then a shape appeared at my side; whoever it was wore a coverall, the face was covered so nothing could be seen, not even the eyes. They held up a tablet with writing on for me to read. I had to read it twice, as whatever I had been drugged with was still affecting me, making my eyesight hazy; also, I could not believe what I was reading. It told me that from now on I had to be silent at all times; did I understand? After I nodded, the tape was removed, and I was given a much-needed drink through a straw, my mouth was very dry. I was untied and helped to sit on the side of the bed, undressed and injected, who knew what with or what for, I suspected later that one of them was a tranquilliser. Photographs were then taken from all angles, and I was given an intensive series of medical tests – my blood pressure must have been off the scale – temperature, height, and weight. Swabs were taken from everywhere; it was obvious that they were going to do several tests judging from the amount of blood taken. Every part of me was examined closely, including internals. I was led through into the room next door, where there was a shower. I was shackled to two posts, they covered me in gel and took an ultrasound scan of my whole body. Afterwards I was given a shower, all my body hair was removed, and I was rubbed all over with oil. A collar covered with diamante with a chain attached was then put round my neck followed up with a harness, also covered with diamante. You have got to be joking! This must be the invention of a man; the effect was to pull my shoulders back so that I could not slouch and after the shackles were taken off, my hands were put behind my back and handcuffed. Absolutely nowhere to hide if I was feeling self-conscious and embarrassed, which I most certainly was, it was mortifying, never having been comfortable without my clothes. My hair was brushed and plaited, the beings that had been doing all this then stood back while somebody else came in and inspected their work. They seemed happy with what had been done. They then showed me a message written on a tablet telling me not to be ashamed or embarrassed about being naked, that I had a beautiful, desirable body that should be seen and admired, never hidden, and it was essential that it was shown off to its best advantage, much depended on how well I did that, and to be proud of it. I had to keep silent but sounds of arousal were encouraged. Oh shit, no guesses as to what was coming next. My legs were shaking so much that it was a surprise they would support me. I was taken out of the room and with beings each side of me escorted through the building until we arrived at a door that accessed a large room. I was paraded round next to a glass wall, nothing could be seen past that, so there must have been people on the other side

6

that I could neither see nor hear. The harness was removed, the collar left on. In the middle of this room there was a bed, I was told to get on and lie down on my back. The handcuffs were taken off and I was shackled so that no movement was possible. A vibrator that had been inserted earlier was then removed. There was another message telling me that a hood would be put over my head and that somebody was going to be standing close, and did I understand? As soon as I nodded, they put the hood on. The fabric was exceptionally fine and light and I could see vague shapes through it, but not much else, no chance of identifying whoever was around, that possibly being the reason I had to wear it. I was getting even more frightened and panicky about what was obviously going to happen next; I also could not understand why I had allowed all this to happen, without fighting my captors. My assumption that it must have been a tranquilliser that I had been given earlier to keep me compliant was obviously correct. What I assumed to be lubricant was massaged round my vagina, the being next to me moved closer, taking my hand and squeezing it. Just then somebody ran their hand up my thigh; this was, I realised later, used as the signal that my 'client' was there and ready, and then without any warning somebody raped me, and the assault kept on, it felt like forever. I cried out as pain lanced through me, it seemed everywhere, there was no disguising the fact that any noise that I was making, far from being made through arousal, was utter distress, because of the violent assault that was being inflicted on me, in a very brutal attack. Even though I had had lubricant applied, it didn't help much. I was cleaned up, and it was the same routine where I was raped four more times in quick succession. By the time that they had all finished I was left sobbing and so sore with pain inside and out. I was released and had to stand very shakily for a few minutes. Suddenly there was a stinging sensation in my thigh, after which I was led out into the corridor and taken to a bedroom. I was taken into the shower where all the oil was washed off and cream was massaged into me where I was most sore. The pain inside did not diminish, however, and I was given a shot of what I assumed was painkiller. I was then dressed in a pair of pyjamas. I never stopped crying while all this was going on, and then some food was put in front of me. There was no way that I could eat anything after all that had happened over the last few hours, although it did look tempting. They made sure that I had drinks regularly by using a straw and squeezing into my mouth from a bottle. Before they put me to bed a tablet was held up for me to read, saying, "You have done very well on your first day. Welcome to your new life and job, which is to show that superb body off to its best and be admired, allowing men to share it. And you will now be known by your new name, which is Scarlet."

My name is not Scarlet, it is Chloe! This became a mantra that I repeated frequently. I tried to sleep that night, but the discomfort and pain kept me awake. Somebody stayed with me all night and they made me drink frequently.

Images of the life that been taken from me kept coming into my mind; I tried to push them away, they were just too painful.

The next morning, I was woken up and breakfast was put in front of me. I pushed it away and sat staring at it. I just wanted to go home. I put my head on the table and started to cry. Again. One of the beings that seemed to be looking after me put their hands on both sides of my face and wiped away the tears. I pulled away from them, pushing their hands off me as I did. I hated everybody in the place. I was taken into the shower and shackled to the posts in the shower room and washed. They put the collar and chain round my neck, handcuffed my hands behind my back and led me out of the room and down the corridor with two of my 'minders', one on each side of me. Did they think I was going to escape? How? Wearing nothing but the collar and handcuffs? I had to stop my thoughts on escaping; I did not think there would be any escape routes open to me, why torture myself? But the thoughts were still there. I needed some hope. We arrived at a door, and I was taken through, handed over to another team, still dressed the same way. Whatever happened next couldn't be as bad as yesterday, could it? Oh, but it could. And it did get worse, much, much worse, that day became both the weirdest and terrifying of my life yet, one that I would never want to think or talk about, ever.

I was taken through yet another door, and shackled to two posts, the same as the shower, but strangely, facing the wall, and then the wall moved back revealing bars, behind which was a large gorilla chewing on greenery of some kind. We stared at each other, with me in shock. He looked at me and came over to the bars, staring at me very closely. I froze when he put his arm through the bars and started touching me, examining me all over. He stared into my eyes and sat back on his haunches, not taking his eyes off me. I did not dare speculate about what was going to happen next. The shutter was then pushed back, and the beings came over to me and held up the inevitable tablet with a message. Oh. My. God. What I read was unbelievable. I started shaking, they had started to unshackle me from the posts and one of

9

them had to catch me before I collapsed. I was being told that this ape was going to mate with me! I started to fight, biting and kicking to get away from them and screaming hysterically, but they brought in two more of the beings and had a very firm grip on me. I was tiring so was easily overpowered, there was simply no way of avoiding this. At some point in the fracas, I threw my head back and hit one of them in the nose. There was a muffled curse and one of them used what I thought was a whip or stick across my back two or three times, it hurt like hell. I was still sobbing hysterically, they had quite a job to force me to lie down, this time on my stomach, and rubbed some foul-smelling stuff onto me. They then left the room, no doubt to give the bruises that I must have inflicted a break. I did get a few good punches and kicks, all of which connected quite satisfactorily. I felt proud of myself at what I had done. The shutter and the gate were then opened to let him in. All he did at first was to give me the once over, stroking me surprisingly gently. After he had done what they wanted him to do he was let out, no doubt having been given a treat by the people outside. After he had left, the people came in, they obviously had no intention of me fighting them again. I was given a shot of what could have been tranquilliser. I was taken to three more apes, the second one being aggressive, I was even more terrified of him. I was numb with shock as I was handed back to what I assumed to be my original minders.

When back in my room, still in a state of shock at what had happened to me, I desperately tried to cut all emotion out of my life, and I was taken to have a shower. It must have been midday, because I was given something to eat but it tasted of cardboard, and it was hard to swallow. After

I had pushed it round my plate, I gave up. I was taken to the room I had been in the day before and raped by more men. Something else I wanted to forget and not face.

That must have been the end of my working day because I was given something to eat, which I again couldn't manage, and after the inevitable shower was dressed in a pair of pyjamas and literarily put to bed, as though I was a child, and then the door was closed and I was alone with my thoughts and memories, again.

THREE

My thoughts went back to the day I had been abducted. Maybe it would make the conditions worse, reliving my 'old' life, stirring up my emotions.

The day had been an enjoyable one and I had been on time for once; I am always late, it is not something I am proud of. We had spent the day in the shopping centre and shops in the larger town, just a short train ride away, with good friends, plenty of chat, and of course a great deal of shopping. We finished off back in our hometown, with coffee and homemade cakes in a teashop that we all love because the cakes are to die for. The owner of the teashop was waiting to close – we had been there for so long and Mark would be at my house soon. Oh dear, I was going to be late getting back. I did not like to think of his reaction. We all spilled out onto the pavement where hugs were exchanged. Still smiling I set off towards the car park, turning to wave to them as I left. One of our friends at work was getting married soon and we had decided to buy her a present from all of us. It would be my turn next, but would I go through with it the way I had been feeling? I was getting more than cold feet. However, after I left my friends, my life changed completely.

Coming back to the present, I lay on my back, looking up at the ceiling. I must not cry. After all, what good were tears? But I could not stop thinking about my folks and my friends, wondering what they were doing and missing them desperately, wondering how they were, despair, utter loneliness, and revulsion engulfing me. I hated the life I was being forced to live.

The days passed, the same routine. After they brought my breakfast, when I was finished, I was undressed and taken for the inevitable shower, and then to the apes. A vibrator was inserted and only taken out just before the first man in the afternoon.

I had no way of keeping a check on the time, or what day it was, even what month; when I was brought a meal was the only time that I knew it was lunchtime or evening. The days seemed to blend into one another, the routine being the same. Every few days somebody came and gave me a manicure and pedicure. My nails had never looked better but some of the colours were not ones that I would have chosen. I suppose it was for the benefit of the clients. Every night the carers rubbed cream all over my body to keep my skin soft. I asked for some to put on my face as well, and they left me some. My skin was benefitting from the regular application of the cream, something I had never bothered with previously. I do not know who it was that did the work on my nails, but they always did a brilliant job and they looked well cared for, which made a change.

I cut myself off from what was happening to me, trying to make my mind blank or think about anything rather than my previous life. Or this one. Most often I pictured a barrier that was too high to see over, and it acted like soundproofing, so I heard nothing either; it became easier and easier the longer I was held in the place, to put up these barriers in my mind and be as emotionless as possible.

One day the routine changed, and I was told that I had been booked for an evening, and I am dressed, if you can call it that, in my favourite harness and, oh no, those awful nipple clamps which have decoration hanging from them, ugh, and they're so painful. Oh joy, what will this be, how many times somebody can fuck me? But it just gets better, because joy of joys it was for a threesome, never really my scene back in the real world. Before I am taken into the room the hood is put in place; he or they must be there already, waiting. I am nervous about this situation. It turns out to be another female, and a man. So, there are more females here. He takes me first, roughly pulling off the clamps on my breasts. The pain was excruciating and what can I say about him, he was not exactly a turn on. He rolls off me at last, thank God, and then inflicts himself on the other girl. He is exhausted and lies there between us, panting, sounding as though he is going to expire any minute. Oh. I. Wish. I am lying there, waiting to see what will happen next, when to my surprise the girl comes and lies next to me and starts fondling one of my breasts, the other hand exploring. When I push her off me, she lands a punch to my side followed up with her knee into my stomach, which doubles me up, and then she rains one punch after another all over me. By this time, I have had enough and turn my back on her and curl into the foetal position. I am not going to fight back. I think then one of the minders comes and breaks it up. I sit on the side of the bed with my head in my hands, I ache all over where she has punched me. They take off the hood and both the others have gone. One of the minders holds up the inevitable tablet with a message saying that

I am going to be punished for non-co-operation. I nearly shouted at them, what about the way I have been punched, I am the injured party in this, why do I have to be punished? What about the bitch that did this to me? Is she getting the same treatment? They make me bend over and hold on to the post of the bed, a probe is inserted into me, and I am given a shock. The pain explodes everywhere inside me, it makes me double over and I end up on the floor with the pain; it seems to take a long time to subside. I suppose he is watching from somewhere, enjoying what he is seeing, no doubt, and I wonder if he has done this deliberately so that he can watch. Sadistic bastard! I am helped to limp back to my room, I suppose in disgrace. That girl certainly packs a powerful punch, I will have bruised badly after that. The care staff take a lot of time to massage cream of some kind into my skin. It helps to reduce the pain, and I am grateful to them for their care and the gentleness.

After some days I am told I have been booked for another evening session, with one man this time. I am dreading it. This man was rough, taking me more than once during the evening. I lost myself, imagining myself far away from this place, and I ended up with a lot of bruising because he also beat me up. He must have had something with him that the 'minders' couldn't see, because whatever it was must have been on his fingers, as when he pushed a finger inside me, I felt him using something abrasive. I was in a lot of pain. He also must have complained about me, and I am punished in the same way, only this time the charge is stronger. It ended up again with me on the floor of the room in agony, but this time I am not able to walk, so I must be carried back to my room. They find I am bleeding, no doubt from whatever he used inside me. I am taken to the medical

15

room and anaesthetised. When I come around, I am back in my room, and one of the care team keeps me company that night. I am kept in my room for about a week because of the damage that he had done needing to heal. Why me? What had I done to make them punish me? Again?

The nightmares, in the form of memories of my past life, surface again, of before I ended up in here.

I should have been getting married soon. Mark and I had been looking for a house. We had decided to sell both our properties and buy a larger one. He had already sold his flat, sooner than we expected, and was in the process of packing up, preparing to move in with me. Until we found somewhere new, we had taken a storage unit until then. I loved my house and had put a lot of work into it. I was not looking forward to selling. I could not bear the thought that all my possessions would be lost to me, my house sold and other people living there. Thank goodness that I had rung the estate agents the day before I had been abducted, and taken it off the market, calling in to confirm my decision. I could have cried myself to sleep, but I do not think I had any tears left. I realised I had something else to worry about. What would happen to me when wherever I was had no further use for me? Where would I end up? All sorts of unwelcome scenarios kept coming into my mind.

FOUR

It is possible to feel lonely, even surrounded by people. I was never on my own apart from when I was in my room at night. I thought cameras could be, and probably were, watching my every move. The feeling of isolation was so strong. No one to talk to, I did not know who I was seeing because all the staff wore those suits, no doubt to intensify feelings of isolation, and emphasise their complete control over me; it certainly worked. It also made it impossible to become friendly with the staff.

I kept looking for a way out but had long ago lost all hope. There was a small, beautiful garden that I could go into on warm days, with a swimming pool behind glass doors that I could make use of for a short time, which made me imagine myself in a hotel pool, and free. I loved having a swim, and felt really good afterwards. Whenever I was in the garden, I scanned the walls to see if it was possible to climb up somehow, but the walls had no handholds to climb up. Then it was electrified; I could see the wires and heard the current clicking, no chance there. The little garden area was beautiful, it was a joy, the perfume from the flowers so strong. It was good to get the collar off for a while, but that was ended, however, when they came to put the collar back on, and it was time to go back to 'work'.

I was told that I had been booked for the evening; it would be a threesome again, with two men. I found the thought frightening. With much trepidation on my part, we ended up at the room door and I was taken straight in without the hood being put on; they must not have arrived yet. I was told to get up onto the bed and the hood was put over my head, and to take the usual position of what I thought was yoga, discovering later it was called the Child's Pose, and wait for them to arrive. This seemed to be the standard position when waiting. I did not have long to wait and the usual brush along my thigh told me they had arrived in the room. It felt so good to have the contact with them. I had to be a bit of a contortionist at times during the evening but if these two became regulars I did not think I would object because they were kind to me, not that I would have any say in the decision anyway.

That night another nightmare haunted me, again with memories of my previous life.

I lived in Mere Abbey village, the same small market town where I had been born. It is one of those attractive places that are used as filming locations for TV and films and, because of the connection with one extremely popular TV series, is on the tourist trail. People arrive by the coach load, stopping off for coffee or lunch, look round the many gift shops, filming locations and then go on to the next port of call. It is quite busy all the year round, the winter weekends being a great attraction, and plenty of visitors at Christmas. It is also in a conservation area, one of those places where house prices are high. I worked in the offices at Mere Abbey, the local stately pile, so my wages were not exactly high enough to indulge in buying a house in that area. However, when I had been looking for a property, before I met Mark, I had been extraordinarily lucky; a large sum of money had been left to me in a relative's will. This came as a complete and very welcome surprise. I had not known her well and I found it very touching that she thought of me at all. It made all the difference to me because it gave me a chance to buy a run-down house near where my parents live. Also, I got a good deal; the people who owned it were emigrating, and they wanted to get all their arrangements done with soon, as they would need the money as soon as they arrived. I could not believe my luck. I would have struggled to buy anything without that bequest, and would be able to pay for it outright, so I would not need a mortgage. I had some left from the purchase to cover some of the renovations. It turned out that the house, despite how it looked, was very sound and was not going to collapse; it would only need cosmetic work doing. There were issues that would need attention, of course, but nothing major. As the house was in a conservation area, although not listed, I had to consult with the planning people as to what they would allow, or possibly not! I had not intended making any changes to the outside, I loved it as it was, but it would be the replacement windows that could have been a sticking point. The architect was brilliant and suggested a few alterations inside that would make improvements that I had not even thought of; they proved to be very much to my benefit. And much to my surprise, planning accepted all that I had put forward without insisting on any changes. Amazing! The architect had a firm of builders in mind and brought them to look at what needed doing; they did a fantastic job. As they obviously knew what they were doing

I left them to it, looking in every day to see what progress had been made and taking pictures. Considering how close to the centre of town it was, there was a surprisingly spacious garden and, miracle of miracles, not only a large, decrepit old farm building that had been used as a garage, but off-road parking for at least two cars in front of it. This was like gold dust where many houses had no parking at all. When I bought the place, my neighbours asked me if I would sell some of my land to them. I turned them down. All the time that the work was going on in the house I tried to get some order out of the chaos that was the garden; it was more like an archaeological dig sometimes, and who knew what remains might be found under all the skip loads of years of vegetation and clutter that had to be removed.

As always, I had to unwillingly drag myself back to reality. It was so upsetting, and like most times I ended up curled up in a protective ball, unable to cry and relieve the tension. I was starting to feel light-headed, probably due to the fact that I had hardly eaten anything in what felt like weeks. I just wanted to get out of the place, I wanted my life back, I did not want to live like this anymore. I had thought that the only way out was to kill myself, which was not going to be easy. I was watched the whole time, and everything had been designed with nothing that left any chances. I had worked out that, if I could find some means of cutting my wrists and managed it early after they had left me, by the time they came to wake me in the morning too much damage would have been done, too late to do anything. As if that would happen anytime soon! I was kidding myself. However, one night I went through to the bathroom just after they had left me. I could not believe what I was seeing, I did not take my eyes off the razor left on the sink. My chance to escape. Maybe? When I went back to bed it went with me. I made sure that any cameras would not show that I was carrying anything, by keeping it close to me, and when I got into bed kept it under the bedclothes. I sat up in bed with my knees up and my arms wrapped round them with my forehead resting on my knees. I did not really want to end my life, however bad it was. I became aware that the door had opened and one of the beings had gone straight into the bathroom, no prizes for guessing what they were looking for. The one who had been to look in the bathroom shook their head. Both heads turned towards me, and one came and sat on the bed. I had nowhere to hide it anyway, they would soon have found what they were looking for. By this time, I was sobbing, and one of them reached up and wiped the tears away. They then started to leave the room, but one turned and pointed towards the bedside table and there was a treat. I turned my back on it; no doubt that was a thank you for not committing suicide on their watch. I did not want to play that game. I did not fool myself that I had been close to my goal. I knew that I would not have had a chance to carry out what I had planned.

Next day when I had finished, I was taken to another room. It was bigger and had a window, low enough that I could sit in a chair and see through it easily, also with a better view. There was also a room off it with exercise equipment in it and, wonder of wonders, a vase of flowers that smelled beautiful. I covered my mouth because I did not want to give away that I was happy to see them and smiling. Flowers were a permanent fixture from then on and were replaced regularly. As I lay in bed that night it occurred to me that I could have an advantage, and they might, just might, grant a request if I acted soon on my idea. I had been so bored and had far too much time to think. I needed something to keep me occupied and remembered that I had taken my tablet computer, both e-readers, charging cables, MP3 players, and hard drives with music, audiobooks and converted films that I could play on my tablet. I had taken them with me because I was not going home after meeting my friends. What a good thing that I had not left them in my car. Maybe I would be allowed to have them, but not the internet, of course. When they came with my breakfast, I asked for the tablet and wrote my request, not with much hope of it being granted. I could not believe my eyes when I was taken back to my room that night; everything I had asked for was there. Chargers as well for my MP3 players. I really could not hide my joy, and so soon. The internet was blocked, as I expected, but I had got what I wanted, which was enough for me. They wrote a message on the tablet that I could only keep them if I made sure that I ate more of the food that was brought to me. Blackmail! However, I was willing to go with that, but my appetite was not large. I asked for the tablet again and wrote, "Thank you so much", putting a row of smiley faces, and yes, I would try, I underlined try, to eat more. They seemed happy with that; I could almost hear a sigh of relief when they read it. I curled up in bed that night listening to my music; it had been well worth dragging everything round the shops that day.

The next morning, I was awake before my breakfast was brought, and I lay staring up at the ceiling, coming to a few conclusions. What was I getting out of this arrangement? Nothing, it seemed to me. This had to change, as much as it could, which would not be much, but hell it would be something. I decided that I would maybe get some entertainment value out of the situation, and a bit of revenge. I would give the men marks out of ten for their performance, starting today. It might give me a bit of a laugh, for a while at least. The first man, well what can I say? I nearly fell asleep, wake me up when you have finished. How many points? Maybe one, and that is being generous. What for? He tried, sort of.

The second one could have farted for England, bring me a gas mask please, ugh! That is disgusting. It seemed to go on forever, playing a sort of tune as he moved inside me. It took me all my strength not to laugh out loud. I wished I could stuff my fingers in my mouth, but of course that could not happen. I must have made a noise because I got a tap on my hand from my minder to tell me to cut it out and no doubt to behave. They were in the firing line as well, and I was sure that they were laughing behind their masks too; I could feel them shaking. Well, he got a minus eight, and I thought that was generous; the smell was so foul it should have come with a health warning. The next two got minus eight for being so boring, yes, I know. I think today at 'work' was acceptable, maybe. I had the impression that my minder got what I was doing, perhaps he or she got some entertainment, who knows. What will tomorrow bring?

FIVE

The next four days I was laid low, as I was every month. I had suffered a lot of pain and it seemed much worse since I had been brought in here, maybe because of the stress that I was under. I always took to my bed for at least one day. The staff must have kept records of my dates as I had absolutely no idea where I was in my cycle; it did not matter to me anyway. They were brilliant and kept me dosed up with painkillers so that I was reasonably comfortable, but still not feeling very well; the phrase 'feeling like death warmed up' described the feeling. The staff seemed to like keeping me company on those days, I did not know why, but it was nice to have company, even though we couldn't talk, although I wasn't particularly good company as I mostly slept, as I always felt exhausted. They mostly sat and read a book or the paper, sometimes they would stroke me, which was nice; it was contact, of a kind, it seemed more that they were looking after a pet, or a child, or possibly a bit of both. Whenever there was a break in proceedings normally one of the beings would be stroking me. In my previous existence I would not have wanted this, but I was so starved of any contact that I willingly accepted anything I could get.

I am afraid that the entertainment value of rating the men was short-lived, and I stopped. What was the point?

As well as memories of my former life back in the real world, I was plagued by the worry of what would happen to me when, wherever I was, they had no further use for me. Where would I end up? I had read enough about slavery to be really worried. Sometimes women would be starved and beaten into submission. A description by a member of an organisation which helped rescued victims kept coming back to me. Women sometimes needed reconstruction surgery, because of the damage done to them due to the unbelievable number of men involved each day. Also, what would happen to those women in that situation? Would they ever get out of that life? Or more likely, I thought, their life would end tragically. I felt cold all over and shuddered at the thought.

One night my memories were of when we were trying to organise the wedding. All I wanted, all we both wanted, was a small manageable ceremony and celebration afterwards, we were not exactly asking for the moon. The family that owned the estate made me an amazing deal on having it there; we accepted with alacrity. The setting was photogenic, we would have some wonderful photographs to look back on. I have to say that I was getting heartily sick of trying to sort out menus and seating plans; well, we could not put auntie so-and-so next to auntie somebody else because of the trouble that would cause. After all, they had not spoken for twenty years, the reason, of course, forgotten by everybody else but them. Give me strength! I did suggest that we eloped to Gretna Green or abroad. Mark just laughed at me, not taking me seriously. I was deadly serious. And then, there was 'The Dress'. And what an epic that turned out to be. And the price! How much? I felt faint, I needed a chair to sit on. To spend as much as they were asking, for one day, and then it would probably sit in a wardrobe in a dress bag for years. Something that was going to cost an arm and not just one leg but both, and that only the down payment. Then, of course, there was the cake, and the photographer had to be arranged. My employers told me that they would give us the cake as their wedding present to us, I was so touched. The photographs were going to be taken by a friend of Mark's who was a professional photographer. He was popular, also extremely good and in demand, and he charged a fortune normally. So, finally everything had been coming together slowly. I finally saw a dress in a shop window when I was out with my friends, and they pushed me into the shop, insisting that I try it on. It was beautiful, just what I had been wanting, exactly what I had been looking for. They all loved it, it needed a small alteration and I arranged to go back a few days later for a final fitting. What a miracle. Unfortunately, the doubts that had been plaguing me for a while kicked in big time, and it made me finally come to the decision that had been on my mind, so I made an excuse to leave my friends for a while, going back to the bridal shop. I was also near to the estate agency that had my house up for sale, and when I met up with the gang later, without saying anything to them, I had cancelled the sale of the dress and signed the confirmation to take my house off the market. I had no regrets about my actions and felt happier and more settled than I had for some time.

SIX

Paul could not believe how nervous he was feeling. He had looked forward to this evening so much, would it live up to his expectations? And would she find the evening something to look back on with pleasure? If that was even possible in here. He walked into the room. Scarlet was standing next to the bed, her minder next to her. He ran his hand down her thigh to tell her that he was there. She flinched away from him when he did that, and then he indicated to her minder that he wanted the harness taken off. After the handcuffs and the chain had been removed, there seemed to be a doubt whether the collar could be taken off as well, but he insisted, and it was gone too. He stood gazing at her. He had been shocked at her reaction when he had touched her, and also at her appearance. He knew she had lost a lot of weight but had no idea how much until now; she was close to being emaciated, and looked so fragile, as though she would shatter at a touch. She had some nasty-looking bruises, older ones, and others more recent. When he took her hand in his she gave a sharp intake of breath, obviously afraid of what he would do to her. He had been told about how badly some of the other members had treated her; she had been beaten up on many occasions, no wonder she was scared. She was so tense when he touched her, seeming to hold her breath. That would have to change. He wanted her to enjoy the time with him, and to relax; this evening was all about her.

*

I had been told that I had been booked for the evening with one man. I was frightened about what would happen after some of my previous experiences. The harness was put on me, oh joy, they seemed to take extra care with me that day. Why? I was then taken out and through a door into what must be the old part of the building, into the same beautiful room that I had been taken to before, and I wished the circumstances were different. There was a large original old four-poster bed with elaborate carvings on the posts. The curtains on it were fabulous, being heavy and sumptuous in dark shades. The walls were panelled and intricately carved, they looked authentic. The windows and floors were definitely the real deal, the squeaking floorboards certainly, I would not have thought the sound of those could be replicated easily. This must be a part of an old building. The whole feeling was of comfort and opulence.

It wasn't the same routine. Usually I had to get onto the bed and kneel, the hood was put on me and then I had to take up the usual position and wait, and it wasn't long before I felt the inevitable stroke down my thigh, which told me that my 'client' had arrived, and it was time to turn on my back ready for him. This time, however, they made me stand next to the bed. The harness was taken off; what a relief. The collar stayed on at first, but after a short time that, too, was

28

removed. He didn't touch me at first, what was he doing? He took one of my hands in his, it made me jump. With the other he was fondling my breasts and stroking me. I was moaning with pleasure at what he was doing, it felt so good. Usually none of the men cared whether I got satisfaction, this man was different. He put his arm round me, pulling me close. With his free hand he reached round and started to fondle my breasts again, moving downwards between my legs, gently caressing and stimulating me, pushing one of his fingers inside. It was getting difficult to breathe. He lifted me onto the bed, and lay down beside me, kissing me all over.

What followed was the most extraordinary experience that I have ever had in my life. He was so gentle and tender, it was amazing. From what I could feel he was slim and toned, possibly from time spent in a gym. I took some time examining his face with my fingers, getting to know every part of it; he was clean-shaven and his aftershave smelled wonderful. He would always use the same one when he booked me; I didn't know whether it was on purpose so that I would recognise him easily or because it was his favourite. He ended up curled round behind me, with his arms holding me in a tight embrace that was wonderful. I did not want the evening to end. A knock at the door signalled that I had to be taken away from him. I was desperate to see him and tried to pull the hood off. Realising what I was doing he took my hands and held them on each side of his head and shook his head to discourage me, knowing I would probably get into trouble. Before he left me, he kissed each of my breasts, got off the bed, and then left. When I arrived back in my room, for the first time in a while I was crying. The staff wrote on the tablet, asking what was wrong? Had he hurt me? I indicated that I would like to write a reply. The tablet was passed to me, and I put a smiley face, trying to tell them the tears were of happiness, not pain or sadness. They seemed pacified by that.

*

Paul was just going back to the room he had booked for the night when Maia, the carer who had suggested he book Scarlet for the evening, called to him. She looked serious. "She was crying after you left," she told him.

Paul was upset. That was the last thing he wanted for her. He wanted to try to make her as happy as he could; he was mortified, this was not what he wanted to hear. "Why? Did I hurt her?"

Maia suddenly grinned and showed him the tablet. "You made her happy, she actually smiled, we have never seen her do that before, and the tears were of happiness." He gave a deep sigh, thank goodness she was happy; if she was, so was he. He had wanted the first time he spent with Scarlet to be a good experience for them both; after all, he had waited so long for this. The evening had been every bit as good as he had hoped it would be. He didn't think he would forget it for a long time.

He and some of Scarlet's clients had talked about her often, and discussed an idea they had, and before he let Maia carry on with her job he asked if she could tell him who, of the men who booked Scarlet regularly, she seemed most comfortable with. He knew the men whose names were mentioned, there were two of them that booked her as a threesome, also separately, and quite a few others, and after making a note of them all, went to the bar. After a quick drink he went to his room, where after a shower, and some time reliving the evening, had a good night's sleep.

The next morning, as he ate his breakfast in the dining room, he wondered what Scarlet was doing and looked over the list of names from the night before. He and two of the men had talked often about Scarlet, and he was aware how fond and protective they both were of her; at least she had the three of them and quite a few others of her 'clients' who were looking out for her interests as well. They also were as concerned, as he was, when he had told them what Maia had informed him about the way that she had been punished. None of them were happy about that and they decided that the situation would have to change for her. As the others could not carry out the plans that they had made for her at that time, Paul had volunteered. When he had finished his breakfast, he made his way to reception and asked for a meeting with the three men who were running the club, but not for much longer if Paul had his way. The more he found out about what was happening the angrier he became, and it was these three that were guilty. He was in luck; they were all there and were able to see him straightaway. He had told Bette, his PA, that he would not be in the office that day, to give him time to carry out the plan. He was shown into the boardroom and was greeted warmly by all of them. How long would that attitude last?

He came out of the room satisfied with what he had negotiated for Scarlet, but it still felt very wrong for something to be decided for her, when she was locked up, with no say in her life whatsoever. He was hoping that her life would change soon, and for the better; it couldn't come quick enough for him. There had been a cost to the new arrangement, a big one to them all, but despite the amount he looked on it as being worth every penny. How the other men would view this was unknown, because they would have to pay a larger amount to book her as well.

*

Again, the memories came back to haunt me in the nightmares that were making my life infinitely more challenging. Some of the friends who I had been out with on that fateful day worked at the same place, in different sections. I worked mainly in the office but could be asked to fill in at other parts, if the need arose. I liked that because it gave me a bit of variety.

The estate had been a wealthy monastery until Henry VIII had closed it down and all the wealth from it plundered. It had been turned into a house, like a lot were in those times, or the building materials taken to be used in other places. It had been sold not long after it had been converted because of the debts incurred by the transformation, and the estate had been bought and owned by the same family ever since. The estate was managed in a way that made it a haven for wildlife, being filmed for many wildlife programmes. I loved taking a walk round part of it when I was on a break or at lunchtime. I never got tired of it because there was always something interesting to watch. I often met up with the people who worked outside; I enjoyed seeing them because I was kept up to date with what they and their families were doing. I knew most of them, many of them had worked on the estate for years. My favourite area was round the lake. It was so peaceful, it was no wonder that the area attracted the large number of different species that it did.

The next booking was for the night, another threesome. Oh no, would it end up with more bruises for me? It was the two men who had booked me before; I breathed a sigh of relief, as the time before they had treated me well.

My routine suddenly changed. I was left in my room for the morning, men coming to me now in the evening, and about half the number. That worried me, what was going on? The afternoon, well, that did not get any easier. I could not sleep very well for worrying about the future. Why the change? Was I being phased out, was my time in here coming to an end? Or was it something that had shown up in the regular tests that had just been done? As usual I was kept in the dark. I lost my appetite again and it was obvious that the staff were wondering what was happening and worrying.

I was booked again for the night with the same man; they were at least giving me hints about who it was at last. These nights were precious to me and the enjoyment I got from them stopped me worrying for a short time. The harness, collar and handcuffs were left off, and I was just escorted to the room without them. The hood stayed; oh well, you cannot have everything. I was always emotional when the nights ended. These nights were getting very regular, I would guess once a week, occasionally more frequently, but I hated being kept from him every month. While we were together, I had started to hold two of my fingers up to my mouth and then make a loud kissing noise, then hold them up to him. He put them to his lips and did the same, well it was kissing, sort of, and it became a regular part of every night that we spent together.

There were no repeats of me getting beaten up or punished; mostly the people who booked me were the two men and the single man, but apart from them my 'client' list was reduced.

My hair had grown very long, and I don't know what the carers had been using to wash it with, but it was looking and feeling very dry, so I asked them if I could have some better shampoo. Much to my surprise I was brought some that made it very shiny and feel so soft.

The second ape had been extremely violent again, and I had received more bites and bruises; they had to be treated and I was given another injection as well, what for? I had no idea; all I could do was accept the treatment in silence as always. But that was the last time that I was taken to the apes, without any explanation.

The next night I had been booked with the same man. I gave a sigh of pleasure when they told me, and when I got to the room, he was already waiting for me because the hood was put on before I was taken inside. I had only just been taken into the room, and before I had moved away from the door, I was stopped; he was standing next to me. He took my hand, there was no need for the stroke down my thigh, and he led me across the room. We were standing close, and I only realised when I reached up to put my arms round his neck just how tall he was. I felt the bed behind me, and he spent some time kissing, nipping, and suckling my breasts, caressing my body, it was absolute heaven. He then pushed me down onto the bed.

He must have been exhausted at the end of the night; I certainly was. His attitude seemed different this time, there seemed to be more urgency about him, what was happening? Something was different, but what? I did not like things to change in here; if they did; it was invariably for the worse. He kissed me all over and then lay behind me; holding me close, I could hear his heart beating as I lay with my head against his chest. My heart sank at the inevitable knock on the door. I kissed my fingers and held them up for him to kiss me back. He started to get off the bed but leaned down and, for the first time, spoke to me, whispering into my ear, "Thank you." I had hold of his hand and did not want to let go, but I had to in the end. Those two words really got me worried, had I lost him for good? Was that the last night that we would spend together?

SEVEN

Paul stood in the shower for a long time after the wonderful night he had just spent with Scarlet. He had a big smile on his face thinking of how good it had felt when they had been lying with her wrapped tightly in his arms, exhausted after another passionate night. Her breathing told him that she was dozing, he had kept her busy so that she did not have much time for sleeping. He had made sure that he had booked her for the night before the raid, so that if she would not have anything to do with him when she was freed, he had some amazing memories of her. He hoped that she would have some good memories of him and remember it as a good night afterwards as well, leaving her with the last memory of him being positive. The smile was replaced with a look of regret when he remembered when the knock at the door had told him it was time for him to surrender her. He had not wanted to leave her, and she had held onto his hand for as long as she could. The vision of her lying there looking so desirable and vulnerable stayed in his mind. He wanted to say more to her when he was leaving, but the carers came in far too quickly for him to risk any more. He gave a big sigh and looked at his watch.

Time was short, he was going to be late, and it would not be wise to miss this, too much depended on what happened later. One way or another. However, he wished, not for the first time, that he could miss what was going to happen before the meeting; it would not be pleasant to witness the introduction of this next girl, he was dreading it. He hoped it would be cut short and not last long for her. Just as he left the room after his shower, he met his friend Josh. "You must have been here early, Paul, I saw your car, where were you? Nearly everybody has arrived, we had better go."

"I spent the night."

"Did you, who with?"

"Scarlet."

"Again? I did not really need to ask. You have been with her a lot of nights, no wonder you had that smile on your face. What will the lovely Maria say when she finds out that you have been lusting after another woman? Especially one of the girls in here. After all the wedding is, what, only three weeks away? Last minute nerves? Second thoughts?"

"I thought everybody would have heard by this time. I called it off a while ago. There is no way that I could go ahead when I am in love with another woman, and can't get her out of my head. It just wouldn't be fair to Maria, would it?"

"Oh, here we go again. How many more times am I going to hear you say that you are in love? That this is the one! This time it is forever! It was a surprise to everyone when you got engaged to Maria, especially when before it was unusual for you to appear with the same girl twice, and I had begun to think that you should be known as Mr Paul one-night-stand Knight. First that I have heard about the wedding being off, though. Is it a complete break, or just temporary? Maybe Maria is giving you some time, thinking that you'll change your mind before she says anything."

"I made it quite clear to her, Josh, that I wanted to end the relationship completely. If she is hoping that… well, it just is not going to happen. And I do not think you are being very fair to these girls, Josh. They didn't ask to be drugged, abducted and then expected to accept the way they have to live now; this isn't the way they lived before, they didn't choose to earn their living this way, being kept as slaves, which is what they are, making their situation worse."

"No, you're quite right, I'm sorry." By now the two friends had arrived in the meeting room. It was very full, but Josh managed to find two vacant seats away from everybody else. "I wanted to have a word with you before the meeting. The general opinion is that this girl should be rejected. Personally, I think it is a good idea. The plans that are in place for her, and they are not just a suggestion, if she is accepted are all going to happen. After today she will not be available to anyone. If the medical tests have come back okay, she will be rented out as a surrogate. There are a couple already signed up. If it all works out, in a couple of days she will have the embryo implanted in her, and after she has had the baby, she will be implanted again as soon as possible for another couple, and the poor kid will be on a treadmill. She will be kept here because there are the medical facilities already in place and one of the members is a doctor who will oversee the whole thing, for a share of the profits, of course. It will be an expensive exercise for the people involved, they will be able to see the girl online through the cameras, but there will be no contact with her. It will be a very lucrative venture, and it doesn't take a genius to guess who will benefit!"

By this time Paul was looking at his friend with horror. "You're joking! She will not be told what they are doing to her? Surely, they will have to tell her at some point, it will start to show eventually! Will she have to figure it out by herself? That is sick."

"I'm afraid there's more," Josh told him. "The situation gets worse, much worse."

Paul groaned. "Go on, tell me."

"Have you noticed there have been more girls brought in just recently? The girls have not been given contraceptive shots for a while, and some of them have fallen pregnant. They are kept away from the other girls in a separate part of the building, I have no idea where. They have DNA profiles of all the girls, also of all the members, so that when the baby is born it can be tested and it is taken away from its mother straightaway. There is a list of people wanting babies who are willing to pay for them. They will be paying serious money. When the babies are a few days old they will be handed over to their new family. And the girls are not going to be told anything after the birth, kept ignorant, it will be as if the months before never happened. How cruel will that be? There are also other angles to this as well, blackmail and extortion. Can you imagine the hold that they would have over some of these men who are members? The positions that some of them hold, the damage that could be caused, and there is a question of whether they are mixed up with organised crime."

Paul exclaimed, "That crowd have got to be voted off, I thought that it was bad enough before, but they have got to go!"

Josh looked at him. "I thought that you would feel that way; apparently they are not going to let all the men have a turn, it's going to be stopped after one." By this time, a girl had been led in; she looked terrified.

"And that is one too many," said Paul. "I don't want to watch this, she is just a kid, how old would you say? She looks underage, what would you say, fourteen? You can see her shaking, poor kid, and if she is that young how many babies will she carry before she is worn out, and old before her time? Poor kid, knowing that lot she will always be kept pregnant. I wish we could get her out of there." The girl in question was being paraded round in a circle for the members to get a good look. It was obvious how much she was shaking, even though she would have been given a drug so that she would be compliant and not fight against what she was going to be subjected to. She had been helped up onto the bed and the restraints fastened to keep her still. The first man had just raped her and there was no doubt that she was finding the experience painful and frightening. Paul wasn't looking; he was finding it hard to watch the spectacle of this girl, who most likely had been a virgin, being raped in front of everybody, and stay where he was without leaving the room. It sickened him.

To Paul's relief the doors opened and a group of police entered, the one in charge shouting, "Stay where you are! I have warrants for the arrest of everybody in this building and a search warrant. Get that stopped and the poor kid out of there," he continued, pointing to the area behind the glass partition. A group of the men with him, who had been watching the events going on with distaste, were only too happy to comply with the order to get the obviously distressed girl out. The rest stayed by the doors to prevent people trying to leave. The officer in charge then went through a long list of charges. A female officer went straight

40

to unfasten the restraints, helping the girl, who was sobbing hysterically, get off the bed and covered up. Her colleagues had the men in that area under arrest and after they had been given time to get dressed, they were taken into the main meeting room where everybody else was being held. Paul looked round with satisfaction, watching the reaction of some of the members. There were men from all walks of life, among them cabinet ministers, a shadow minister, MPs, also well-known faces from the law, film industry, stage, television, finance, and the press, as well as charities. Most of them people whose reputations would be tarnished when this became known, especially the connections with people trafficking and some of the other practices that had been going on, and would cause, he speculated, a few heads to roll, as well as the end of some careers and marriages. They were all sitting in stunned silence, some with their heads in their hands, others trying to pull rank, demanding to be allowed to leave. Paul heard, "Do you know who I am?" announced by someone in a loud voice who was being politely but very firmly told to sit down; nobody could leave yet. He and Josh also sat in silence for a while, thinking after all a bit of scandal wouldn't be too harmful to either of their businesses.

Josh said, "I wonder how the police found out about what was going on? The club is usually keen to keep under the radar. I suppose it might have come to light if they were investigating the traffickers and the trail led here."

"Could have, couldn't it?" Paul said, as noncommittally as possible. He hated having to keep his part in this a secret from his friend, but he had been sworn to secrecy by the police when he had taken his concerns to them. Not that Josh would have said anything, but he thought it better to keep quiet.

When the police had first entered the building, they saw, ranged round the entrance hall and reception, what was known as The Harem; eight of what could only be described as display cases. They had a curved glass exterior, behind which was a life-sized picture of one of the girls with her Harem name written on it. One was empty and had no picture or name, but there was a picture of Scarlet, although she was missing. And in all but two of them was the girl herself. They were standing with their hands handcuffed behind them. They each had the usual diamante collar and chain round the neck. All of them were wearing the harness, covered in diamante, that pulled their shoulders back so that they couldn't slouch and showed their breasts off to full advantage. They wore nothing else, and there were spotlights inside these booths, illuminating them.

The men were entranced and stopped to admire the view, because they were all good-looking girls, of all colours and nationalities, until the officer in charge shouted at them to get on with the job, they weren't here for a peep show. Apparently, they were told later that all the girls took their turn at being put on show for at least half an hour at a time every day. But when there was a meeting of the members, they were all displayed like that, showing the property that was owned by the club. When the officers went to take the girls out, they realised that they could neither see nor hear what was going on the other side of the glass. The police took them to their rooms, which had their names on the doors. When they had done that, they had found Blue, Crystal, Amber, Sapphire, Ruby and Violet. There was a door without a name which obviously had no occupant, but none for the girl called Scarlet, and they were puzzled about where she was. It was suggested that they spoke to the people who looked after the girls, they would know.

It was a warren of corridors and rooms that they passed. Finally, their guide stopped at the room, with Scarlet's name on the door, that they had been searching for. It was isolated right at the far end of the building.

When Anna, the police officer who had been assigned to Scarlet, finally opened the door gently, she found a very scared, very sleepy-looking girl sitting up in bed, watching her come through. She was visibly shaking, her knees drawn up and her arms round them, the bedclothes pulled up to her chin. She had long thick hair with a narrow face which was pale, with high cheek bones and large green eyes, which at that moment were opened wide with fear and had dark circles under them.

EIGHT

I had woken with a start, my heart pounding. It only seemed to have been a few minutes since I had been brought back to my room and fallen into a deep sleep. What woke me was the noise; noise in here? What was going on? I started to shake as I was so scared about what this meant and by having been wakened so abruptly. The noise was of feet in the corridor, and where was the shouting coming from? Doors banging as well. It was all getting too much for me. Just then the door opened, and two females came into the room. They were not wearing the coveralls but were dressed in black trousers with a white shirt that had epaulets on the shoulders. Uniforms? I could not believe what I was seeing and sat there trying to make sense of it all. Another thing that I could not believe was that I could see their faces. I could see their faces. One of them came towards me and was talking; I could not seem to hear what she was saying. Could they possibly be police? I was in shock, and realising that, she repeated what she was saying. "Hello Scarlet, I'm Anna and this is my colleague, Sophie. We're police officers and are here to rescue you so that you can go back home again, back to your family and friends." I hadn't spoken for so long, and when I tried to speak nothing happened.

I cleared my throat and swallowed, but I don't think that my reaction was what they expected because I looked towards the door very fearfully, saying in a quiet voice, obviously not wanting to be overheard, "I'm not allowed to talk to anyone. I have to stay silent, and I will probably be punished if I'm caught talking to you." Anna and Sophie looked at each other.

"The boss will want to know that," Sophie commented.

Anna sat down on the side of the bed and took my hands in hers. "You will not be punished for talking now, everything has changed. The people who were running this place have been arrested and will be charged with many serious offences. You're free of all that. What we would like to do is take you to a safe place and then we would like you to tell us what happened to you, how you were treated, as much as possible. Sophie is going to see if she can find all your belongings. We found the other girls' clothes in lockers, still intact, so I think yours will be too."

"So, there are other girls here as well?" I asked.

Anna looked at me with raised eyebrows. "Yes, of course there are," she answered, looking at Sophie. "Surely you would see each other?"

I shook my head. "We were kept isolated from everyone, didn't know who we were dealing with, forbidden to talk. I thought that it was probably to stop us forming attachments with our carers and trying to get them to help us to escape. Or identify anybody." I shook my head and yawned; I felt quite overwhelmed. "I'm sorry, I have only just been brought back to my room and only been asleep for a short time. I was with someone all last night." Suddenly I realised what all this meant. "So, am I free?" There were tears running down my face. I put my head on my knees and started sobbing. Some of the tears were because I was so relieved to be rescued after I had convinced myself, so many times, that there was no chance of this happening, but some were because I realised that I would never have such a wonderful night ever again, as it had been last night and every other that I had spent with this same man. Anna came and sat on the bed, pulling me into her arms and holding me tight while I cried, rocking me like a baby. Sophie came back into the room, carrying my handbag and holding bags containing my clothes and it seemed to be everything that I had with me the day I had been abducted.

When it seemed that I had no more tears to shed, Anna held me away from her, so she could speak to me face to face. "I'm sorry," I said to her.

Anna looked confused. "What have you got to be sorry for?"

"You've got a wet shoulder," I said with a weak smile. Anna laughed and hugged me again.

"She's used to that," Sophie put in, adding, "I have found all your clothes, your handbag and all the shopping you must have done when you were abducted, they had been put in a locker. My, you must have been seriously hitting the plastic. Surprisingly, your credit cards haven't been used, your phone is here and was switched off, also there is a bag with jewellery inside your handbag. Are all these yours?"

"Oh, yes they are mine." All that I had with me that day that I ended up in this place was still all together.

"When you've got dressed, and there is absolutely no rush, take as much time as you need. We'll take you somewhere we can talk to you and you can be checked over by a doctor at a private hospital. Our boss would like to hear all that has happened to you since your abduction. I know that you will be desperate to get back home to your family, but if we can get it out of the way, apart from maybe checking on a few points we may want clarifying, we will bother you as little as possible." I think that, although they didn't make it obvious, both kept watching me, because when it came to fasten my bra, I was shaking so badly it was proving impossible for me to manage.

Anna came towards the bed. "Can I help you with that? You're shaking so much no wonder you can't get it fastened." I nodded gratefully, and she came and sat on the bed so that she could see better. As she was about to fasten it, she paused and said nothing. Sophie looked at her questioningly. Anna said quietly, "Come and look at this." Sophie gasped when she looked at my back. Anna said, "I'm so sorry, I should have asked you if it was all right for Sophie to look. You have what look like old scars left from what look like bite marks, and several old ones that could have been inflicted by a cane on your back. Also bruising to your stomach and back. Did the man who spent the night with you do any of this?"

"No definitely not, I have been with him many times and he has never shown me anything but kindness," I said defensively.

"Don't try to cover for him," she warned me. "We need to know if he did."

"I am not covering for him, I told you he has been good to me. I wouldn't recognise him anyway."

"What do you mean, about not recognising him?" I explained about the hood and they both looked at me in surprise when I told them. They didn't press me further, but I could tell the two of them hadn't let the subject drop completely and would ask more later. "I would like to get my boss to come and look at your back. I think he might want photographs taken as well, if that is okay with you?" I nodded my agreement and suddenly found that I felt very self-conscious about keeping myself covered up, pulling the bedclothes up under my chin again. Sophie left the room and came back a few minutes later with their boss. When he got to the door he knocked before he entered, and as he came over, he pulled a chair up to the bed so that he was sitting more on a level with me. He held his hand out to me and took mine very gently in his, saying, "Hello Scarlet, I'm Dave, and for my sins their boss. We don't know what else to call you because we haven't found out what your real name is yet, we can't find any records to tell us."

"I'm Chloe, Chloe Winters." It felt so good to speak and say my name out loud at last. "Hello, Chloe, at last I know who I'm talking to. I am sure that Anna and Sophie have told you that we would like to talk to you before we take you back home." I nodded, not taking my eyes off him, and still shaking, but not as much. "And that's all right with you?" I nodded again. Anna put her hands on my shoulders and said to her boss, "Chloe isn't used to talking much yet, because she was forbidden to talk while she was kept here."

"Well, you will get plenty of practice talking to us," he said, smiling at me. Everybody was being so kind, I felt my eyes filling with tears, again. "Now I am told that you have what look like bite marks on your back, that look very nasty, and you have said that it wasn't the man you spent last night with. Have I got that right?" I nodded and said, "I've spent many nights with him, and he has never treated me badly."

"If you let me have a look, I won't keep you any longer." I moved round so that he could see for himself. He made a sharp intake of breath before saying, "I would like some photos taken, it will help when we take these people to court if we can show some of the injuries that you have. The photographer is just down the hall, will it be all right if I call him in?"

"That's fine," I said. "Take as many as you want."

"Thank you. I'll leave you in the safe hands of these two, they will look after you. If there is anything that we can do for you, just ask, and no doubt I will see you again soon." After shaking hands with me he left the room. The photographer came in just after he left and took quite a few pictures. When he had finished and gone, I finally managed to get dressed but I needed help, because I was still shaking. I must have lost a lot of weight; my clothes were very loose on me. It felt so strange to be wearing clothes again, it was going to take some time for it to feel normal. Sophie took my jewellery out of my bag and handed it to me, and as I put it on, she came upon my engagement ring. "This is lovely, is it an engagement ring? I should think that you will be looking forward to seeing your fiancé," she said, admiring it, and then handed it to me to put it on, but they looked at each other in surprise when I put it into my bag and not onto my finger. They didn't comment, however, and I had the feeling that it would be enquired about later. I made sure that I picked up all the gadgets that I had had restored to me; they had made such a difference to my life, I was not about to leave them behind. I was feeling some trepidation about getting back into the real world again; it was, I realised, going to be extremely difficult. "We're going to take you out of a back entrance that we found, and which I think will be quieter, not so many curious eyes watching," Anna told me. "The press hasn't picked up on the story yet so it's mostly just police, but a lot of them, and some other agencies as well.

There have been a lot of rumours circulating about some of the things that have been happening here and so a lot of speculation. We want to try to save you from some of that."

I was still a little shaky on my feet, so Anna walked with her arm around me as we left the room and made our way down the corridor. The door to the room that I had been through to the apes in the afternoons was shut. I expected it to open and to be dragged through it as we passed. I breathed a sigh of relief to get past it without anything happening. A young policeman came around the corner. "The car's ready for you," he said, smiling kindly at me. "It's just out here." I found myself coming to a stop. If I had thought about what I would do if, a big if, I ever found myself in the position I was in now, I would have envisaged myself running out of the door, celebrating. How odd to feel the way I did, I couldn't understand myself. Anna and Sophie looked at me enquiringly. I stared at the open door; what was on the other side was the unknown, and danger lurked out there, and I would be punished if they found that I had escaped and they caught me again. I turned around and unbelievably looked longingly back the way we had come. I still couldn't understand myself. Back there was what I had got used to, my life, such as it was. I was looked after back there, I wanted for nothing, did I? My meals were put in front of me, I could have anything I wanted. Everything was done for me. How would I cope back in the real world? I really didn't think I could, I was incapable. And I wouldn't have 'him' in the real world. It was all so confusing. Suddenly Anna's voice came through the fog that was affecting my brain, saying gently, "Come on, Chloe, what's the matter? When you get through that door, that leads to your family, home, your friends. To freedom. This place isn't home to you, it's been your prison, come on, it's just a few more steps." It felt more like a few miles. I took the steps out into the fresh air and sunshine; it was a beautiful day, and I was free. There were two policemen stationed outside, and as I walked through the door an alarm started to ring loudly. I jumped at the noise, my heart beating hard, looking around in fear. *Somebody might come running to take me back inside*, I thought as I panicked, feeling terrified about what could happen. Anna put her arms around my shoulders to comfort me and we all looked to see what had set it off. As we were looking confused one of their colleagues came from the back of the building. "Don't worry about that, it will stop soon, we're working on it. I'm afraid that it was probably you that set it off," he said to me. "I think that you will have had a microchip, that also had a tracking device, implanted in you, that caused the alarm to go off when you came out of the door."

"I think I was given that little present on the first day that I arrived here." I stood by the car just looking up at the blue sky, the little white clouds, the sunshine. I turned my face to the sun, letting it warm me, enjoying the feeling of it on my skin, and hearing the birds singing. When I turned back to Anna, she was watching me, a look of sympathy on her face. "Feel good?" she asked. I nodded, and with tears not far off got into the car. I sat in the back of the car behind the driver with Anna next to me and Sophie in the front. The car turned the corner of the building to a scene of apparent chaos. The place was filled with police and vehicles. The driver stopped, to speak to one of the men on duty. That gave me a chance to see the outside of the building for the first time. I couldn't believe how beautiful it was, part of it looked incredibly old. "It's such a beautiful place, I never saw it from the outside," I commented to Anna. She put her arm round me. "Yes, and now you are out and free of it, especially once you have had that awful tracker removed. Where is it, do you know?"

"Just about here, I can't feel it anymore," I said, pointing to my thigh where there was a small scar. "I will try and organise the operation to remove that as soon as possible," she said.

"It will be so good to get that out of the way, thank you." I was still looking at the building when I was vaguely aware of someone staring at me. He was standing by one of the cars in the car park. Just then the driver closed his window and set off onto the drive that led to the main road. I breathed a sigh of relief. Freedom at last, how wonderful that was. I thought that maybe I would wake up and find that it had all been a dream but prayed that scenario never happened. I found my phone in my bag, but the battery was, of course, dead. I would have to wait until I could charge it before I spoke to my parents.

After a long drive, the car turned into a police station yard. Anna had told me that we would be going there, and that after something to eat they wanted to get me checked out by a doctor at a nearby hospital. Then later I would be taken to a hotel for the night. The next day they wanted to talk to me and take a statement. I would then be taken back to the hotel for the night and probably be taken home if they had finished with me the day after. I was taken to the canteen when we arrived. I was so hungry; I hadn't had any breakfast. When I had finished, Anna put her arm round my waist and guided me through the throng of officers that were assembled. I felt dwarfed and rather intimidated by them all, and I was so glad when we got outside and into a car. When we arrived at the hospital, I was shaking. It seemed to take hours, but at last I was told they had finished all the tests, and after I had given my parents' telephone number to Anna, so that she could ring them with the good news of my rescue, I was taken to the hotel for the night. I ate my meal and then retreated up to my room and decided to have a shower. As I was getting ready to step under the spray, I caught sight of myself in the mirror. There had been no mirrors anywhere, so it came as a shock when I looked at my reflection. I stood looking at the mirror in disbelief. The woman who stared back at me was so different from the way I had looked before my abduction. I was so thin, with dark circles under my eyes; they looked huge in my face. I looked almost unrecognisable. I dried off and even though it was a bit early to go to bed, I was tired and thought that I would fall asleep easily. How wrong I was. I couldn't settle, and lay looking up at the ceiling, until I gave up trying and put the light back on to read for a short time. Eventually I did sleep, but only after I had cried over the mystery man who had made me fall in love with him.

The next morning, after I had eaten my breakfast Anna came and took me back to the station to give my statement. It took most of the day, and by the time that I was taken back to the hotel for the night, I was exhausted. I rang my parents; I needed to hear their voices. My mother and I cried, and my dad sounded choked with emotion. I couldn't wait to get home to them again.

NINE

Three members ran The Newford Priory Club and were voted into the roles as managers. The three men who had run it for years had decided that they wanted to step down from the positions; they didn't want the responsibility anymore, and all stepped down at once. Paul had been abroad when the management changed but was kept informed of what was happening and didn't like what he heard. There were two parts to the membership. General members had no voting rights; the fees for this included an excellent restaurant with a superb reputation, which was open to the public and was extremely popular. There was talk of going for a Michelin Star, but nobody seemed to want that, preferring to keep it as having good food accessible to all. There was also a spa, health club, and a casino. There were extensive grounds, with a network of paths covering most of the large parkland; members had free use of that area also. The gardens were a big attraction and open to the public, they were well known, well patronised, and profitable. There was a golf club attached which had held some large tournaments.

Full members paid for a share of the club, including membership of the golf club, and paid large fees every year for the privilege. Also included was a small high-quality hotel and, very strangely, a brothel, open only to full members and known as The Harem. It was illegal, everybody knew that, but the girls were well looked after, and on the payroll, who knew under what job title. They employed a gang that was usually engaged in people trafficking to recruit the girls, the main stipulation being that they weren't to have been sex workers previously, be good-looking with a good figure. How they persuaded the girls to apply for the job wasn't known, but if the girls that were approached showed an interest, they were taken to the club to be shown round. They were paid very well and were given a luxurious room for themselves. The men were generally kept out of these; it wasn't a rule of the club, but the girls liked their own space. They had a dining room of their own, the food being the same as that served in the main restaurant. They were given an extensive medical examination before they were employed and tested regularly. All the members had to have tests done regularly, so everybody was hopefully protected. When a new girl was employed all the members were there to see her introduced. There was a ballot for them to put their names forward to try the new girl out, and the first had to pay a premium to the club for the privilege. She had to walk in among the members, showing herself off, and after the winner of the ballot had finished with her, there was a vote. There had to be a majority to decide whether she should be employed or not. A strange interview for a job!

After the new management team took over, everything changed, drastically. The girls that had worked there previously were let go. Some of them had amassed quite a large amount of money, through some of the members giving them sizeable tips. The new girls were brought in by the same gang as before; the specifications were the same, but the girls were not taken to the club for a job interview this time. When the traffickers found someone they thought would be suitable, the gang notified the club that a possible target had been found, and photos were sent to them. The girls were then followed for two weeks, and regular reports were sent back about where they went, where they worked and who they were meeting. When permission was given to go ahead, the gang decided when the pickup would happen. The club was then notified, and she was picked up, sometimes from the street, drugged, and delivered to the clients. When they arrived at the club the gang members, usually two, would stay that night, because full payment would only be handed over after the members had accepted her. If for some reason she was rejected, they would only get expenses and a bit extra. This only happened the day after she had been brought in, and after she was accepted, she was injected with a microchip that was also a tracker. And only after that would the traffickers be paid their money. The girl then became the property of the club and its members. When the gang were told to check her out, the members were sent a message saying a new girl was being brought in in two weeks, and anyone wanting the chance to try her out should put their names down for the ballot in the usual way. When it was known on what day she would be picked up, the members were notified that the meeting would take place the next day, and who had been lucky in the ballot; these men paid a large sum of money. The girl would be taken to the meeting room after she had been put through rigorous medical tests and be paraded round the room to let the members see her, and then had a hood put over her head, so that she couldn't identify anybody. After they had finished with her introduction there would be a vote to decide whether she was accepted or not. If she was rejected for any reason she would be cleaned up and handed back to the gang. She would then be taken back near to where she was picked up and it was staged as though she had been assaulted where she was found. She would be given drugs that had hallucinogenic effects so that whatever she told the police would not be believed. The managers told the members that the apparent changes were to improve the whole experience; that there were no actual changes to how the place was run. The girls had been told, it was said, to act as though they were badly treated and downtrodden. They were very persuasive and managed to con everybody, until one or two members started to hear whispers of impropriety and illegal activities. These were not spoken about to everybody, because those that had found out some of what was happening didn't want the men alerted to the fact that what they were doing had been found out.

After Paul had seen one of these 'introductions' he decided that he didn't want to be a member anymore and nearly ended his membership; but he decided to go to the police instead. However, he needed to find out more about what was going on before he did. As Paul had been out of the country when all the changes had taken place it made it less suspicious for him to ask a lot of questions, using that as an excuse. He dragged himself unwillingly to the next one, which was when it was Chloe's turn. This time they treated her brutally, which didn't go down well with all the members there that day. The members that had carried out the 'introduction' had been barred from the club and stripped of their membership, as well as being fined an eye-watering amount of money into the bargain. The other members had insisted on these measures being taken so that the men running the club couldn't go against the decision.

The next day he went and spoke to the police about his concerns. He talked to them for most of that day, giving his statement. He was asked if he could get any more information, and he promised he would do his best. He then discussed what other information they would need. What he told them was taken very seriously and they wanted to set up a raid as soon as possible. He was told, in confidence, that concerns had been raised previously about what was going on, including people trafficking, and this gave them another reason for the raid. Paul explained that there would be another meeting coming up because the members wanted to get the managing team voted out of the job, so that everybody who could get there to vote would do so. Rumour said there might be another girl being brought in to fulfil another of the management team's money-making schemes. Schemes that the members knew nothing of, and most of the money would, of course, be going into the management team's pockets. Paul had notified the police the day before the meeting, and of the best time to stage the raid, and he hoped that it would all take place smoothly.

As he sat there in the meeting room, waiting to find out his fate, Paul thought back to when he had first really noticed Scarlet. He had been at her introduction; he was appalled at what had happened to her and concerned about how she was after the treatment she had received. She came into his thoughts regularly; was he in love with her then? Certainly, he was strongly attracted to her, but love? He had asked to have a tour of the club, needing to know the layout so he could relay it to the police. He had never asked to tour the place before; it never seemed necessary, until then. When he was on the tour, he was taken to an area on the far side of the building. They were just going down another corridor when they passed a window which looked out onto a garden. He stopped to admire what a beautiful area it was, and he saw that there was a swimming pool over to one side, accessed from the garden through a glass sliding door. One of the girls had been having a swim. She came out and stood enjoying the sun on her, and she was free of the collar and handcuffs. "Is that Scarlet?" he asked his guide. "Yes, it is, she loves to come out here when they will let her." The effect she was having on him was startling, standing there, naked in the sun, looking incredible, but much thinner than he remembered. He had been in the room for her introduction, and he hadn't been able to get her out of his mind since then, but he had frequently seen Maia, one of her carers, and she gave him information on how Scarlet was. He never thought that he believed in love at first sight, but he had never experienced a feeling like it before. He couldn't take his eyes off her and it wasn't just her beautiful body but something about her attitude that attracted him so strongly. If he had been asked, he couldn't have put it into words. Just then one of her minders came to take her back inside and the pleasure she had shown, and the look in her eyes both died when the collar was put back on, and she was taken over to the shower where she was washed. There were two of her minders with her, as always, one holding the chain that was attached to the collar; they kept stroking and fondling her, almost as if she were a pet. Paul was getting more and more angry about the way that they had their hands all over her. He could have wept for her the way she just stood there and seemingly accepted what was being done to her with resignation, despite the lack of dignity; treating her as if she were an animal, where lack of privacy wasn't an issue, and that she couldn't do anything for herself, or understand anything that was said to her. He wanted to rush in and take her out of there, to take her to safety. *I'm going to get you out of here, soon,* he told her in his mind, but it wouldn't be soon enough for him. "Where are they taking her now?" he asked. "Can you take me through there?"

"No, I am afraid that is off limits to everyone. Look, they're handing her over to the team who work on that side, they don't work for the club, no connection with us at all." With some trepidation Paul asked his guide, "What happens through there?"

"All we know is that somebody put up a large amount of money for an experiment to be carried out," said his guide. "And what does this experiment entail, exactly?" he asked, knowing full well that he would hate the answer. "Nobody on this side really knows what goes on in there. There was another girl called Blanche, who was involved before Scarlet. I don't know what happened to her, she suddenly wasn't around anymore, and there hasn't been any mention of her since. We were told to drop the subject in a very threatening way, when we asked. There has been speculation that Blanche died, but we don't know that for sure, or how. I had better not say anymore. I think I have said too much already; you didn't hear anything from me."

"Of course not, I won't say a thing."

"She's beautiful, isn't she, have you ever booked her?" asked his guide, changing the subject. Paul shuddered with distaste. "No, I don't like the way the club is run, the way the girls are shackled."

As he made his way back, he met Maia, one of the carers

who looked after the girls. He always asked for a progress report on how Scarlet was doing because he knew he would get an honest answer. "How is Scarlet? Is something wrong? I have just seen her, and she doesn't look very well, she's lost quite a bit of weight, hasn't she?" Maia gave a big sigh. "We are all concerned about her, she isn't eating much, not enough to keep her going. She isn't happy in here, which isn't a surprise, she is grieving for her old life. She seems to be fading away before our eyes, and we can't do anything about it. She is so lonely because of the way they are kept in isolation; she needs someone to make love to her, hold her in their arms, not just have sex with her." Paul asked, "Could that happen, would it be possible?"

"You could book her for the night, but they would only let you have her for an evening for the first time. She would still have to wear a hood though." Paul leaned down and kissed Maia on the cheek, making her blush. "Oh, Mr Paul, are you going to book her?"

"I am on my way to do that now and thank you." He then headed off in the direction of the office, but before he had gone far, he turned back to Maia. "Is it true that a bid can be made on any of the girls for when the club want to move them on?"

"Absolutely, they will tell you how in the office. Good luck."

TEN

When Paul arrived at the office, he was referred to the clerk he needed to speak to and had to wait, getting more and more impatient until a phone enquiry was sorted out. "I'm sorry about the wait, what can I do for you?" she asked with a dazzling smile. Having seen him around she had always hoped that a chance to meet him would happen. "I would like to put a bid in for Scarlet, if that's possible?" He couldn't believe that he was contemplating putting in a bid to buy another human being, in this day and age; it was so wrong on so many levels, not to mention highly illegal. "Of course, it is," she said as she found the screen she needed on the computer. "Now let me see, there are bids already in for her, she's a popular lady." He had hoped that there wouldn't be any. She turned the screen round so that he could see the competition he faced. He wasn't sure if she had the right to show him the details, but he had no intention of questioning what she was doing. As he looked, he knew the men involved and they had all put down large bids, so he outbid them by a big margin. He was prepared to go a lot higher if necessary; he had no intention of losing her now. He then asked if he could book her for the following evening. As the clerk looked at the screen she said, "Yes, that will be all right, oh, wait a minute, it's just come up that she will be indisposed for at least four days. I'm sorry, you'll have to wait and book her later." She saw how disappointed he looked and told him, "There is a way that you can spend the afternoon with her; she is always poorly and suffers badly for the first two days, poor thing, and the staff sit with her. She mostly sleeps but we think that she appreciates the company. Would you like to do that? I could arrange that for you, and you would only be able to sit with her." He would also see a bit more of what went on behind the scenes, what her room was like as well. As he left the desk the unfairness of the girls' lives hit him hard. The fact that other people knew more about them, because all the regular tests that were done on the girls and the results, what injections, any treatment they needed plus a great amount of other details about them were put on their pages on the club's website, including cycles and every intimate detail of them than probably they did. And that it was common knowledge and talked about freely among all the people who worked there, including the office staff. He was sure that they would hate that if they knew. On their pages were pictures of them, obviously taken when they had been booked; he wondered if they were released as pornography and would probably bring in a lot of money, even used as a blackmail tool. The faces of the men were blanked out on the website, but the original photos would show who they were very clearly. He couldn't bring himself to look at Scarlet's webpage. These girls were just captives with no rights, it made him even angrier than he had been before. He also wondered what the girls in the office thought was going on. The real reason must be cleverly hidden from them, and from almost all the members.

63

The next afternoon, after putting on the obligatory outfit that he was provided with – he felt so weird wearing it – he was taken to her room. He had been told that he could touch her, that sometimes she liked that. It wasn't that she needed supervision because she might need medical help, only that the staff sat with her purely to give her company, she mostly slept anyway. She was lying on top of the bedclothes and was wearing a pair of what looked like silk pyjamas, she looked so beautiful. When he looked down at her lying on the bed, he was shocked at the difference from two days before, when he had seen her last, and how ill she looked now. His companion who had entered the room with him asked her, using the tablet, if she needed more painkillers, at which she nodded and was given another shot. The other person left the room, leaving him on his own with her at last. She seemed to have dropped off to sleep; her breathing sounded as if she had. While he was sitting next to her it gave him a chance to survey her room. He was very impressed, everything was of top quality and very comfortable, and would not be out of place in any of the top hotels where he had stayed; at least she had something positive. He got up and looked out of the window, not a lot to see but trees and farmland but not a bad view. From what he had been told by Maia, for meals the girls were given the menu from the restaurant to choose from. When he sat down again after looking out of the window, he noticed an e-reader on the bedside table and took the liberty of switching it on to see what she had been reading. It was then he noticed that the battery was running low and found a charging cable, so he put it on charge for her. Next to the book were MP3 players; they, too, were running low, so he found charging points for those, so that they would all be fully charged when she was ready to use them. He felt that he was intruding but hoped she wouldn't mind. He suddenly realised her eyes were open and she was watching him, albeit very sleepily. She sat up and he picked up the tablet that he had been left and wrote on it, "Sorry did I disturb you? I didn't mean to". She shook her head and her mouth turned up a bit, in what appeared to be a slight smile. Turning over on her side, she took his hand in hers, and having done that closed her eyes, still holding it tightly and close to her. He longed to take her in his arms, but he doubted that would go down very well, and he would not be allowed to have this, as he looked on it, privilege again, not that he wanted her to suffer like that, but it gave him a rare chance to be close to her. He tenderly pushed her hair off her face, wishing the circumstances were different. It only seemed to have been a short time that he had been with her before his companion was back, to tell him that time was up. As he turned round, before he left the room, she was sitting up in bed and mouthed, "Thank you" to him before he left, her mouth turning up slightly in another sad smile that melted his heart.

Thinking back about what he had seen, when he was sitting in the bar with a drink, he thought that the best way of describing the way that the girls were kept was that they were in a gilded cage. Their surroundings were luxurious, but as for the rest of their lives, well, what could he say?

Paul thought that he ought to see what happened when the girls were booked, how it was conducted. He did not want to do this, he knew that what he would see would be upsetting, but it was, he was sure, a hundred percent worse for her. When he could see that she had been booked next time he visited the club, thankfully by no one that he knew, he had a stiff drink and then made his way to the meeting room. Looking round the room there were many men there watching what was going on. Scarlet hadn't been brought in yet, he was a bit early.

When he left the room sometime later, he felt almost nauseous. The reaction of the men watching made it a lot worse, making it a spectator sport. He was glad that none of the girls would be able to hear what was being shouted from that side of the room, these men obviously were getting off on watching.

Coming back to the present he sighed. The two friends sat in silence until Paul said, "I'm afraid that I have a confession to make, and I am so sorry to have dragged you into this." Josh looked at him in surprise. "Confess? About what?" Paul looked uncomfortable. "No one else is to know what I am going to tell you, this is strictly between you and me, okay? But I went to the police about what is happening here. I thought that the way they treat these girls is abhorrent and should be stopped. It's slavery, there are no other ways to describe it. I am even more glad that I did after what you have just told me. I have been talking to some of the members over the last few weeks and I don't think that they realise just what has been going on, thinking that all the business with the collar and handcuffs is just for show, that the girls are treated as they were before, that nothing has changed. I am afraid that I didn't put them right about the truth." Josh looked even more surprised and didn't say anything for a moment. Paul said, dreading the answer, "Well, say something. I'll totally understand if you never want to speak to me again. After all, we will be arrested, just for being here."

"I was just thinking, good for you, and for staying here, because you are going to be arrested as well, aren't you?

Being involved in this. You certainly kept that quiet. How long ago did you go to them, and did Scarlet have anything to do with it?"

"I'm so glad you have taken it that way. I didn't like the set-up when I went to Blue's introduction. I thought that was bad enough, and I decided then that I would go to the police. It was that far back, but I thought I needed more information before they took it seriously and more questions needed answering. And yes, I decided definitely after Scarlet's introduction; they treated her brutally. I wasn't in love with her then, that came much later." Paul filled Josh in about the circumstances of how he had fallen so much in love, and so quickly, with Scarlet. "I don't believe, no, correction, I didn't believe, in love at first sight, it didn't seem possible to me. What did I know? But it just seemed to physically hit me, I can't put it any better than that. I couldn't think of anything else but her, she came into my mind constantly. I did think that it was maybe just a phase, but in the end, I had to call off the wedding. I didn't think it would last, myself, but then it became imperative to me that I get Scarlet out of here. I couldn't stand the thought of other men with their hands all over her, and she could have vanished from here. Her health was deteriorating, she was looking ill."

"Lust," said Josh. Paul laughed. "Yes, plenty of lust, I am not ashamed to admit to that. I know this sounds crazy, when I haven't even spoken to her, but I don't want her just as a mistress. After time for us to get to know each other, I want to marry her, if I feel the same way after we get to know each other, and if she is willing, hopefully feeling the same." Josh was silent for a few minutes, thinking, then he said slowly, "No, surprisingly, it doesn't sound crazy. I have

67

been your friend for long enough now to know you, I think very well, and none of the girls you have had relationships with, including Maria, seems to have had the effect on you that she has. Sounds like you've got it bad, but you'll have to be prepared for if she refuses to meet you."

Just then they were called to give a statement and it was some time before Paul finally stepped out at the front of the building. He had been seen by one of the officers whom he had spoken to when he had visited about what was going on in the club; he was thankful that he didn't have to explain his part in what had happened all over again. He passed on what he had heard from Josh, one of the police admitting to him about the rumours they had heard about what was going on, and he took plenty of notes. Apparently, the police hadn't found the area where the girls who were pregnant were being held in the first search, but after questions were put to some of the staff they were directed to the area where they found the girls, four of them, all at different stages in their pregnancies. Before he left the building, one of the police came and thanked him for the information, and told him that they had been found, and were all in good health, and were being transferred out of there.

Paul had had a vision earlier of them all being taken out in handcuffs and carted off to the local nick, maybe to spend the night in the cells. He breathed in, enjoying the fresh air and freedom, thankful that he was finally out of there. He wandered to the car park. Josh had parked his car not too far away, so he stood leaning against his, enjoying the sun, watching what was going on while he waited for his friend. The place was swarming with people, mostly police, and as he stood there a large car came out from round the back of the building. He was on the alert in case some of the people who had been running the club were trying escape, but of course that couldn't happen, because they were all in the room when the police raid took place. The car stopped next to two of the police and the driver lowered his window to speak to them and the fact that he was wearing a uniform was obvious. Paul glimpsed the person behind the driver, and he gasped. There she was: Scarlet. "Oh, my beautiful girl, you're free at last, but will you want anything to do with me later?" He couldn't bear to lose her now, the thought that he might, depressed him. She seemed to be staring straight at him, but she was perhaps looking at what was going on outside. She wouldn't be able to recognise him anyway, he reasoned. It was probably Anna, the policewoman, who said something to her and put a consoling arm round her shoulders. He wished that it was he who was sitting next to her and wondered, not for the first time, what her name was, and what her voice sounded like. The driver closed his window and set off at speed down the drive. He watched until after the car was out of sight and turned at the sound of footsteps in the gravel behind him. "No handcuffs," commented Paul. "No handcuffs," laughed Josh. They both had papers in their hands and spent the next few minutes comparing court dates. "I don't think that I am going to be able to keep this from the family," said Paul ruefully. "Did you ever tell them about the changes that were made?" asked Josh. "I thought it better not to."

"Very wise," came the reply. "Your mother hated you having money in this place before, didn't she?"

"Oh, I dread to think what I will have to face when she finds out what it has become, can I take refuge at your place, please?" They both ended up giggling like naughty schoolboys, trying not to laugh too loudly. "Did I see the lovely Scarlet being driven away just then?" Paul nodded and gave a sigh. Josh patted him on the shoulder, and they were both quiet for a few moments. Paul said, "You know what? I'm starving. I wonder if the restaurant is still open, or if everything has been closed. I could eat a large meal right now, how about we see what the state of play is?" Josh licked his lips, discovering that he, too, was hungry. "Now that you mention it, so am I. It works up quite an appetite, being arrested." They made their way to the main entrance, which was being guarded by a policeman. Surprisingly, it appeared the restaurant had been allowed to open and there were many members in there already, and after they had ordered, they joined some of the others until it arrived. There was, of course, only one topic of conversation. Some of the people were just there for lunch and hadn't been to the meeting; the news of what had been going on in the club had come as a shock to many of them, because very few knew about the different money-making schemes, most of which were illegal.

ELEVEN

Paul and Josh were sitting at a large table which was nearly full. Paul suggested, "We will have to have a vote very soon for people to run this place. There is the day-to-day running, ordering for the bars and the restaurant. We might have to have a temporary management. There are quite a few of us here, maybe we can go some way towards making a decision now?" This suggestion was met with approval from everybody there. "Is anyone willing to put themselves forward? On a temporary basis, of course?" asked Paul. "What about you, Jim? You're used to that sort of management, aren't you, can we twist your arm? Please?" There were nods of agreement from everyone and all the other members present were now standing round, joining in. Paul and Josh were eating as the discussions carried on around them. The member called Jim said, "Well, if you all agree, that's all right with me, but I don't think I could do it long-term, or on my own; how about the job, Pete, are you up for it?"

"I would be happy to," said Pete, who received a pat on the shoulder from the members around him. "Maybe we had better have a vote. Is everybody in favour of Pete and I running the club, until permanent managers can be found?" The vote was unanimous; the two men in question were looked on as safe pairs of hands. Pierre, the chef, had arrived by this time and, having been put in the picture about what had happened, became the third member of the temporary management team.

Later in the day, as Paul drove away from the club, he slowed as he approached the gate, and the policeman on duty waved him through. He gave a sigh of relief as he left the place behind, and the nearer to home he got the more his mood lightened, as it was finally sinking in that Scarlet was at last free, and safe. He needed some food. It was always an option to call in to see his parents, there would be a meal there for him, but he decided against, and after he had parked the car in the garage went out to the shops. There was a good selection near to his apartment, and he came back loaded with the supplies he needed. He hadn't a housekeeper at present so had the kitchen to himself. That didn't worry him because his mother had insisted that he learn to cook when he was a teenager. At first, he couldn't see the point, but it wasn't long before he started really enjoying cooking. It proved a particularly useful skill to have when he was at university, and a skill he excelled at. He also enjoyed cooking for himself, it was very calming after a busy day at work. His previous girlfriends had been thrilled that he cooked for them and were more than happy to eat at his apartment. After loading the dishwasher, he remembered a bottle of whisky, a rather expensive one, that a friend had given him for his birthday. Tonight was the ideal time to sample it and celebrate Scarlet being liberated from her captivity. Taking a sip he closed his eyes, revelling in the superb taste, and, taking the book he was reading over to the sofa nearest the windows, savoured both the drink and the view. He started wondering again what Scarlet's real name was. Where was she? What was she doing? What did she wear to bed? A nightdress? Pyjamas? Nothing? Now that thought woke his body up! She wore silk pyjamas when he had spent time with her when she wasn't well. He hoped that he would find out the answer sometime in the future, and also why she had all the gadgets with her; how had she managed that? He stood, saying, "Sweet dreams, darling girl." And drained his glass in a toast to her.

Paul dragged himself into the office the next day, but his mind was elsewhere. Nobody could get a word out of him, the staff speculating about the cause. He was well respected by everyone, and they didn't like the fact that something had upset him. He was always willing to help if they had problems and treated all who worked for him fairly. He stared moodily out of the windows in his office, but he wasn't seeing the spectacular view; he was deep in thought, his mind firmly on a certain young woman whom he had helped rescue the day before. Bette, his PA, was asked many times if she knew anything, as she was the one who had all the information about what was happening. She was in her forties and had worked for him for a few years. Paul looked on himself as being very lucky to have her working for him, and they had a very good relationship. She could ask him questions that nobody else would dare; she was also the only one on first name terms with him. There was a glass wall around the offices, and she was keeping a close watch. There were some letters that needed signing, so she took them into his office, hoping to possibly find out more. He signed them without checking what he was signing, which was totally out of character; he was always keen to check all that went out, despite knowing how efficient she was. She drew that to his attention. He looked up as though coming out of a trance. "Oh, yes you're right, I don't know where my brains are today."

"I've got to ask, Paul, but are you okay? Nothing wrong? We're all worried about you." He smiled at her. "I'm fine, thanks for the concern, but I'm waiting for an important phone call." He didn't enlighten her any further. "What are you doing at lunchtime? If you are staying in the office, do you want something ordering? There's that nice little takeaway that you like." His face brightened slightly at that. "Yes, that's a good suggestion, you know what I like off the menu, and see if anybody else wants lunch from there; it's on me."

"That will be very popular, thank you. Is the meeting about staffing levels still on this afternoon?" she asked, and after he had told her it was, she went to pass on the good news. There followed a discussion over the menu. Watching from his office it made him smile, and when they saw him looking, they gave the thumbs-up and mouthed their thanks. They were an excellent team, small considering the amount of work they did for him, and he had decided it was about time he increased the number. His company was growing both in profitability and size and was on course to expand; he was being careful not to expand too fast too soon and put the business at risk.

Paul's parents were both in finance, and wealthy. Before Paul started at university, he had borrowed money from his parents; they were very sceptical as to whether they would see it again and wrote it off. Some of his parents' aptitude must have rubbed off on him, because very soon he made enough through investing astutely to be able to repay them, and pay his way through university, as well as buying a large house, turning it into good-quality student accommodation, for him to live in and let out the rest. By the time he left university he had made a large amount of money and had added another larger block of good student accommodation.

Paul's parents had offered him a place in their business, but he wasn't sure that he wanted to be in finance exclusively, although the investments he had made were very profitable. Property had always fascinated him, so he went into developing. Quite unexpectedly one of his uncles died and left him a small airline, which was failing, but that just put another direction for his life in his way, even though the future for it looked bleak. There were six planes and two helicopters. The planes were old, looked run-down and every bit their age, and were costing the airline a fortune in repair bills. He sold the aircraft cheaply and negotiated a deal on two much newer second-hand ones, this time going for the private hire for higher end customers, had them resprayed and refitted with high-quality fittings. He kept the staff who had worked for his uncle, because, with a few courses to upgrade their knowledge, they were an experienced team. The helicopters were kept busy with private hire and contracts with film – and documentary – makers, so much so that it wasn't long before another one arrived, as well as another small jet to join the growing fleet. The business was getting a satisfying amount of work as private hire was becoming more and more popular with companies rather than using the bigger airlines. Limousine hire came next, so that the customers could be picked up at the door and taken to the nearest airport, to join either the helicopter or jet, whichever had been booked. The helicopter numbers had now risen to four, all of which were kept busy, and another plane, this time a new one, had been ordered. In one of the meetings Leanne, who dealt with bookings, said she had been asked if any of the planes had a bedroom, and she suggested that was considered when the decisions concerning the specifications for the fit-out were under discussion. The suggestion was received with enthusiasm from all the team assembled, and it was decided that would be a definite addition. The new jet had a much larger capacity for fuel and the engines were the latest models and much more energy efficient, so that it could take on longer flights without needing to refuel as often, so the bedroom could be a popular addition.

For some time, Paul had been buying run-down property in areas that were likely to be on the upwards trend, renovating and selling most of them on, mostly making a decent profit. The apartment block that he lived in had just been finished when he looked around the penthouse, thinking of buying, and he fell in love with the view over the Thames, and as there was no chance of anything being built to spoil the view it appealed to him. The building had fewer storeys, the height being one of the reasons that it had got planning approval, because the buildings behind would have lost their view of the river if the height had been greater. He asked if he could view the rest of the apartments, and later, after a bit of research, put in an offer for the whole building, and after a bit of haggling, bought it. He never got bored with the view; the change of light over the river was spectacular and seeing the city lit up at night reflecting in the river was just as amazing. A few of the buildings that he bought he kept and rented out – income from these was well worth the occasional trouble with tenants – as they were the ones where the value was rising quickly. Over the last few years, he had bought two old warehouses and converted them, with the advice of charities, into accommodation for the homeless. One of them was for families and the other for single people. He turned the running of them over to the charities – he felt that it was better for them to do that because they probably had more experience – but he kept monitoring them and visited every few months. He had gone down that route because when he saw people sleeping on the streets, the unfairness that they had nothing, and he had a luxurious lifestyle, made him want to give people a chance to move out of that kind of life, providing help for them to beat addiction, which seemed to be the reason many of them had ended up on the streets.

The warehouses were good-looking buildings and had been deteriorating through vandalism – there had been numerous fires in both – so he saw the purchases as saving two fine buildings from demolition. Losing buildings like them always spoiled the area, it never looked the same to him. The renovations were spectacular, making them good investments for the future, the building company having done a beautiful and sympathetic renovation, to an extremely high level of finish externally.

The meeting about staffing levels had come to an end, and it was nearing time for him to leave the office when his phone rang. This was not missed by Bette and the staff who were left.

TWELVE

Paul was tempted to snatch the phone up, but he closed his eyes briefly, took in a deep steadying breath, let it out and then, standing, went to look out over the city as he answered, "Anna, thanks for ringing, how is she?"

"She's fine, a doctor has checked her over. He did quite a few blood and swab tests. Apparently she had the same done a few days ago in her regular checks. The doctor commented in his report how underweight she is, but he said that being back with her family and friends should solve that problem, hopefully with no lasting damage. Her name, we have found out, is Chloe Winters. She's very subdued, but despite that has told us what went on in there in detail, an unbelievable amount of information. Even if the case against these people wasn't strong already, what she and the other girls have told us would convict them, just from that. The whole team collected to watch and listen to what she said on the video link, taking a lot of notes about more possible leads. It was a very emotional time for her, and for us. When we all discussed what we had heard afterwards, everybody had the same opinion; that she didn't tell us everything, that she was holding something back. But I'll be keeping in touch with her, so maybe she will eventually tell us more that can be used against these people. She is quiet and nervous around people, especially a crowd; I have had to be careful who is around for the moment, but she will come out of it. There were obviously going to be some issues created from being kept so isolated. I have been in touch with her parents, they can't wait to have her back. They had feared the worst, of course. She spoke to them briefly and broke down completely. I don't think she got much sleep last night, partly because she's not used to any noise, but mostly from excitement about seeing her family again. She is so restless, never sitting anywhere for long, but I suppose she will settle down eventually, when she gets home to familiar surroundings." She paused. "There's some good news and I'm afraid some bad news, which do you want to hear first?"

"Best get the bad news out of the way first. Go on, tell me the worst." He dreaded the answer. "She's engaged and would have been married by now. She had bought her wedding dress the day she was abducted. But things can change; you don't know how she will react to being back home," Anna added quickly. He was silent. It devastated him to hear that news. The fact that she might not want to meet him was a definite possibility, and he shouldn't forget that. "Are you still there?" Anna asked gently. She was only too aware of how he felt about Scarlet, that his feelings for her seemed to be very deep, and because of the way he had pushed to be able to meet her later. "Yes, I'm still here," he replied quietly, sounding totally dispirited. "What's the good news?"

"She wants to meet you."

"She does?" There was suddenly hope in his voice. "Oh,

that's something to look forward to, I suppose, but why would she want to meet me? When I'm part of what kept her imprisoned after all?"

He had asked Anna if she would find out how Scarlet would react to meeting up with him, because he wanted to apologise face to face for what she had been put through in there, in his name, as a member and therefore part-owner. Well, that was his story anyway. If he kept telling himself that enough times, it might sound true, even to him. The main reason was that it would give him a reason to meet up with her, maybe it could be stretched to several times. He wanted to know just what she was like; he hadn't heard her voice, didn't know her likes and dislikes. There was so much he wanted to find out. They didn't know each other at all and he wanted that situation to change, but he had to be prepared; they might not be compatible, which was a possibility, and a worry. But it would be a pointless exercise if she got married. It would have to be after he had been up in court himself, although the police had promised to ask for a lesser sentence, because what had been going on had been brought to their attention by him. It would also have to be carefully handled not to advertise that fact, so that there would be less chance of reprisals. "She wants to meet you to thank you for giving us the information that led to her rescue. I think that the isolation that she was kept in has affected her. We are a bit worried; she has said more than once that she has a vision of the place still having a hold on her, almost like a curse, ending up killing her in some way or other eventually. There have been some very dark thoughts going through her head. One thing always on her mind was, when they had no further use for her, what would happen then? Where would she end up? It sounds as if that preyed on her mind continually. I think that she was envisaging herself ending up somewhere that didn't look after her the way that she was cared for in the club, and that a great many more men would be involved. Oh, yes, she did appreciate the care that was taken of her. She did try to take her life one time, when an opportunity was put in front of her." Paul gasped in horror. "Fortunately, they were usually careful about not leaving anything that could be used in that way around, and the rooms were designed so that there were no opportunities; they got to her before she had time to do herself any damage and carry it out."

"Thank God for that!" Paul exclaimed. "She had all those worries before she was rescued and she thought that all the worries would be in the past, but I'm afraid that another one has taken over. She has commented that she thinks that no man could possibly want a relationship with her, because what could she say? Tell them the truth about what she had been involved with and have them run for the hills, or not say anything, and it end the same way when the story comes out, which it will in time, of course. I told the rest of the team what she said, and we all think that is connected to something else, to whatever she is keeping from us." Anna hoped that she wasn't talking out of turn, but while Paul was so keen, she thought that he ought to know what he had just been told, keeping her fingers crossed, hoping there wasn't any comeback. "I feel terrible hearing that, knowing I was part of it all," he said quietly. "But you didn't use that part of the club, until Scarlet! You also didn't know what was going on behind the scenes, did you? And you helped stop it when you found out, didn't you?" Anna told him. "Well, yes, I suppose I did. When will you be taking her home?"

"Tomorrow, as far as I know. I'll ring you again later, sometime after I get back, although it might not be this week."

"Thank you, you're being so kind to me, and I appreciate that very much. It's not as if I'm her family."

*

Anna and her colleagues had investigated Paul thoroughly before they agreed to introduce Paul to Chloe, after they had asked Chloe how she felt about the introduction. They wanted to be as sure as possible of his character, that they weren't introducing her to someone who would drag her back into the type of life she had just been rescued from.

Anna picked Chloe up from her hotel the next morning and, as she pulled out into the stream of traffic, asked, "Sleep well?"

"Not too bad. I was surprised to get as much as I did. I was so wound up, and my brain was too active to sleep all night, looking forward to seeing my mum and dad, catching up with my friends, I woke several times. It was noisy as well. I'm not used to that yet, the slightest noise disturbed me, after the quietness in there; it's strange because it's quiet where I live so really, I should be used to peace, but in there it was different, it became so oppressive. It will be so good to wake up in my own bed with the birds to wake me up. I wonder if anybody has been feeding them for me while I've been gone. There are so many varieties it's lovely to see them. I loved sitting watching what they were up to." The enthusiasm and animation in Chloe's voice as they travelled was so different from the subdued attitude since she had been rescued, as she talked about her home, family, and friends, making it evident how much she had missed them all, although Anna did think that she was not saying everything. Chloe hadn't mentioned Mark once while she was talking, and she still wasn't wearing her engagement ring. Anna turned off the road and stopped at a small café. "Let's stop for a drink, shall we?"

*

When we were settled with a coffee, Anna looked at me; oh dear, the Anna interrogation look, what now? "What's wrong? You seem worried about something. You can tell me if you are – you've been through a hell of a lot. It's only natural that there will be some worries for you. If I can help you, tell me." I said nothing for a minute, looking at my hands, tears suddenly rolling down my face; oh no, not again! It was time that I stopped acting like a victim; I had survived and needed to remind myself of that constantly. Anna took my hands in hers. "Tell me."

"It's Mark, my fiancé, soon to be ex-fiancé when I see him next time. He has been drinking a lot; he has hit me when he was drunk." This came as surprise to Anna. "How often?"

"A few times."

"Have you told anyone about this?"

"No, I haven't."

"Why?" I shrugged. "I don't know."

"What are you going to do?"

"Finish it. I don't want any more to do with him. I have put up with enough, both from him and when I was in there."

"Good for you, when did you make up your mind?"

"Before I was abducted. I called into the estate agents when I was with my friends and called off the sale of my house."

"But hadn't you bought your wedding dress that day?"

"It was beautiful, just what I had been looking for," I said, remembering it with sadness. "I went back to the shop and stopped the sale going through. My friends didn't know about that. I was going to be late back, and he was sending me some dreadful messages, so I knew he had been drinking and that I would end up with a lot of bruising, always where they wouldn't be seen, of course. I had decided that morning that I wouldn't go back home anyway, and I had been going to ring Mum and Dad when I got back to the car to clear it with them, but I was sure that it would be okay. I was going to tell him to move out the next day, that it was over between us, hopefully when he had sobered up. The thought of us living together really brought it all into focus, and I couldn't stand the thought of it, all the love that I had, or thought that I had for him, well, that was lost some time ago."

*

Anna felt very sorry for Paul, because it was so obvious how strong his feelings were for the beautiful, troubled girl sitting opposite. She wished that the situation was different for him. He had sounded so upset when she had passed on the bad news that Chloe was engaged, and they might have been married by now if the abduction hadn't taken place. Although after what Chloe had just told her, Paul might have a chance, but she wasn't going to say anything. She thought that he was hoping that the meeting would lead to at least friendship, although she was sure that he wanted much more than that, marriage was not out of the question the way he spoke about her, keeping that thought to himself.

*

We reached the turn from the motorway and eventually ended up driving down the main street of the small town, with me navigating. I couldn't wait to see my parents, the time since I had been freed seemed to have dragged. "This is a beautiful place to live, no wonder you were impatient to get back, is this yours?" Anna asked, indicating the house we had stopped at. "No, my parents'. I live just around the corner. Mark has been living there, thank goodness, he has done something useful, keeping it from being sold. I was so upset thinking that it could have been and there would be other people living in it, because a good offer had been made, that's always assuming that I had got free of that place. Although from what my mum told me she had no intention of letting it be sold. Are you okay with dogs? They have two sweet Labradors that will lick you to death given the chance." Just then the front door opened and the two dogs in question erupted out of the door and down the path, jumping up at the gate enthusiastically, their tails wagging madly. They were followed by my mum, who rushed up to me and threw her arms round me, hugging me tightly to her, sobbing into my neck. They had sent a small suitcase of clean clothes for me, so Anna took that out of the back of the car as well as the shopping that I had done. My dad finally managed to give me a hug, and then he surveyed me critically. "You have lost so much weight, we'll have to fix that." I grinned up at him; oh yes, a few of my mum's meals would hit the spot. I introduced Anna to the three of them. Mark hovered in the background, saying nothing, not so much as a hello! He was tasked to bring all my luggage into the house and upstairs. When he came down, he stayed in the background, looking sulky; I didn't want him around. When my mum heard that we hadn't stopped for lunch she insisted on making a meal for us all. Anna hadn't realised how hungry she was and was grateful. The talk was mostly between my parents and Anna. Mark sat there looking sullen, and I was getting sick of his attitude. I didn't add much to the conversation either, feeling withdrawn, listening, but not taking in much of what was being said, feeling as if I was in a world of my own, not really part of what was happening. I walked out to the car when Anna decided it was time for her to leave. She put her arms round me, giving me a big hug. "I don't know how to thank you. You've done so much for me. I wouldn't have coped without you." I was crying. Again! "I am such a crybaby these days."

"Give yourself time, you'll get there; it might take a while, but you will, I promise. I'll ring you tomorrow, and dry those tears, you're home again with your family, where you want to be."

THIRTEEN

I went back into the house after Anna had left and I felt somehow that my support had been taken away. She had been with me so much over the last few days, I had started to depend on her support, probably too much. I sat down and looked at my parents, feeling nothing but love coming from them and feeling so blessed; it hadn't been that long ago that I had almost resigned myself to never seeing them again. I wasn't sure how Mark was feeling; his face was a mask and unreadable, he hadn't said anything to me or hugged me, nothing. "What happened?" asked my mother very quietly. "If you don't feel like talking at the moment we'll understand, only when you're ready."

"I might as well tell you all of it now and get it over with." I then told them everything, well, almost everything, leaving some things out. They listened in stunned silence, wiping their eyes at times, and when I had finished, which was much, much later, just sat thinking about what they had just heard. It was a lot to take in for them and upsetting to hear. Mark sat with his head in his hands, staring at the floor. Finally he roused himself and said, in an aggressive voice, "But you didn't even try to escape, did you? Surely there must have been someone who would have helped you, wasn't there? Did you want to stay? Because it sounds to me as if you didn't make much of an effort to escape." At that my parents got up and went into the kitchen, no doubt to talk about what I had told them, and to leave us alone to talk, or not as it seemed now. I thought it was time I told him how I was feeling. "You were treating me very badly before I was abducted, and I got sick of being treated like a punchbag when you got drunk. That day I was going to end the engagement anyway. I had been going to come and stay at my parents' that night, I was afraid to go home. Imagine that; being afraid to go back to your own home! And how dare you accuse me of not wanting, or trying to escape, how dare you!" I repeated, and getting up, slapped him hard across his face. He staggered back, looking shocked, it was almost funny. I took the engagement ring out of my pocket, held my hand out, palm up, put the ring on it and said, "You had better have this back. As far as I am concerned the relationship and engagement are over, I never want to see you again. And I want you out of my house by the end of the week."

"But…" he said. "What?" I snapped. "I don't think can move out that soon, I haven't anywhere to go," he whined. "Tough. I want you out by the end of the week, deal with it. I don't care if you end up on the street." I held my hand out to him with the ring on it; I was proud of the fact that my hand didn't shake. He stretched out his hand to take it from me, thought better of it, and then taking a tissue out of his pocket, picked the ring up with it, wrapped it up, got his jacket and walked out of the house, and out of my life. He had treated me as if I was contaminated, that he would catch something nasty from just touching me. My hand chose that moment to start hurting, badly, my palm was red from the force I had slapped him with. I suddenly felt sick; my worst fears that I had told Anna about were coming horribly true. Was this how all men would feel about me? At some time, it would all come out about what had happened. Would I ever have a relationship again, of any kind? I didn't think that I would ever have the confidence to take the risk of being treated like that again and accept any invitations.

My parents came back into the room with cups of tea for the three of us; tea is always the thing to drink in times of stress. I told them what had gone on, that Mark and I were finished, and why. Neither of them said a word but they both came over and we had a group hug, which felt marvellous. I was crying, again, and we ended up sitting on the sofa, with me between them, their arms around me, just letting me cry. At last, I felt safe, for the first time since I had been abducted. "Will you stay with us for a while so that we can look after you?" my mother asked. "It's wonderful having you home again. We had almost given up hope of you ever being found, and I was expecting when the police rang for them to say that your body had been found. I couldn't believe it when they told me that you were alive. I just don't want to let you out of my sight." There were tears running down her cheeks. "I would love that, it will be great to spend time with you both, and I told Mark I wanted him out of my house by the end of the week. He told me that he had nowhere to go, that it might take him longer; well, I told him I didn't care if he ended up on the streets, I wanted him out, that I never want to see him again." My father found that funny. "That's my girl. We hadn't realised that you had taken your house off the market until Mike showed me a letter from the estate agents, confirming your decision.

The people that were buying it looked as though they were going to make a fuss about it and get nasty until I met them and explained the situation; they were very understanding after that."

Again, that night I lay missing my mystery man, this happened every night. However, I slept better than I expected, waking feeling rested and ready to face the world, well my small part of it anyway. There was a gentle knock at the door and my mother came into the room with a cup of coffee. She sat on the edge of the bed. "I can't believe that you are back with us again." And leaning over, gave me a hug, kissed me on the cheek and then went back downstairs, wiping her eyes. While sitting drinking my coffee I started planning and coming to a few conclusions. When I finally got downstairs for breakfast my mother told me she had decided to stay at home for a few days, to spend time with me. I appreciated that; it would be lovely just the two of us. I love my father dearly but sometimes it's good to have mother and daughter time together. "Mark rang earlier," she commented. "He said that he will move all his things out of your house today; a friend is coming with a van to help him. He's going to take another storage unit somewhere else and move all his things out of the one you both have. I didn't ask anything. It might be a good thing if you stayed here until he's finished and gone, unless you want to see him? He will put the keys through the letterbox here when he has finished. Is that all right?"

"Yes, that's quite all right, and no I don't want to see him again, I might contaminate him, I wouldn't want that, would I?" I replied bitterly. "We had no idea he was treating you so badly, why didn't you tell us?" She put her arms round me, and we stood like that for quite some time before I answered, "I don't know, I suppose I blamed myself. I usually kept out of his way when he was drinking, when I could. When he was moving in with me, it made me realise that I was going to have to do something, not just leave it as it was, because he would be with me all the time, and I didn't think I would cope. The messages he was sending, when I was late back with the girls, were unpleasant. It was obvious he would start when I got home, so I was going to ring and check if I could stay with you two when I got back to the car. Well, you know what happened." During the morning I think she was watching me very closely; I couldn't settle to do anything. "Do you want to talk about it?" she asked. "About what?"

"Whatever is making you so restless. If you know what's causing it, talking about the problem might help a little. If it's something that embarrasses you, I have a broad mind, I won't be shocked, but I think you know that. It's just the two of us." We had always been close and been able to talk about any topic, including sex when I was younger. I decided to tell her what was on my mind. "No drugs showed up on any of the tests that were done on me at the hospital, after I was rescued, thank goodness, but I feel as though I have been hooked on drugs and gone cold turkey – not that I have any experience – and I feel as if part of my life is missing, not necessarily a good part. Do you think, and I know this sounds odd even to me to say this, don't laugh, but do you think that it's the sex that I'm missing? I would have thought it would be the opposite, and not want anything to do with men ever again. Several men were having sex with me every day, it was the regular routine, no days off; surely, I haven't become addicted, that's too weird to contemplate." She looked at me, a thoughtful look on her face. "I don't really know what to say, did you ask when you had therapy? It might be something to ask the doctor, see what he says. But whatever your dad and I can help you with, we'll be here for you. I'm sorry but I don't feel that I have been any help." I went and put my arms round her; it was so good to talk to her about my worries and know she wouldn't ridicule me about what I had told her. I told her more about when I was booked by the men, what went on. There was also the subject of the mystery man – I refused to think of him as a client – who I had fallen in love with. I took a deep breath and told her about him. "There was a man, he started booking me for the night, the first time for the evening. There were no handcuffs, no restraints, no collar when I was with him. The hood stayed, but…" I couldn't say anymore, the tears had started again as I spoke. I closed my eyes, thinking back to those nights, to those surprisingly wonderful nights. My mother just held me close, saying nothing until I could speak again. "I spent the night before the police raid with him. He had never spoken to me before then, but that morning when they came to take me back to my room, he leaned close to my ear and said, Thank you. That was all. I got the feeling he would have said more, but the carers came into the room. The problem was that I had fallen in love with him. How? We had never spoken to each other, I didn't know anything about him, I wouldn't have recognised him because of wearing the hood. I always thought that because I was so starved of any kind of contact or affection, that was to blame."

"And?" asked my mother, looking at me with, I thought, a knowing look on her face. I looked at her and giggled, did she know, or was she fishing for more information? "Well, the sex was pretty good," I said, hardly daring to look her in the face, it was a bit embarrassing after all. "No, it was more than that, I can honestly say that I have never had nights like those, ever!" When I looked at her again her face was unreadable, and she said quietly, "I never saw that look on your face when you were with your other boyfriends and talking about them. He must have been incredibly special. Do you know who he is? If you are likely to see him again?" I shook my head. "This is what's been bugging me, the fact that I might not, but strangely the police informant has been in touch with the police several times to ask me if I would meet up with him. He says he wants to apologise face to face for what happened to me in there. It makes me wonder, but I daren't think along those lines, I could get very hurt." My mother must have decided to change the subject because I was getting upset again. "I rang the estate to tell them you are back at home at last, they were thrilled. They will be glad to have you back, but the message is to take as much time as you need." We left the talking at that; I felt as though it had helped, discussing my thoughts with her.

Sometime later in the day I had taken the dogs out for a walk, going in the opposite direction to where my house was, when my phone rang; Anna. I was so pleased to hear her voice. "Hi Anna, how are you? How was your drive back?"

"Good thanks, the traffic wasn't too bad, I'm glad to say. How about you?"

"Well, I ended the engagement, like I said I would. But when I told them about what had happened, he treated me as if I were contaminated. There was so much revulsion on his face, it was, it was horrible! It made me realise…" I was sobbing by this time. "It feels as though that place has put a curse on me, I know that sounds crazy. What would

I say to any man about what happened? If I told them, was honest, they would leave me, heading for the hills without a backwards glance, probably calling me all sorts of names, and if I didn't say anything and it came out, which it will at some time, well…" I didn't want to finish the sentence. Anna didn't say anything for a minute. "I can't imagine what that must have felt like. I don't know what to say, I am so sorry it turned out like that, but you sound as if you have done the right thing. How do you feel? Now that you have."

"A bit numb surprisingly, but I haven't any regrets."

"Good, when are you going back to work?"

"Next week. I wanted a chance to get used to being back at home again and spend time with my parents and friends. My mother has taken a few days off, but my dad couldn't because he had a big case to work on."

"That sounds like a good plan to me. I'll ring again if there are any developments this end, look after yourself." I remembered a question that had been on my mind, and I had always forgotten about it until after I had finished talking to Anna. "Before you go, can I ask you something?"

"Yes, anything."

"How did the gang pick on me? Or was it just random? Has anything been found out during the investigation?"

"Nothing has been said about that, but the two who abducted you haven't been let out on bail, or been up in court yet, so I will make enquiries. I had better make a note, otherwise I will forget. I'll tell you if I do."

*

After Anna rang off, she made a note about Chloe's question. And then sat tapping her fingers on the desk in indecision, looking at her phone. It rang before she picked it up, she looked at the number and smiled. "I was just going to ring you, Paul. What can I do for you?" *As if I didn't know*, she thought to herself. "Just to know how Chloe is, that's all. It was yesterday you took her home, wasn't it?"

"It was, and I have just spoken to her. She's doing all right and taking some time off before going back to work. Her mother is spending a lot of time with her, taking her out and about to get her used to being back home. She has a lovely family, and good friends, very close, they will help her a lot."

"Spending time with her fiancé I suppose, planning the wedding again," he said bitterly. "No, actually it's off."

"What, the wedding?" he said, not sounding all that enthusiastic. "No, she's ended it with him, both the engagement and the relationship, so she's a free agent again." She thought it was probably better not to mention what else Chloe had told her. Anna was nearly deafened by the whoop of joy that came over the phone, she was laughing at the reaction at the other end. "Have a care for my ears, please, I'm surprised I can hear anything after that."

"You really have made my day, and yes, I understand it might not come to anything anyway. But thank you." He was mightily pleased that he was alone in the office; they would think he had gone mad. He went home and slept better than he had for a while. After a celebratory drink of course.

*

I had just finished talking to Anna when my phone rang again. This time it was Stephanie, one of my closest friends.

"I couldn't wait to speak to you. I was wondering… if it's too soon, say so, but we are all desperate to see you, tonight, if you have nothing else planned. Will you? Please say yes." It didn't take long to decide. "That would be wonderful, just what I need, a catch-up with you all. After all that's happened to me, getting back to normality will be good. I'm not back in my own place yet, Mark is moving out today, and I am at my parents' until he's gone."

"I'll pick you up, and then you can tell us about Mark, and we want to know about what happened after you were abducted. Is seven all right?" I realised I was going to be thoroughly interrogated about what had happened between Mark and me; it could get uncomfortable, and how much to tell them? I decided that I would tell them everything about what had happened between us. And there was what happened after I was abducted. I decided to keep some of what happened to myself, for now. Naturally, they would want to know all the gory details. I was going to have to get used to talking about my experiences. I had only spoken to the police, my parents and, of course, Mark, so far, and as they were all good friends it might be easier to start with them.

Stephanie picked me up and took me to a friend's home which was a short drive away. When I walked into the room there was silence as they looked at me. "What's the matter?" I asked. "My God, Chloe, what did they do to you in there? The bastards! You look so thin and pale, not like you looked before, and your hair, it's grown so long, but it looks fantastic and suits you." They all crowded round me, and I got a hug from each of them. It was wonderful to be back with them all, it was an emotional reunion. Sandra tapped her glass for attention. "Girls, I think our mission, if we choose to accept the challenge, is to help Chloe put on more weight, what do you think, are we up to the job?" There was a deafening shout of agreement. After glasses had been refilled and food handed round, all eyes focused on me; a rabbit in the headlights came to mind, and I almost expected them to shine a light in my eyes to interrogate me further. I hate being the centre of attention, even with a group of my dearest friends, and as usual it was Beth who came and sat next to me. I love them all very much, but we seemed to gravitate towards each other, possibly because we were a bit more alike in our thinking and were the quietest of the group. It was usually Beth who would be at my house or I at hers for coffee. Sometimes we met up at the little coffee shop we had all met at the day I was abducted. "Before you talk about what happened after you were abducted, we want to know what happened to you and Mark. Come on, we need details, spill the beans." This was Melanie, always the bossy cow, trust her, but swallowing hard I told them everything, including the abuse. Get that out of the way. They were horrified, and there were many comments about what they would like to do to him. It got rather gory at times, and of course a lot of asking why I hadn't finished it earlier, which was a fair point. There was a silence after that as what had been said was absorbed.

FOURTEEN

"What happened after you were abducted?" asked Sandra. Her husband was a policeman and I wasn't sure whether he had got any information that he had passed on to her. It was her wedding present we had met up to buy, the day I had gone missing. After another mouthful of wine, I told them all that had happened, well, almost everything. Telling them about being drugged, that the first thing I was aware of when coming round was a very clinical medical room, being tied down, gagged, told to stay silent, forbidden to talk anymore, about the many medical tests, not to mention the collar and chain, handcuffs and the vile sparkly harness, and the name I had for myself when wearing it. They found that hysterically funny. "But how did they tell you what to do? Where to go? What was happening?" asked Beth. I told them how any messages were relayed to me, and nothing about what was going on. "So, what did you wear?" asked Louise. "I was dressed in either pyjamas or a nightdress when I was put to bed and after breakfast I was undressed, given a shower, and they put on the collar with the chain attached, my hands handcuffed behind my back, and that was it."

"Nothing else?" Louise asked, looking horrified, her eyes looking even larger than they did normally. "Nothing else," I replied, trying to keep a straight face at her expression. "I would die of embarrassment," she said with a shudder. "I wouldn't be able to cope with that."

"I wasn't exactly thrilled. I have never been happy naked, I had no choice." I told them about losing all control of your life, you were there to do with what they wanted, and everything was geared to make you realise who was in control. I told them about the isolation, no communication, and about the suits the care team wore, with hoods and masks over their faces, so that it was impossible to know who I was dealing with. About two people escorting me everywhere, and when the men were having sex with me, being shackled, a hood over my head, probably to protect the identities of the men; apparently there were a lot of influential men who maybe would lose a lot through the connection to the club. My 'client' list, apparently containing the names of some immensely powerful and wealthy men, that they gave me a copy, and it was sitting unopened in a drawer, and did I really want to know? "It must have been weird wearing a hood, what was that like?" asked Stephanie. I thought about what to say. "Yes, it was weird at first and I assumed it was all about identities, but in a strange way it made the whole thing a little easier to cope with, surprisingly. I found I wasn't as embarrassed as I expected, because I didn't have to look them in the eyes when they had sex with me. That does sound odd to say, but it did deflect some of their bad breath as well." They all laughed loudly at that, pulling faces at the thought. What I didn't say was that it also helped to hide the looks of revulsion and hatred of them all that must have been on my face at the time. "What were the hoods made of?" Stephanie asked. "Was the fabric very thick?"

"It was light, and I could see shapes but not details through it. I had thought it would be hot, but it wasn't. I did realise that the life I had was not as bad as girls usually have who are sex workers, sometimes being beaten into submission or starved until they did what their pimps wanted, and many more men than any of us did, and becoming addicted to drugs, so keeping the girls in line. The rooms that we had were beautifully furnished, they were like a five-star hotel. As for the meals, we had a choice from the same menu that was used in the restaurant, the food was beautiful. We had brilliant health care, and regular blood and swab tests done, as did all the members that used that part of the club. If they couldn't produce an up-to-date certificate, they weren't allowed access to us, so that hopefully everyone was protected. The medical room was very well set up with equipment, and I think that they could do small operations. Apparently, we each had our own page on the club website and all the results were put on that. Another thing I was very thankful about was that we weren't given drugs, so we didn't become addicted, that would have been dreadful, but I suppose we were controlled very closely, and weren't going anywhere, so drugs weren't necessary." There was silence after I had stopped talking: they all looked stunned.

The atmosphere lightened, however, when we started talking about more general topics, what had been happening while I had been away, and looking at Sandra's wedding video, which made us all laugh at times. It was sad not to have been there, a part of the celebrations. Altogether it was a good night, even if it had been more than a bit upsetting. After I was dropped off at my parents' I went straight to bed, and after a short read, settled down and slept very well, waking feeling refreshed, although my head was a bit fuzzy, but not too bad considering how long it had been since I had drunk anything alcoholic.

The next day Mark dropped off the keys to my house with his key to the storage unit, and I made up my mind to go and see what needed doing before I moved back. It was good to be staying with my parents, and I loved it, but I was getting too comfortable. So, after a quick lunch I found myself at my front door, and if I was honest, surprisingly, feeling a bit reluctant to open it. I had decided to go on my own, even though my mother had offered to go with me. Taking a deep breath, I unlocked the door and crept in, almost as if I expected him to be waiting, letting the breath out when nothing happened. I was listening to the silence; here in my own home it was welcoming. I stood leaning against the wall, looking round, taking everything in, making a mental inventory of all that was there, nothing had changed, although there was a small box in the top corner with a light on; an alarm sensor? I tried not to make it obvious that I was looking at it, but where had it come from? Was it an alarm? I thought that it might be, but it could have a camera inside. I walked further into the living room; all was as it should be, nothing out of place, looking just as it had done, like my home again before Mark arrived in my life, but with another alarm sensor? I walked around touching everything, picking things up, getting to know my home again. I checked the kitchen, looked in the fridge and made a list of shopping that would need doing. The freezer was almost empty and needed defrosting, so there was more to add to the increasing number of items to be bought, and to be done. There was an alarm in there, too.

Looking outside, the garden showed signs that my parents had kept it in good shape, and the feeders for the birds had been filled up. It was good to be doing things that seemed so normal and every day, I felt that I was relaxing a little bit. I went upstairs; the bed was made up with clean bedding. The bedroom looked wrong to me and then I grinned to myself. Of course it didn't look completely normal, it was tidy, which wasn't usual when I was around, there was after all nothing on the floor waiting to be hung up. Oh well, when I moved back in, normality would be restored. I am not naturally a tidy person, I have only to be in a room for a few minutes and it ends up untidy. There was an alarm in there, too. I suddenly caught a smell that I had noticed downstairs that I couldn't identify, and then it came to me: Mark's aftershave. I went into the bathroom; it was stronger there. I would open the windows wide when I was going to be here longer, I wanted that gone. An alarm sensor in there too? Really? I looked in the bathroom cabinet and then the bedroom, looking in drawers and wardrobes, giving a sigh of relief when I realised he had left nothing, not a trace of him remained, apart from the aftershave, which would soon fade, as it was only slight. All that was left were my own clothes. I looked in the second bedroom, a sensor in there, also on the landing; they were everywhere. I caught sight of myself in the bathroom mirror; the changes in me were small, but there, most of them in my head, but there were bound to be changes after what had happened to me. For some reason I kicked off my shoes and went and sat on the bed, leaning against the headboard, looking out of the window. It had been a long time since I sat like this, looking at the view of the garden; so much water under the bridge. Suddenly I started to cry and curled into the foetal position, not just a few tears but in a way I couldn't remember ever doing before, sobbing hysterically it seemed at times, really letting go of my emotions. When it seemed that there were no more tears to come, I felt exhausted, both mentally and physically and I must have gone to sleep, because my phone woke me. It was dark, how long had I been asleep? When I answered, my mother, sounding worried, was on the other end. "Where are you? The meal is ready."

"I am so sorry, I called in at home, I'll be there in a minute." I made my way back. *I must go to the storage unit next and get my things delivered back to me*, and so thinking arrived at my parents' front door. Another thing that I must do was to get that alarm removed, and probably replaced, not a bad idea to have an alarm system, but one that I had put in. I knew I was being paranoid but there had been cameras all over the club, watching; I felt that although I knew that I was being totally irrational I wouldn't feel comfortable living back at home until they were gone. There might be cameras inside the sensors; I didn't trust Mark at all. I would have the locks changed as well; I didn't want him to have any access.

The next day I called the locksmith to ask him for a quote; he would be able to see me later that afternoon. Now, about the alarm system, I didn't get the company Mark had employed, obviously, but one that had been recommended to me. They could come just before lunch as they were working not far away. When the man came about the alarm system, he introduced himself as Mark! Oh dear, another Mark. He walked round the house with me, looking at where the sensors were placed, a puzzled look on his face. "Why are there so many?" he asked. "I have no idea; these were installed by somebody else."

"They are very new; they don't seem to have been in long. Do you really want them all taking out?" his look saying this woman is mad if she does. "I could use some of what is here to save you some money." "I want everything taking out and a completely new system putting in, starting from scratch." He looked at me again as if I was crazy; let him think what he wants. We toured the house again, with him telling me where he recommended the sensors were to be placed. His suggestions seemed logical, so he left, promising me he would get back to me quickly with a quote for the work, as I had told him I wanted the job to be done as soon as possible. The locksmith called me not long afterwards to ask me that, if it was all right, he could come around in about ten minutes, rather than later. After he had given me a price, he told me the job could be done the next morning, which was fine. I would have to be there later because the storage company were delivering what I had been storing with them that morning, so there was only the alarm system to sort out. Mark had rung to tell me the cost; he would give me a written quote and be able to do the job for me in two days.

Mark was fitting the new alarm system and I was sitting talking to one of my friends on the phone, when he knocked on the lounge door. I told my friend that I would ring her back. "Sorry to disturb you, but I thought that you should see this." He put the pieces of one of the sensors on the coffee table and picked up one of them to show me. "There are cameras in quite a few of them, both bedrooms, bathroom and the shower room downstairs among them." I went cold inside. What had Mark been doing while I was away? And was he hoping for something to see later? What a scary thought. I was so glad that I would have no further dealings with him. "I was afraid that there was a possibility, you can see why I was so adamant to have the original alarm out, can't you? I didn't trust the man who had them put in. Were those put in as a later addition? Or were they bought like that?"

"Put in later," he said. I made him a coffee and then he went back to work. After he had gone, I rang my mother. "The man putting the alarm in has just shown me one of the sensors he had taken out, and I was right to be worried, there were cameras in some of them." She didn't say anything straightaway; my parents had thought I was being more than a bit paranoid about the subject but had been careful not to say too much. "I don't know what to say, but you are definitely better off without him. Will you move back as soon as the work on the alarm is finished? Not that I want you to move back yet, we love having you back home with us again."

"This is going to sound even more paranoid, but do you think that Dad knows anybody that can scan the place for more hidden equipment?" I had moved out into the garden so that nobody could overhear me. There was a pause at the other end of the phone. "I'll ask him, how much longer will you be?"

My dad came up trumps with the name of somebody who could help and some days later, when I crawled into bed, it was my own bed this time, the first time that I had slept in it since I had been abducted. So much had happened to me since then and the house had been given a clean bill of health, no further equipment had been found.

I decided to call into work to see everyone and get the initial meetings over with before I went back. My colleagues and I had spoken on the phone often, so that I had been brought up to date with all the happenings, but I hadn't seen some of them face to face since I had returned home. They were all stunned to hear about Mark and I having broken up, and wanted to know if we would get back together again later. I told them it was finished between us, his treatment and reaction having made it impossible for a reconciliation, as far as I was concerned. Wondering what was going on, the boss's son put his head round the office door and as soon as he saw me, with a smile on his face came and gave me a big hug. "We have all missed you so much. Have you got time to come up to the house? I know my parents will never forgive me if I let you go and not tell them." He then apologised to everyone for taking me away. We made our way up to the house and as we walked, I enjoyed seeing the gardens and the surrounding area. It seemed like years since I had been here last. As the gardens were open to the public, they were busy with visitors, there were plenty of photographs being taken. We made our way to the kitchen, which was always the gathering point. He opened the door and announced, "Look who I've found!" and then opened the door dramatically so that they could all see me. As soon as they saw me, I was ushered in and it was hugs from all of them, it was a little embarrassing. I was made to sit down and a mug of coffee and a plate with a large piece of delicious cake were put into my hands. I was overwhelmed with the attention. "It was horrible after you went missing, wasn't it, Phil?" said Jane, my employer. "The atmosphere was so sombre; everybody was expecting the worst news. Sandra had been trying to ring you, about something she had forgotten that she thought you ought to know, but your phone was switched off. Mark had got worried when he had tried ringing your mobile as well and had come to the same conclusion. He went to look for your car and found it still in the car park, so he went back to your house for your spare keys. But you will have been told all this, won't you?"

"I haven't heard any of this side of the story, please tell me what was happening."

"Mark started ringing all the friends you had been with, including Sandra. Of course, she told him about trying to ring you as well, and after he heard that he rang the police. I don't think that they took it too seriously at first because it hadn't been all that long. They did check the car, nobody had touched it. The cameras on the street showed you leaving your friends and walking along the street towards the car park. The film does show somebody, leaving the coffee shop before you all did and walking towards the car park, it also shows another man who had been standing across the street follow you. There were no cameras after the turning off the main street, but because of what happened, cameras have been installed. When they looked at the cameras in the car park a white van was shown parked behind you when you left your car in the morning. One man got out and followed quite close behind as you went to meet your friends, and then onto the train. The two men joined up later in the town, and when the police started to investigate seriously, they looked at the cameras in the shopping centre and they were following you. They thought that the two men hoped to have a chance to snatch you if the opportunity arose. The van was picked up much later where it had stopped on the side of the road. There could have been an argument between the two men because the one that had been in the back was dragged out by the driver onto the road and then got into the front. The van wasn't seen again. There were searches and appeals for information on the television and social media and following that a woman came forward to say that she thought that she saw you with two men, you seemed to be finding it difficult to walk. She had stopped to ask if you were all right and was fobbed off by one of them with an accent, telling her that you had drunk too much at lunchtime. She accepted that and went home, but she couldn't give any descriptions unfortunately. When your friends thought about it, they all checked the photos that had been taken that day, and one of them in the coffee shop showed a man sitting at the back, seeming to be taking pictures as well as talking to somebody. The police think that he was one of the kidnappers." I had been listening to this in silence, it sounded like a plot for a crime drama. "They were getting nowhere with the investigation, so the search was scaled down. The police have been wonderful and so supportive of your parents and Mark. Until eventually, much, much later, when the future looked very bleak, there was an excited phone call from your mother saying that you had been found safe and well, that a brothel had been raided and you were found there. We were all very thankful. There were a lot of tears shed about you, prayers had been said in church when you went missing and more said again to celebrate your being found."

FIFTEEN

Walking back home, I couldn't understand why I was feeling so depressed again. I should be revelling in being back in my own home, thrilled to be back with my family and friends, something I had desperately wanted for so long. What was wrong with me? There was a bench by the path round the lake, my favourite, where I sat on many occasions to have my lunch, and I sat down looking at the view and the tears began to fall. Again. It was as I had talked about to my mother, that I was suffering from withdrawal symptoms. It was hard to think that maybe I was missing the sex. I couldn't make any sense out of that idea, the fact that those men raped the other girls and me, I really didn't think that I would want to have a relationship of that kind ever again. Maybe it was time to have more counselling? I had been offered more; I might get some answers. I had been told by the police doctor that the blood tests showed no trace of any drugs. Thank goodness I hadn't ended up addicted, which had been entirely possible. I was so relieved. I looked up the phone number that I had been given, and I felt better having made a positive decision. I hadn't mentioned how I was feeling to anyone before, apart from my mother, so I suppose it was good to talk to somebody else again. Maybe I was starting to heal at last; it had been surprising to me how unbelievably difficult it had been settling back into home and life. It had been in my mind that once home all my fears would go away, but how wrong I had been. The old fears were replaced with new ones, along with hallucinations, flashbacks, violent nightmares, and panic attacks. The person that I spoke to was kind and made an appointment for me with the person that had seen me before. I had found her quite easy to talk to. I hoped that it would help speaking to her again.

Anna and I spoke on the phone quite often; she was keeping me up to speed on what was happening with the case. One day she rang to tell me the court cases concerning the other members had just finished that day. "How did your informant go on?" I asked. "Like most of them, he was sentenced to a jail term which was suspended, but if he behaves himself, he will be in the clear. You are still all right about meeting, aren't you? He has been on the phone already, asking me to set up the meeting between you two as soon as possible. He is so keen to see you. We checked him out very thoroughly before agreeing to ask you, all checks came back clear. He seems to be one of the good guys. How do you feel? You can say no to this meeting."

"I have so much to thank him for, I have my life back because of him, the other girls have, too. I just can't figure out why he would want to meet me, and just to say thank you to him seems a bit inadequate for what he has done." I still couldn't figure out why he was so insistent on meeting me, and the possible reason popped into my mind, again. I didn't dare dwell on it too long, I could be completely wrong, upsetting if I was. "There are some other people desperate to meet you as well," said Anna, breaking in on my thoughts. "Really? Who?" I asked, mystified. "Your care team from The Harem. You don't have to, but I know that there will be some disappointed people if you don't. They say they loved looking after you and tried as much as they could to make your life easier. They had all come to love you and wanted to see you as you really are. They do know that seeing them could bring it all back and could upset you, so they will understand if you don't feel strong enough." I thought back and smiled when thinking of the small but important things that they had done for me, and yes, their help had made my life much more bearable; the smallest things they did were magnified many times. I hadn't been able to see them anyway, so I wouldn't recognise anybody. "I would love to meet up, to put faces to the people who did so much for me. I don't think they will ever realise just how much difference they made to my life. I owe them a big debt of gratitude, I don't know how I would have survived without them and their care."

"There are a few things that we would like to talk to you about, tie up some loose ends, so you could meet them all then if you would like to come down here?" We decided on the following week and I would take a couple of days' leave. We discussed which train I would get, and she told me she would meet me at the station.

I surfaced from the nightmare that kept coming back regularly and shot up in bed, panting as though I had run a marathon. My pyjamas were soaking wet and my hair was plastered to my head. I shivered; the bedroom was warm, but the cold feeling went all through me as I looked around at the familiar surroundings of my home. My heart rate finally slowed, from feeling that it was going to jump out of my chest, and my breathing slowed as well. Peeling my pyjamas off, I had a quick shower, took a clean pair out of the drawer, and put them on. That felt a million times better. These nightmares were becoming more frequent, and it was mostly the same one. After reading for a short while my head started to nod, so without much hope of getting any sleep, I put my book down. I woke up later having slept quite well, much to my surprise.

I walked up the platform to the gate from the train and saw Anna waiting for me. It was so good to see her again. We hugged and then set off to the exit. "I got a taxi, the parking is non-existent both here and at the hotel, and talking about the hotel, I have a surprise for you." I hadn't heard the address she had given to the driver before we left the station, so I stared when we stopped outside a very smart hotel and looked at her with raised eyebrows. "Here?" I asked. "How is that possible? I am sure that funding for accommodation would never cover somewhere like this!"

"No, it's being paid for by our informant, as a thank you for agreeing to meet him. Well, say something!" I was speechless, what could I say? But why had he done this? By this time, we were standing on the pavement outside the hotel, the taxi having driven off. "What can I say but wow! I don't think I am dressed well enough to stay here." After I signed in, we went to find my room. It was beautiful and turned out to be a small suite. I was speechless, again. "It's a bit like the room I had at the club, bringing back memories," I said to Anna. She looked at me with a frown on her face. "I hadn't thought of that," she said. "Will you be okay? It won't be too much of a problem, will it?"

"Oh, just ignore me, I'm just being silly. I'll be fine. But what is this about? What does he want from me? Has this man got an ulterior motive? Are there strings attached to this generosity?" Again, I got that feeling, but pushed it out of my mind with difficulty. Anna came and put her hands on my shoulders. "Slow down, and let me get a word in. All I know is what I have told you. And changing the subject a little bit, will you meet your care team tomorrow morning?" I took a deep breath. "Sorry about going off like that, but you know how scared I am about ending up back in that place, or somewhere like it, ending up as a slave again, and yes, it will be good to meet them."

"I can't imagine what you must go through, and will you meet our informant in the afternoon?"

"I am so nervous about meeting him, how old is he? Has he got a girlfriend? What does he look like? Not that it matters, I suppose, it's only a meeting." Anna looked at me and grinned. "What did that look mean?" I asked. Anna pushed me into a chair and went to get a bottle of orange juice out of the fridge, holding it up for my approval. I nodded and, pouring the orange into a glass, she handed it to me. "Drink it and calm down. We checked on everything he told us and it's all good, no lies. I can say he is not married; he was engaged and like you, not far off getting married, but he called the marriage off and ended the relationship some time ago. He hasn't got a girlfriend at the moment, and, as for what he looks like, well, you will have to wait and see, won't you?" she said, laughing. I told her she was a spoilsport. "What are you going to do for dinner? You could eat in the restaurant or order from room service, and whatever you want charge it to the room number." I grinned and commented, "I could run him up a large bill, couldn't I? I'll probably order from room service, and then have an early night." I decided to mention something that had been on my mind just lately. "I've been getting paranoid thinking that I'm being followed. I don't feel safe going out on my own anymore, it always feels as though I'm being watched, probably followed as well. I did think that it comes from hearing about the way that I was abducted, they managed it so easily, and I think it has been preying on my mind. There have been some strange messages on my phone at work, and on my mobile. How they got my phone numbers and at work as well I really don't know, it's a mystery. They have been text and voicemail. I handed her the phone so that she could read and listen to them for herself. She looked thoughtful, saying, "Some of these are quite nasty, aren't they? Have you any idea who is sending them? Any clues, do you recognise the voice, or from what they are saying that could pinpoint somebody? How about Mark? Leave it with me, I'll see what I can find out." It was arranged that she would come for me after breakfast to do the introductions and I would wait for her in reception.

I ventured down to the dining room for breakfast and was shown to a table where I could indulge in one of my favourite pastimes, people watching. I find it fascinating, and something that I had missed doing when I was locked up. Looking at the time I suddenly realised time had moved very quickly; Anna would be coming soon but I had no idea where the meeting would be held.

We went to a small café just nearby and were shown through to a private room where we wouldn't be disturbed. As soon as we entered a group of people got up and came over to us, crowding round me. Anna had stepped back out of the way. They all hugged me enthusiastically. There was a lot of emotion on both sides. It seemed strange that these people had cared for me so well for so long, and I didn't recognise any of them. One of the women stepped forward, she seemed to have taken on the role of spokesman. She stood looking at me and I smiled at her. She put her hands to her mouth and said in broken English to the others, "Oh, she's smiling, how wonderful." One of the others was translating what was being said for those who obviously couldn't understand. She came and took my hands, gently wiping away a tear, it was such a lovely gesture it made me cry more. "My name is Maia, and we never saw you smile. You always looked so sad, it broke our hearts to see you like that, being kept and made to live as you were, with no freedom. We hope that you can smile all the time now. You were very much loved by all of us. We felt your loss after you were rescued, but to think of you being back with your family made it easier." I struggled to say anything at first, the lump in my throat was so big. I swallowed and squeezed Maia's hand. "I can't tell you how happy I am to be back with my family and friends, so yes, I can smile now. I can't thank you enough for making my life so much easier with your care. I don't think you realise how much getting my gadgets back helped. You must have had to fight extremely hard to get them back for me. I was going mad with boredom, I had far too much time to think. They made such a difference." Maia smiled at me. "We did possibly exaggerate just little, but not much, because we said that we were worried about your mental state, that you were not well, which was not a complete lie, because we were."

"Oh, bless you," I said. "The flowers you put in my room were always beautiful and very welcome. I loved those, as well as everything you did for me, I did notice. I was always so touched by all you did, and I don't know what to say. I am so grateful to have met you all, so that I can thank you face to face." The tears were flowing again, and I had to look for a handkerchief; of course, I hadn't got one, had I? I shouldn't go anywhere without a box of them these days. A tissue was found, and by this time the drinks that Anna had ordered had arrived. "I'll pay for these," I said to Anna. "No, they are already paid for."

"Let me guess, or do I need to?" The smile on her face said everything. It appeared they were in this country illegally, having been, most of them, trafficked from eastern Europe. Their cases were under review as to whether they would be allowed to stay. Most of them wanted desperately to get back home and would be helped with that; the others, including Maia, were waiting anxiously for the decision. I felt so sorry for them, they were as much victims as the other girls and myself and I knew exactly what they must be feeling. Anna and I left after we had all had lunch. Talking had lasted longer than planned. It was nearly time for me to meet 'My Saviour' as I had started calling him.

SIXTEEN

Paul was feeling a mixture of excitement and anticipation about seeing Chloe; he was also surprisingly nervous about the outcome today. He had held many important meetings for his business, but for him there was far more depending on this personally than any of those. He knew what he wanted out of it, but would she feel the same way? He had been restless and had arrived early, not having been able to settle to anything during the morning, unable to put the thoughts of seeing her out his mind, spoiling his concentration for anything. Finally, giving up, he told his PA that he would probably not be back that afternoon. When he arrived at the hotel, he was still a bit early but scanned the lounge to see if Anna and Chloe were there. He spotted them; Anna was sitting blocking his view of Chloe. Anna looked at her watch and got up to leave the room. As she did, he stepped forward to meet her. After they had exchanged greetings, and just as they had reached the doorway, her phone rang. "I'm sorry but I'll have to answer this." Paul looked across at Chloe, and gasped. She looked, if possible, even better than he remembered. She had put on a little weight and had a healthy glow about her that she hadn't had before. He hadn't seen her with her hair loose, as it was now. It had always been in a single thick plait, and he had never noticed the colour because of that. It was very thick and a red-gold colour, and as it flowed over her shoulders it caught the shaft of sunlight coming in through the window nearby; it shone, looking like silk as it hung over her shoulders. What would it feel like to run his hands through it? It looked silky and soft. The effect that seeing her was having on his body was unsettling. While he was waiting for Anna to finish her call, he couldn't take his eyes off Chloe and stared at her hard across the room, willing her to look in his direction. She must have felt his eyes on her because she turned to look at him, her eyes widened, and she seemed to take in a deep breath. Then she looked straight at him. Paul smiled at her, and she returned it, tentatively at first but with one that lit up her face, making her even more beautiful. He had never seen her smile before, it was breathtaking. They didn't lose eye contact as Anna led Paul across the room to introduce them. There was a look of amusement on Anna's face as she did so, she felt that she was superfluous at that point. *She is a lucky girl*, she said to herself, and if she was honest, she felt more than a bit jealous.

When Anna and Paul arrived at the table where Chloe was, she got up from her chair to meet him, and it surprised him how much taller she was than he remembered. She had seemed much smaller at that time, but then she was always barefoot when she was brought to him. Also, thinking back, her feet were always cold, so he had attempted to warm them for her each time. It was a lovely memory, from a bad situation.

*

I had been left sitting in the lounge of the hotel while Anna went to make a phone call, no doubt to Paul to say where to find us. I was feeling so nervous, and I couldn't say why. It was just a brief meeting to thank someone for doing such a marvellous thing for me and the other girls, nothing more to it than that, was there? Although again, I had the feeling there was more to this meeting but couldn't figure out what. I had had a strange feeling that I didn't want to think about too hard, in case I was wrong, a feeling that had come into my mind every time I thought about this meeting. Well, I might be enlightened after this afternoon. Maybe? I happened to look towards the door because I felt that there was someone watching me. Anna had stopped to answer her phone. The man with her was staring at me. When I looked at him, he smiled, a dazzling, knee-weakening smile. I gasped. I couldn't help returning it. I couldn't take my eyes off him. To say he was gorgeous was an understatement of epic proportions. He was tall, over six foot I estimated, judging from Anna's height, and slim, having what could be described as an athletic build, with broad shoulders. He was very elegant, wearing what would probably be a designer dark blue business suit, a pale blue shirt and no tie, with the shirt top button open. It seemed that we couldn't take our eyes off each other. Everything seemed to be moving in slow motion around us. I was shocked at the reaction I had to him, after thinking that I wouldn't have any feelings about any man after what I had been subjected to. He walked with the confidence that comes from a lifetime of money. I caught the look on Anna's face; she was watching us with amusement as she was going to make the introductions. I suddenly felt short of breath, starting to shake, oh no, not a panic attack, not now please, no. Anna was watching me closely, as she had seen the change in me, and moved to put her arm round my waist. "Are you okay? Take deep breaths. Chloe suffers from panic attacks," she said to Paul. I started to feel a bit steadier.

*

Paul felt unsure what to do, and if Chloe reacted like this, had it been wise to have arranged the meeting yet? He was upset that he had obviously had this effect on her and asked, "Would it be better to arrange this meeting later, when you are feeling a bit stronger?" She looked at him and the stress was all too evident on her face. He longed to take her in his arms and hold her, until she stopped shaking. But he didn't think that would be the right thing to do at that moment.

*

I gave him as good a smile as I could muster. "I'll be all right, thank you."

"Whatever is best for you," he said to me. "Let's carry on, shall we?" I replied and he looked relieved when I said that, and Anna carried on with the introductions.

"Chloe, this is Paul Knight. He asked me to introduce him to you, and Paul, this is Chloe Winters, who, of course, was known as Scarlet in The Harem." I could hardly speak to say hello. I was tongue-tied, my brain had gone to mush, what bit of brain I have. I was just aware of Anna telling me that she would be near the door and that she would have to leave shortly. She would see me the next day unless there was anything else. As if in a dream, reluctantly I held my hand out to shake his. He took it, and leaning down, kissed me on both cheeks. There seemed to be a powerful chemistry at work when we touched, surprising me. "Thank you," I said to Anna, speaking as though in a trance, still not taking my eyes from his. I was mesmerised. I had never experienced feelings like this in my life, even though I had been convinced that any relationships were not going to happen. "It's so good to meet you at last," I managed to say with difficulty. My mouth felt as though it was lined with cotton wool.

*

"Shall we sit down?" he suggested. He could hear her voice at last. It was deeper than he had expected, sounding very seductive. Her eyes were a dark shade of green; he hadn't been able to see them previously. A couple that had come to sit nearby were watching with interest, and quietly making comments to each other, they weren't missing much.

*

We both started to speak at once and laughed at ourselves. "You first," he said, and again I felt tongue-tied. "I don't know where to start. I have so much to thank you for, for giving me my life back, our lives, all of us, just saying thank you doesn't really cover it. I don't think that we would have been rescued but for you. Just to think of enduring life in there for longer, well, I feel sick thinking how it would have been. Oh, I'm crying again, I'm surprised I have any tears left! There have been so many since I was rescued. I know it doesn't sound like it, but they are tears of happiness, I promise you."

*

He had been feeling that he was sitting too far away from her and had been looking for an excuse to move closer; he was longing to touch her. Trying to think of a way to change the situation, her crying gave him the perfect excuse, so he took full advantage, moving to sit next to her on the sofa as close as he dared, their legs touching. It felt amazing to have such close contact.

*

Moving over to sit so close to me on the sofa that we were touching, he took a handkerchief out of his pocket, handed it to me and then put his arm around my waist, pulling me closer to him. I tensed at first but felt surprisingly comfortable about him sitting so close, and I couldn't believe my attitude towards him; not wanting to move away from him in spite of having the panic attack earlier. "I didn't want to upset you, that was the last thing I wanted to do. I am so sorry." I wiped my eyes. "It's just me being a wimp." He dropped his voice so that the couple near us couldn't overhear our conversation. "I'm sure you're not a wimp. How does it feel to be back home? It must be amazing." I nodded. "I can't tell you how much."

*

The look on her face said everything.

*

"Shall we have some tea?" he asked me, and I nodded my agreement. "That would be wonderful, my throat is so dry, thank you." When the tea arrived Paul poured it out for us both and held the plate with the most delicious cakes on it that I had ever seen and laughed at me when I couldn't make my mind up which to take. "I sometimes bring my mother in here and she can't make her mind up either." When we had made serious inroads into the cakes Paul carried on telling me about the club.

"I have been making a nuisance of myself, asking Anna to arrange this meeting, even before they rescued you. I felt that I must apologise to you face to face for the way you were treated, because as one of the members, therefore part-owner, all of it was done in my name, when I had no part in setting it up. I was out of the country when all the changes were made but I was kept up with the news by my friends, and I can tell you that I was not happy with what I was hearing, and I decided to end my membership. But when I thought about the situation, I made my mind up to go to the police instead because I wanted to get that part of the club closed. I needed more information first, before they would take it seriously. So that it wouldn't create too much suspicion, because of the way it had changed I asked for a tour. I had no idea how the place worked anymore, it would be a good cover story."

He told me all about being shown round, partly to get the layout of the place, telling me about seeing behind the scenes.

"When I was being shown around, the guide took me past a window, and I stopped to admire the garden outside. It was beautiful, and I could see the doors to a swimming pool. I was just going to carry on with the tour when they must have come to take you back outside after you had been swimming, and then through into that little garden area. You looked stunning, you looked almost relaxed. I checked with my guide that it was you. I had been in the room at your introduction. Because you looked different then, obviously thinner, I was horrified, you were treated so brutally that day. The collar and handcuffs were put back on, and your expression changed to being... what can I say? Unhappy? Defeated? I don't think that covers what was showing on your face. And then you were taken to the shower, one of them massaging some cream onto you, it was so intrusive. I could have wept for you, and I got more and more angry when I saw the way that you and the other girls were being treated; like slaves, to be bought and sold, kept like animals who can't do anything for themselves, being kept so isolated, I didn't realise how isolated until I asked Maia more. She was my informant in there, giving me a lot of good ammunition to use against the management team. There is a long list of charges against them." I nodded. "I met her and the rest of the care team this morning. They are lovely people and didn't deserve the life that they had to live, either. It was almost funny at times because I was treated more like a pet, stroked and caressed." Paul looked at me, frowning; he paused before he said anything. "Did it ever go beyond stroking and petting? What I'm asking is, did any of the care team have sex with you, abusing their position?"

"No. I don't think that there would have been a chance of that happening anyway, we were monitored and controlled too closely.

"Those outfits, if you can call what they dressed me in an outfit, were ludicrous. You would have seen them, and they dressed and undressed me as though I was a child that couldn't dress myself. I had a name for myself when

I was dressed in that awful sparkly harness affair; I called myself Bubbles. Hello, I'm Bubbles and I'll be your Poodle for today. Well, there was more that was very crude, but you can probably get the drift of what I'm saying." Paul's face was a picture. He was desperately trying, unsuccessfully as it turned out, not to laugh. He failed miserably and laughed so much that he was wiping away the tears that were running down his face. Everybody, including the couple nearby, looked questioningly at us, no doubt wondering what the joke was; I was laughing hard as well.

*

Anna got up at that point and left. They seemed to be getting on all right, she wasn't needed. Now it was up to them. She had done all she could for the moment. She was looking forward to quizzing Chloe on what she thought of Paul; yes, she could have some fun with that subject.

*

When Paul had wiped his eyes from laughing, he looked at me, and it set us both off again. "I would like to hear what happened to you, from when you were abducted to when you were freed. If you are willing, and as much as you want to tell me at a time," he added hastily. "Would you do that?" If he strung it out it would give her time to get to know him and give him more time with her. "I would like that," I said. He seemed to breathe a sigh of relief. "You could come for weekends? I could book you into here again." I couldn't think of anything that would give me more pleasure. "That would be wonderful, thank you, you're very kind, and I understand you have done that for me this time, as well?" He gave me the most brilliant smile. "It's my pleasure and thank you for agreeing to this meeting. Just charge whatever you want to your room number."

"I might go on a spending spree; you are taking a risk." He laughed. "Be my guest, make yourself comfortable." I got up when he did, he held out his hand to me, and taking it hesitantly, walked into reception with him. It felt so natural, and surprisingly, I didn't want him to leave. He bent down and kissed me on the lips very gently before he left. As he walked towards the door he turned back and took a card out of his pocket and handed it to me. "That's my mobile number, ring me, anytime, and I mean anytime, even if it's only to talk, or if you need help in any way." He was so insistent, that I wrote mine down and he put it in his pocket. This time he put his arms round my waist, pulling me into his arms, kissed me again and went out of the door, turning to smile at me before he did so. I kept staring longingly after him, wishing he could have stayed longer, giving a sigh. I didn't want him to leave, he certainly affected my heart rate. I had to grin to myself when I looked at his card; Paul Knight. Oh yes, he was my knight in shining armour all right. I felt so emotional. A voice brought me back from my thoughts of Paul. "I'm sure he will be back, don't worry." When I turned around it was the wife from the couple that had been sitting near us.

"We thought you made a lovely couple. Have you known each other long?" "We only met for the first time today."

"The way you looked at each other was lovely, so tender, it seemed as though you had known each other for much longer. Are you having dinner in the restaurant? We would love to invite you to eat with us."

SEVENTEEN

I was touched by their kindness, but I had an idea that it would be to get more information. "Thank you so much, that's an extremely sweet offer, but it's been a long day, and I think I will have an early night. It's going to be another long one tomorrow. But thank you again, I do appreciate the thought." I made my escape upstairs and ordered from room service; the meal was delicious. I had just finished the last mouthful when my phone rang. It was Anna. "Hi Anna, you're not still at work, are you?"

"I am just going to head off home. I'm shattered, but I had to know how it went this afternoon. What did you think of him?"

"Oh. My. God." I exclaimed. "Why didn't you tell me what he looked like? Why did you do that to me? I thought I was going to have a heart attack."

"Why would I spoil the fun and miss seeing the expression on your face? I just wished that I had a camera with me, it was priceless."

"I was speechless with shock."

"I noticed. What was that about relationships that you told me again?" she laughed. "You got your speech back and appeared to be getting on okay. Any more meetings arranged?"

"Not yet, give us a chance, we only met for the first time today." I heard her yawn at the other end of the phone. "Right, I am off home, and I will see you tomorrow. Let me know what happens between you two; I want details, I will be asking questions." After I had finished on the phone I did as I had intended and went to bed early, although I didn't get to sleep so easily. I couldn't get Paul out of my mind. Could I trust him? He was, after all, a member of the club and part of the system. I had the strange feeling that the club hadn't finished with any of us yet, and that in some way they would try to get us all back somehow. I did think that just possibly I might be being a little irrational.

I had never had the reaction to any other man that I had had to Paul. It was almost as if there was an electrical charge when we touched. I pictured his face; cheerful is how I would describe it, not one that I could picture with a look of anger, but I had only just met him and didn't know him at all. He was clean-shaven and his face was angular with high cheek bones, dark blue eyes that positively twinkled, dark blond hair, longer on top and short at the sides, very fashionable, and the style suited him. As to age? Thirtyish? I am no good at guessing people's age. I found myself going on a flight of fancy about the future, pulling myself up, telling myself, don't go there, it will be upsetting if it doesn't turn out the way I would like it to. It wouldn't turn out the way I hoped; it was, after all, only in stories that things worked out, not in real life. I gave up trying to sleep and sat up reading, trying to concentrate, but failing. I had just started to nod over my book when my phone rang. Paul's name showed up. "Hello, Paul."

"Chloe, hello, I hope that I'm not disturbing you. But I had to say thank you again for meeting me, I enjoyed talking to you. Will you see me again? I want us to get to know each other, and I wondered if you would have dinner with me tomorrow night?" My heart did a back flip in my chest. "That would be wonderful, thank you. I'll look forward to that very much."

"Shall I meet you in reception at seven? Good night, Chloe, sweet dreams." Well, I just sat there looking at the phone with an idiotic grin on my face. That sounded to me as though he wasn't intending to stop seeing me, yet, if he wanted us to get to know each other. I fell asleep with a huge grin on my face and dreamt of twinkling dark blue eyes.

*

Before Anna had time to leave her office her phone rang. It was Paul. "Thank you for arranging the meeting this afternoon," he said. "That's all right, what did you think?"

"I couldn't believe how she is looking now, she's stunning, even better than when I first saw her. But I suppose at that time she would have been drugged and very scared. She certainly is better for being back home. I hope you don't mind my ringing you. I had better ring off now, but I wanted to thank you again."

*

The next morning Anna was picking me up and taking me to see her boss, and I stood on the steps to wait for her. Traffic was bad, as usual, but we made it eventually to her office. We had to walk past where most of the team who were working on the case were based. I had met most of them, so they weren't all strangers. They came over to speak to me, they were so kind. "You're looking so well now, a great improvement on when she was rescued, isn't she?" the sergeant said, to someone who had come into the room behind me. It was the inspector. "What a difference, being back home is certainly agreeing with you," he said with a warm smile. "Come into my room and we can talk there." I smiled at the team as I left, with a chorus of goodbyes following me. The sergeant and Anna followed us into the room and sat in the corner, out of the way. "There are a few things we would like to clarify, if you can help us with them?" We went through items on his list and finally that part was finished. "What we would like you to do is to write an impact statement. We hadn't mentioned it before, to give you a chance to settle back home. We thought you might be able to think more clearly now. There isn't any rush, but if you let Anna have a copy then she will send one to the prosecution barrister. Don't leave anything out, this is your chance to say how this has affected your life, and all you girls are in line for a generous amount of compensation for what you went through. You will be expected to sign a nondisclosure agreement to say you cannot talk about how much the award was. Anna has told me about your worries concerning any future relationships, and that is a very valid point that should be put into your statement.

"My life has already been affected," I said, tears coming into my eyes again. "My engagement is off, partly because of what happened, although there were other reasons as well." The inspector looked at me with sympathy on his face. "We were all sad for you when we heard. And that needs to be included in your statement. I believe you had an implant injected into your leg after you were abducted, and it hasn't been removed yet." I told him it was still there. "I have spoken to my boss and if you want, it can be arranged for the next time you come down here. Will you set that up for Chloe?" the inspector asked Anna. "I will be glad to," she replied. "It's time that it came out, you will probably feel better when it's gone, another connection to that place severed."

"Thank you for coming to see me. Is there anything else that you may have remembered? Or you haven't told us about? However small it might seem to you; it could make the case stronger." I said that I couldn't think of anything else that might be useful. The inspector looked at me as though he suspected I hadn't told him everything, and then he said, "I think that is it. If there is anything more, I will contact you myself or Anna will." When we left the inspector's office we went through into another room and Anna asked, "Do you still feel unsafe, that you are being followed?" I nodded. "Yes, I do, it hasn't changed."

*

Anna had mentioned Chloe's fear that she was being followed to Paul, after Chloe had told her. What Anna had said gave Paul a cold feeling of horror every time it came into his thoughts. He had come so close to losing her. Paul already knew that somebody else was intent on owning Chloe, and that the club was playing Paul off against this other man. What he hadn't known was that the deal had already been done and evidence showed, from computer records found after the police raid, that the money had been paid and the sale would have been completed the very day she was rescued. No doubt she would have been taken out by helicopter. That wouldn't have raised any concerns because there were always one or two parked on the club's landing area. She would probably have vanished without trace. The possibility that she was being followed with the intention of trying to snatch her was very great; the amount of money that had been paid making it impossible for them to give up without a fight. Paul contacted John, the man who Anna was going to talk to Chloe about employing to act as security. They met up at Paul's office to talk. The meeting ended in Paul offering John a job with his company because John could prove useful to him as well, and there were more benefits for him. Paul was going to give John time to think about the offer, but he accepted without needing any time to think about it. After all, the job included a room in the staff quarters of Paul's apartment, which was a huge bonus, as well as many other benefits. Both Paul and John were pleased with the outcome. Because John couldn't start straightaway, Paul had arranged for protection for her, keeping her under observation. He had hesitated to mention that fact to her before he could see whether it would work. He would tell her later.

*

Anna looked thoughtful and then said, "If you are feeling that way, do you feel that maybe somebody to act as security for you might be the answer?" I must have looked worried. "Why, have you heard something that backs up that feeling?"

"Possibly," she replied slowly, sounding evasive. "What does that mean, possibly?"

"There is a chance that you might have a problem." I swallowed. "Will I ever truly be free of that place? It seems as if it's still got its hooks in me, and they will drag me back at any time. I don't feel as though I ever really escaped." Anna came over and gave me a hug.

"There is somebody that you can employ for protection. He hasn't been out of the force for long and the job he has been doing will be coming to an end very soon. He knows your story and was in the station when you were brought in and was listening to your interview. All the team had gathered to watch the video feed and he was asked if he wanted to sit in. You had quite an audience. He had come in to pick up some paperwork, and he has taken an interest in the case ever since. He is here now if you would like to meet him?" I did wonder how I was going to pay for something like that, because it certainly wouldn't come cheap. "Okay," I said hesitantly. Anna left the room to go and find him. When she came back, she introduced me to John. I felt dwarfed by him. He was tall and muscular, good-looking but with a very forbidding look. I could imagine him being able to deal with anything, being more than a little intimidating, looking more like he should be in the boxing ring or a bouncer at a club. As he took my hand to shake it, he smiled at me, and he immediately changed from being forbidding to stunning. We shook hands, mine feeling tiny and fragile compared to his, and the three of us sat down to talk. This was mostly between Anna and John, as they had a better idea of what I needed. The discussion took a little while, as we had to talk about terms of employment and what would be expected, both from him and from me. His present employment was ending soon, which was when the family he was working for left to go back home. It was left that he would contact me when his employment ended. We exchanged mobile numbers and after we had shaken hands Anna and I left the building. It felt so good to be outside again, it seemed we had been in there all day. "You're very quiet, what's on your mind?" asked Anna as she drove me back to the hotel. "I was just going over what was said, about the impact statement, just remembering the revulsion on Mark's face. It will happen again; I'm not looking forward to facing that." Anna didn't say anything for a while. "What did you think of John?" I considered my answer. "He seemed okay, but it's going to seem strange getting used to having somebody around like that most of the time. I am worried about how I will be able to pay for it before I get any compensation money."

"Don't worry about that now." It was up to Paul to tell Chloe about the arrangement between himself and John. "Are you seeing Paul again before you go back home?" I sighed and smiled at the thought. "I am, we're having dinner tonight."

I was impatient to see Paul again and it seemed as though time moved very slowly; I went down to reception early so that I was there waiting when he arrived. That night he took me to another restaurant. We never seemed to stop talking, telling each other about our lives, families, work, many more topics as well. We were sitting in the lounge of the hotel, and he commented, "I keep in touch with Anna, to see how the case is going, and she told me that you were feeling that you were being followed. She also said that there was evidence that proves it's not just in your imagination. So, if it's okay with you, my company will employ John, because there will be more benefits for him, and he can live in the staff quarters of my apartment. He will also be extremely useful to the company. How do you feel about that?" I didn't know how I felt about it because I still hadn't got my head around the fact that I needed security. "That sounds okay to me," was all I could think to say. "The last time that Anna and I talked she mentioned the tracker, that it still hasn't been removed."

"It was mentioned by her boss when I saw him today." He took my hand in his. "I know a clinic that is very good, and I can get you booked in to have it done there. I would like to do that for you, if you will let me?" I was silent for a minute or two, thinking. He gently ran his hand down the side of my face. "What are you thinking?" he said softly. "I was just wondering what I have done, for you to be so generous? And what strings are attached?" He looked troubled. "I realise that you don't know me very well, and you have issues with trusting people, and I'm probably rushing you, expecting you to trust me far too soon, but believe me there are absolutely no strings, and I do not expect anything in return."

"Okay, thank you." He beamed at me. "Good, I'll set it up tomorrow and ring you to check when it's convenient." He was as good as his word and it was arranged that I would go down the following week and it would be done then, after scans and tests had been done to find where the implant was. He surprised me by offering to come with me and hold my hand, as it would be done with a local anaesthetic. I thought that was very sweet of him and surprised myself by accepting his offer, hoping he had a strong stomach. I didn't want him passing out and regretting the whole thing. I couldn't believe that he had made the offer, but his plan to hold my hand was rejected very firmly by a very officious nurse, who appeared to have had a sense of humour bypass. But when the surgeon was asked, he agreed. The operation went well and didn't take long because the tracker was found very easily and hadn't gone too deep. He held my hand throughout. I still felt that it was a bit above and beyond what I would have expected of him, and as I didn't know whether I counted as his girlfriend, appreciated what he had done even more. That night I slept very well, and my phone woke me; it was Paul. "How are you feeling this morning, did you sleep well? I hope you aren't feeling too sore."

"Not too bad, thanks. I did catch it during the night, but it could have been worse."

"Good, I'm glad, how about lunch before you go for your train?" I looked at the small bottle that the offending implant was in. I would have to decide where I was going to dispose of it, somewhere it couldn't be found easily, but where? I took it with me when I went out for lunch with him, thinking of it maybe ending up in the river, possibly a rubbish bin somewhere on the road, or in some wet concrete on a building site? Hmm, possibly the river, which is exactly where it did end up, from a bridge. Paul found it very funny and laughed at me when I took it out of the bottle and threw the implant into the water. "Try to find that and good riddance," I said, as it vanished below the surface, I didn't think it would ever be found. He took me to the station to catch my train, but before he left me, he asked, "Will you come down here next weekend? You can stay in the same hotel again!"

Every day he made a habit of ringing me to say goodnight. It was lovely to hear from him and I couldn't wait, looking forward eagerly to his calls.

The day Chloe was coming to the city, Paul was restless. She filled his thoughts, wondering where she was. Would she turn up? He had detected some hesitancy about the whole situation from her; he couldn't blame her really. He had asked her to send a message when the train was half an hour from the station so that he could meet her, but he hadn't told her the reason. He was scanning the passengers, looking for her, and there she was, walking along the platform. He gave a sigh of relief. When he realised that she had seen him he smiled at her. Her smile back was encouraging, he couldn't wait for her to reach him.

*

The train was slowing as it entered the station. I collected my bag and checked that I had everything, getting ready to leave the carriage. I was so nervous, wondering why I had agreed to this, that I should have got off at the stop before and got on the next train back. It was the first time that I had been anywhere on my own since I was rescued. I comforted myself, thinking that plenty of people knew where I was. I walked along the platform, deep in thought. I looked up towards the end of the platform. I couldn't believe it; he was there waiting for me. As soon as he realised that I had seen him, he gave me the most dazzling smile. I couldn't help but return it. When I reached him, he surprised me by putting his arms around me, giving me a hug. I tensed at first and then relaxed; he bent down and kissed me on the cheek. He took my case from me and took my hand. We walked out of the station to his car, where his driver was waiting. When we were in the car, he took my hand in his. "Thank you for coming. I wasn't sure whether you would. I can imagine that it was a big step for you."

"I nearly didn't," I confessed. He squeezed my hand. By this time, we had arrived outside the hotel. His driver, Louis, got my case out of the boot, giving it to Paul, who told him he wouldn't need him to get home as he would call a taxi. I checked in and left my case to be taken up to my room. Paul suggested a walk, after stopping at a café for a drink. We arrived by the river and stood watching what was going on for a few minutes. I could tell that Paul was itching to say something, and finally, putting his hands on both sides of my face and smiling down at me, he planted a gentle kiss on the end of my nose. "I am so glad you're here with me. I haven't been able to get you out of my mind since we met up last week. Wondering what you were doing, how you were feeling. This morning was pure torture. Time seemed to go so slowly, I couldn't concentrate on anything. I should have had a meeting this morning, but I cancelled." "I'm glad that I am here, too." He drew me close and hugged me. There was a seat free. I sat staring out over the river but was brought back by Paul asking, "What's on your mind?" I thought about how to put what I wanted to say. Oh well, here goes, before I lose my nerve. "When I was rescued, the thought of having any kind of relationship with a man was out of the question, something I didn't think I would ever want again." Paul wanted to take her in his arms, but he didn't think that would be appropriate. He suddenly thought he knew what she was worried about. "Were you worried that I would expect you to sleep with me this weekend? Is that why you were so nervous?" All I could do was nod; he had got that so right. He put his hand under my chin and turned my head so that I was looking at him. "Oh sweetheart, I won't lie to you, there is nothing that would make me happier than to make love to you. I want you so much. Whatever happens, or doesn't happen, will be your decision. I want you to be happy and not feel pressured into something that you don't feel comfortable with. If ever you feel like taking the friendship further, it's up to you, only when, or if, you feel ready. I want you in my life, and if it is just a friendship, I'll have to live with that, but I'll always be here for you, whatever."

"But that isn't fair to you, waiting to know whether we have a future or not. I might never want anything more than friendship." But I hated the thought of him with another woman. "You would be better looking for somebody else."

"No!" he exclaimed vehemently. "Is that what you want?" he asked, more quietly. "Do you want to walk away from me? You let me decide what is fair to me or not." He pulled me into his arms, hugging me close. "Are you all right staying in the hotel? I have booked you in there because I'm having my apartment redecorated. I wasn't keen on what the designer did so I didn't employ one this time. It was too cold-looking, and impersonal. I chose all the new furniture myself, and I got rid of all the pictures, apart from one, because they really were not my style, and I am going to look for ones to take the place of them myself. I've moved out and I'm living with my parents until it's finished. And I also thought that you would feel better not having me around and be able to relax."

I was so touched that he had been so thoughtful. "The hotel is beautiful. You're going to spoil me."

I went down to London to see him regularly for the weekend, always staying in the same hotel, but he never came up to my room, meeting me in reception. I knew that he was interested in what had happened while I was in The Harem. I think we had exhausted that topic. But when he kissed me, it was very undemanding, no real passion involved, but the way that he looked at me, well, there was desire on his face that made me more than aware that he wanted me, especially after what he had said to me the first weekend. Maybe he was trying not to crowd me. We had been on some lovely nights out to some spectacular shows, and fabulous restaurants. He had introduced me to quite a few of his friends. I did feel that they looked at me with speculation, but maybe I had got that wrong. But they seemed to accept me with no problems that I could detect and seemed interested in me and my life. No one mentioned anything about my abduction; he had probably told them anyway. I was glad; I wasn't really ready to talk about what happened to strangers yet. They were a mixture of people, some wealthy most not, a variety of jobs, professions, and nationalities. He himself spoke several languages, and it appeared was well travelled, and educated.

He took me with him on many occasions to look at some of the properties he was either thinking of buying or had bought already, to discuss with architects, builders and designers what needed to be done. I found the whole process fascinating and made even more so because he included me as well.

I was sitting in the sun at one of the properties while Paul had a long discussion at the back of the house about

140

what needed doing to the outside; there was plenty to be done. I was watching him and thinking. The man that I had fallen in love with, in the club, was rather fading out of my thoughts, and the strong attraction that I had felt for Paul when Anna had introduced us had completely shocked me. It was a feeling I had never experienced before. Paul was the best-looking man I had ever seen and this, coupled with his patience and caring personality, made him irresistible to me. Would this other man have the same effect? I didn't think so.

I talked about my feelings over a glass or three of wine to Beth, one of my closest friends, to get her ideas on the situation. After taking another mouthful of wine she looked at me over the top of her glass. "Sounds like lust at first sight to me." She could well be right!

EIGHTEEN

Anna rang and told me that the court date, when I would be giving evidence, had been set, and what day I would be expected in court. "Will you be all right for getting leave? The prosecution barrister wants to talk to you to go over procedure and your evidence. Have you written your victim impact statement? The barrister wants to read that as well." I sighed. "Yes, I have, it took me absolutely ages, writing and rewriting. I decided finally to put everything down, just how I was feeling. I don't think that I have left anything out; I am hoping I haven't gone too far."

"I'm sure that it will be fine. You can email it to me, and I will make sure that the barrister gets a copy. It might be as well to come down a couple of days earlier than you are needed; that will give time beforehand for the barrister to talk to you. Her name is Tara Wells and you'll find her extremely easy to talk to. Paul is going to pay for the hotel again, and if that's not what you want, you can always say no." We decided which train I would catch, and Anna told me she would meet me at the station. I sent a message to Paul. I thought a message was probably better, just in case he was in a meeting and busy. I didn't want to disturb him.

"Hi Paul, I have been told the date when I will be needed to give evidence. I will be needed on the nineteenth of next month. I'm not looking forward to standing up in court. Love Chloe."

Much to my surprise he rang me back straight away.

"Hi sweetheart." I loved the way he greeted me. "That's come around sooner than was expected. It's not that far off, is it? Can I book you into the hotel again? I'm looking forward to seeing you, we don't see each other often enough, I've missed you so much."

"I've missed you too."

"You have?" He sounded thrilled at that. "Are you sure about paying for me again? It's very generous of you but I don't want to impose."

"You're not imposing, I want to do that for you, you're very special to me." My heart was in great danger, the way it reacted to what he was saying; his voice sounded like a caress, and I tried to ignore how my body was feeling. "Where are you?" he asked. "At work, on my lunch break, sitting on my favourite bench by the lake."

"That sounds wonderful, I wish I was with you."

"I wish you were too."

"What are you wearing?"

"What?" I described the outfit. "What colour is your underwear?" What followed was the kind of conversation where I was glad that I was alone and couldn't be overheard. Okay, so I have had conversations like this before with my ex and other boyfriends, but they have never ever affected me as much as this one was doing. It's a good job that there was nobody around to see my face; it must have been bright red, and not just with embarrassment. My breath caught in my throat. All he was doing was talking and he was seducing me. "Are you still with me?" I could hear the smile on his face down the phone, if that was possible; he knew the effect he was having on me. "Yes." It sounded more like a squeak to me. At that he laughed out loud. I had got to get out of this conversation, otherwise I felt as though I was going to burst into flames. Going back to work was going to be difficult enough as it was without a cold shower. "I need to get back to work, my time is up, much as I would love to carry on this conversation."

"What a shame, I would rather talk to you all afternoon, it would have been far more interesting and enjoyable than the meetings that are lined up for me."

"Good to know that I was an interesting diversion."

"Oh, you're more than that. I can always cancel them, you only have to say."

"Go back to work," I said, laughing. "Slave driver," he accused.

That night I had just gone to bed and was sitting reading when my phone rang. Paul, again! "Hi, just to say goodnight, and I hope your dreams are good ones."

"They will be if I dream of you," I find myself saying. Where in the world did that come from? I'm amazed at myself and know that I am blushing, again, even though I'm alone. "Goodnight, Chloe, dream of me."

"Goodnight, Paul, I'll try." We both switched our phones off at the same time and giving a sigh, I turned off the light. I am sure that I fell asleep with a large smile on my face.

The day that I had been dreading arrived, and as I got off the train in London my butterflies had become huge. However was I going to be able to give evidence? The whole thing could turn into a garbled mess at my end, and the whole case would be damaged. I didn't think that it would be irrevocably harmed, because thankfully I had been told the case was strong anyway, it didn't depend on me and my evidence. Still, I felt the pressure to get it right and not end up as a quivering wreck. Anna was waiting for me when I got off the train, surveying the amount of luggage I had with me. "How long are you staying? That looks like a couple of months at least," she teased me. "I was trying to cover all bases! I didn't bring the kitchen sink though, like I usually do, I thought they might just have one in the hotel, what do you think?" We looked at each other and burst into loud laughter. "It's so nice to hear you laughing like that and looking good at last. I can see that you're getting there."

"Slowly, very slowly," I told her. "There has been a change of plan, and if it's okay Tara has asked if she can see you now, straight from the station. Is that all right?"

Tara greeted us with apologies for having to change the time. I felt comfortable meeting her. She seemed to be one of those people who had a calming effect, on me anyway, someone who I found very approachable. I had no doubt, though, that she could be one scary individual given the right circumstances, and not put up with any nonsense, a good person to have on your side, someone who would fight as hard as she could for whoever she was representing. After we sat down and had cups of tea put in front of us, which was welcome as I was feeling very thirsty, Tara got down to business. Turning to me, she said, "I have read what you told the police after they rescued you and watched the taped interview, and I was sent a copy of your impact statement by Anna. I must say that it is a powerful and emotional read. Anybody hearing that cannot help being affected, as I was. There are some things, however, that you mentioned but didn't go into detail about. I realise that it will be upsetting to talk about, but can I ask you to be totally open with me and tell me more?" I had a nasty suspicion about the subject she was referring to; what she said next confirmed that I was right. "What I am talking about are the mentions of being beaten up. Will you tell me about those, and what you had done to cause them to be inflicted on you? I would like to record what you say." They both looked at me and I felt the tears come into my eyes. Anna took my hand and squeezed it reassuringly. I looked at her and then at Tara, swallowed hard and nodded my consent. "I was beaten up many times, always ending up with a lot of bruising. The first time that it happened I was booked for the evening as a threesome, a man, myself, and another girl. He had sex with me and then with the other girl. He was very rough with us both, he must like it like that. I was very sore afterwards. When it was my turn again, he was even worse, but then the girl started to beat me up. I don't know how it could go on because there was always someone sitting in the room when a member had booked for the evening for the first time. I ended up with massive bruises, she was biting and kicking me. Maybe she was encouraged to do that, possibly he liked seeing women fighting? Maybe it turned him on? Who knows? I turned my back on them both and wouldn't have anything to do with them. I rolled up as tight as I could. I was so sore, both inside and from bruising on my body. Before being taken back to my room... I..." I stopped talking. What happened to me next, I wanted to forget and keep it to myself. "The care team were always amazing and always helped me, they were so caring. The second time when I was booked for an evening, it was with one man. He was all right at first, but became increasingly rough, violent really, he hurt me, and I cried out. I couldn't help it because I think that he had something rough on his fingers. I was in a lot of pain, and it made me bleed and I had to be kept in my room for about a week to let the damage heal. He then started to beat me up, the bruising was still obvious and painful from the last time."

NINETEEN

Tara turned the recorder off. She looked at Anna but neither of them said anything for what seemed a long time. Anna had been holding my hand while I was speaking and came and put her arms around me. I was in tears, again. "Thank you for that," said Tara quietly. "I can't imagine what it must have been like to go through that, and to tell us about it as well. However, I will mention this when you are in court. It should be brought to the attention of the jury. I realise how difficult and upsetting it will be for you, and I won't bring it up if you feel that you can't face it. But think of it as a chance to get some revenge."

"I'll do it, but I hope that I don't fall apart in front of everyone."

"It will just show how much it has affected you, if you do." I remembered a question that I had asked myself several times. "I would like to know why I was apparently treated differently to the other girls. From what Anna has told me they weren't treated as badly. What did they have against me?"

"I will do my best to try, but I can't promise anything. Now I had better go and thank you."

Just as we were leaving there was a message from Paul. "Chloe, I'm at the hotel. Will you be long? I can't wait to see you." I replied, "I have just finished talking to the barrister and we are on our way. See you in a few minutes, can't wait to see you too. Chloe xxx." Anna looked at me speculatively. "Have you been meeting up with him?"

"Oh yes, quite a lot. I've been down here a few times because he asked me to tell him what had happened to me while I was held captive."

"Hmm," said Anna, smirking at me. I noticed her look. "What?" I said, laughing at her. "What's that look all about? And no, I haven't slept with him, he's just given me a peck on the cheek every time. He never comes up to my room, we meet in reception, and he leaves me there when we come back to the hotel. He rings me every night to say goodnight." Anna knew about Paul's feelings. "Maybe he's giving you time to get over being in there. Taking it slowly, letting you both get to know each other." When the taxi pulled up outside the hotel Paul must have been watching for us, because he came down the steps and helped unload my luggage, paid the driver and then gave me a kiss. He went and gave Anna a kiss on the cheek, saying quietly to her, "Thank you, and you know what for." She told me she would pick me up at nine o'clock the next morning, got back into the taxi, waved to us, and then went back to work. I checked in at the desk and we left my luggage to be taken up to my room. "How long have you come for?" Paul asked, eyeing my bags. "Oh, don't you start, it was mentioned earlier," I laughed. When we came out of the hotel it had started to rain. "Do you feel like some lunch? We will have to change our plans for this afternoon with this weather."

"I am starving, yes please. I got up later than I had

planned, so I hadn't time for breakfast. There is one way of passing the afternoon," I said, raising my eyebrows at him. It didn't take him long to catch on to my meaning. I had decided that I would take the initiative as he had told me it was up to me when I was ready. He grinned down at me and put his arm around my waist, pulling me closer to him. "Just a very quick lunch then?" he said, grinning at me. We were just starting off up the road when his name was called from behind us. "It's my mother and her friend, Katy. They're going to the theatre this afternoon." The two people in question were walking down the pavement towards us. "I'll go back to the hotel and then you can talk to her without me around." I turned to go but he tightened his grip on me. "There's no need for that, stay and meet her, please, don't be nervous." I swallowed hard and nodded. He planted a kiss on the top of my head. By this time, they had reached us and, not letting go of me, he kissed his mother on both cheeks. "Hello, how are you, Katy?" he asked her friend, and after some catching up, his mother said to him, "Now aren't you going to introduce us? I don't know where his manners are." She smiled at me and rolled her eyes about him. I giggled. "Mother, this is Chloe. I told you about her, she is in court tomorrow, err, giving evidence," he added quickly. "I am so pleased to meet you at last. I'm Evelyn and this is my friend, Katy, do you feel like going for lunch? We can talk more out of the rain."

"That's just where we were heading, weren't we?" The four of us ended up in the café where I had met my care team from The Harem. After we had eaten and chatted, Evelyn looked at her watch. "I so enjoyed meeting you, Chloe, will you come for lunch the day after tomorrow?" I looked up at Paul. "If it's all right with Paul, I would love to.

That's if they have finished with me in court." A look passed between them, and Paul said, "And why wouldn't I want you to come with me? She'll be there, won't you?"

"Yes of course I will, thank you." We had stopped outside the hotel; we kissed goodbye, and I went inside.

*

Evelyn watched Chloe go into the hotel; there was sympathy on her face. "She is so nervous. She was shaking when I shook hands with her. Was that caused by being kept in that place?" She turned to her friend. "Chloe has had a rough time, she was abducted and treated very badly. I feel so sorry for her." The look of sympathy was exchanged for one of distaste.

Paul said, "She was kept so isolated, no one spoke to her, all the communication was done through tablet computers, the staff all wore suits that covered all of them, even their eyes weren't visible. It's taking a while to get used to being in crowds and meeting new people, but she is so much better."

"Why aren't you going with her?" his mother asked. "I don't want to push her, I want to take things slowly. She's been left very vulnerable; I don't want to take advantage of that."

"Are you the same man who loves them and leaves them, that we usually can't keep up with as far as girlfriends are concerned? Who are you and what have you done to my son? Are you feeling well?" she asked, laughing as she said it. "I know, strange isn't it, love at first sight. Who would have thought it? I didn't believe in the concept. I spoke to the psychiatrist who spoke to the girls after they were rescued, I think that was what he was. I wanted to know how to help her, what to do, what not to do. He could only speak generally, of course, but he was so helpful, and I'm following what he suggested. Hopefully, it's working." After a moment, his mother asked, "You really want it to work out between you and Chloe, don't you?"

"Oh yes," he answered fervently. "I most certainly do. I can't remember anything that I have wanted more than this, I love her so much." His mother hugged him, and then they parted company, the two of them setting off towards the theatre.

Paul stopped in the hotel reception to phone Chloe. He needed to know if she still wanted him to go to her room. She answered quickly. "Paul. Where are you? Is everything okay?" There seemed to be disappointment in her voice. "You do want me to come to you, don't you?"

"Yes of course, I haven't changed my mind. I'll leave the door open for you." He breathed a sigh of relief and with a feeling of anticipation he took the stairs up to her floor. He had realised that Chloe was perhaps giving him a hint that she was willing to try for a closer relationship, after he had told her the decision was in her hands. He had thought that he should check that it was still the case. From the time when Anna had introduced them, he had intentionally put his arm round her, or held her hand, making physical contact between them. She had been stiff at first, but it seemed to be working out well and she seemed to welcome the contact more and more.

*

It had been quite a morning. I had to get up early to catch the train, and then meeting Paul's mother; what a lovely person. As I was going up to my room my phone rang; Anna's number. "Hi, Anna, everything okay?"

"I have just heard that the defence have asked for an adjournment, I don't know why yet, and it could be a few weeks before it happens."

I was feeling nervous and pacing around the room trying to decide whether I had made a mistake, when there was a knock at the door and he came into the room, closing the door behind him, I felt a frisson of either excitement or fear, I wasn't sure which. Was I really ready for this? He took my hand in his, gazing at me. I hadn't taken my eyes off him. I told him of Anna's phone call. He took my face between his hands and, leaning down until his lips were almost touching mine, looked down at me closely, almost as if he was memorising what I looked like in minute detail. I stretched up towards him until our lips were touching. Then his mouth came down hard on mine, kissing me with far more passion than he had shown before. All other thoughts were lost, we both ended up breathless and he rested his forehead against mine with his eyes shut. I looked up at him. "I haven't been kissed like that for a long, long time." *If ever*, I thought to myself. "It was wonderful, and I'm out of practice."

"Not that I noticed," he said, and then kissed me again. "No, definitely not out of practice," he said, grinning at me. "And it was my pleasure, any time."

"Hugs are good, too," he chuckled. "All the hugs you want," he added, tightening his arms around me. He looked down and said softly, "I want you." I could hardly breathe and whispered, "I want you too."

"Shall we take this into the bedroom? Only if you are ready." I nodded and taking my hand he led me into the bedroom, shutting the door behind us. I stopped suddenly, finding I was shaking. Did I trust him? Was this a mistake? I told myself to stop analysing the situation. It was what I had wanted ever since I had met him, wasn't it? Even thinking that I would never want a relationship with any man again, I was feeling surprisingly nervous. It was as if it was the first time that anyone had made love to me, which was laughable considering the life I had been forced to live not too long ago. He was looking at me with concern on his face. "You're shaking. Are you all right with this?"

"Definitely," I replied. Taking me in his arms he said, "I have wanted to make love to you for so long, but you needed to trust me. I didn't want to take advantage of you. You seemed so vulnerable after your release, and I didn't know whether you would be interested in a relationship after ending up in The Harem. I didn't want to put any pressure on you. You can say no to me."

"I think I know that I want you to make love to me." Leaning down he kissed me, gently at first, and with increasing passion. "I have something to tell you later," he whispered into my ear, at the same time unfastening the buttons on my blouse. We undressed each other in haste, unwilling to wait any longer. I found what I was looking for, I was ecstatic, and I gasped, I felt as though I had a volcano of happiness building inside me, that would blow up any minute, making all the firework displays in the world combined, pale into insignificance. He stopped and looked down at me, a worried look on his face. I was grinning like an idiot. "What just happened then?" he asked, looking anxious. "We don't have to do this. You know that don't you?" He obviously was thinking I was having second thoughts, oh, how wrong he was. "Oh, but we do, and let's just say, that the earth moved." He looked at me strangely. "I'll tell you later," I said, and pulled his head down to mine, kissing him. He broke from the kiss. "Now, where were we? And no more interruptions," he said with mock severity, smiling as he said that. Leaning down he kissed me. He was gentle at first, but becoming very rough, taking my breath away. We had waited so long for this, and need took over, we ended up breathless. He put his arms around me and, holding me close, rolled us so that we were lying on our sides, our foreheads resting against each other.

*

He lay with her in his arms, berating himself for losing control, calling himself an idiot. If she left him it would be entirely his own fault, for acting like a teenager.

*

I had my eyes shut, savouring the closeness, thinking how different this situation would have been if Paul had been somebody who didn't attract me at all. When our breathing was back to normal, I opened my eyes. He was watching me, then he sighed and whispered, "I'm so sorry, I just couldn't wait. I'd been wanting you for so long." I stared at him. "Sorry? Why?"

"For losing control, being so rough, and I've bruised your lip. I think that was more a wham-bam-thank-you-ma'am fuck than making love."

I laughed, and stopped suddenly, looking him in the eyes. "Well, I'm still here, not packing up and rushing to get a train home, am I? When I was rescued, I thought that any relationship with a man was never going to happen, that I would never want that. But... I thought I'd lost you when I was rescued. The nights that we spent together; they were wonderful, totally unexpected. You probably don't realise this, but you helped to keep me sane, I think you saved my life. What would have happened to me if you hadn't spent all those nights with me? Well, those thoughts are too horrible to think about! The love that I developed for you was overwhelming. Who would have thought, falling in love in a place like that, under circumstances like that. I didn't think I would ever meet you again. You were so gentle and kind. I was always devastated when the night was over, and I was taken away from you. And here you are. If this is a dream, it's fantastic, and I don't want to wake up. Ever."

TWENTY

When I finally looked at him, he was propped up on his elbow and looking down at me, eyebrows raised in surprise. "This is no dream, I'm glad to say. But how did you know it was me? Were you told? I can't believe that you knew, and that was what I was going to tell you, and you knew." His eyes widened as he realised the full implication of what I had told him. "I knew the same way that I checked who it was every time I had been booked for the night, hoping and praying that it was you. The nights that I spent with you were very special, you made me extremely happy."

"But how did you know?" he asked again, pulling himself up to lean against the headboard and pulling me into his arms. "You used the same aftershave, didn't you? Like you have today?" He smiled. "Yes, I did, hoping that you would recognise me."

"I thought you did, but you have a small scar on your back. When I found that just now you have no idea how incredibly happy that made me feel, because I was desperately afraid that I wouldn't see you again, and if I couldn't have you in my life, I didn't want anybody else. I had had enough of men. The only one I wanted was you. But I had been having this strange feeling about you because of the way you were asking to meet me. Wondering if you were the man I had fallen in love with, but I didn't dare think about that too much. I would have been devastated if I was proved wrong. But I always felt that there was some sort of chemistry between us, and it was there when Anna introduced us. Did you feel it too?" He tightened his hold on me and didn't say anything for a while. "I know, I felt it too, and it means so much to me that we both feel the same. You said you recognised me by a scar?" he mused, looking puzzled, and then he smiled as he remembered. "I got that falling out of a tree when I was a kid. It hurt like hell, bled a lot and needed stitches, fancy that. And the nights we spent together were special and made you happy?" That thrilled him. "I tried to make you as happy as I could, until you were rescued. But I remember you giving me a hell of a lot of pleasure too, it wasn't just one way. So, I think that it was mutual, don't you? I tried many times to rescue you, but they weren't interested in letting you leave, and I was getting desperate. I think they were playing me off against another man who also wanted you. I dread to think what your life would have been like with him. He was a cruel man. You would have been earning him a large amount of money. He was offering an exceptionally large sum of money for you; they were just waiting to see who blinked first. I wouldn't have let you go; I couldn't, I looked on you as mine, because I was in love with you. Also, I was afraid that you wouldn't want me, because you would blame me for being kept a prisoner." I had shuddered at the thought of living like that again in much worse conditions. We lay there for a long time with me wrapped tightly in his arms, just like we did at the club, as though he didn't want to let me go. But from now on there wouldn't be a knock on the door to take me away from him. The feelings that I had been having about why he had wanted to meet me, all made sense; he didn't want to lose me either.

*

He sighed, feeling contented, the feel of her lying in his arms was indescribable. She had made such a difference to his life since she had arrived, and she hadn't been out of his thoughts since he realised how deep his feelings were for her. It had purely been physical attraction until Anna had introduced them. After that the more he got to know her the more the feelings grew in intensity. She had changed since they had first been introduced, becoming more confident, not as fearful. It had been wonderful watching the transformation over the short time they had known each other. Her personality had disappointed him at first; she seemed to be a bit lacking, being withdrawn, not adding much to conversations and hesitant, but that too was changing, the effects lessening as time went on, making him wonder if this was the real Chloe coming back at last. He didn't want to be parted from her, hating it when she went back home. The future looked even brighter for him if she agreed to be in his life long-term. If she didn't, well, he pushed that thought to the back of his mind. He didn't want to dwell on that too closely; he tightened his arms around her, the idea upsetting him.

*

He tightened his arms around me so much that he was threatening to suffocate me, and I pushed away from him.

"I do need to breathe," I said, grinning at him, and he eased his hold, kissing me. I looked at him. "What was that all about?" I asked. "I just had a horrible thought that I could have lost you, and I couldn't bear that."

I needed the bathroom, and I pulled on the wrap that I had by the bed, and when I came out, he was leaning up on his elbow with an appreciative grin on his face. I raised my eyebrows at him. "Just enjoying the view, can't blame me for that, it's pretty good from where I am." I started to feel embarrassed because of his scrutiny. He took my hand and pulled me back into bed, and I pulled the bedclothes over me, trying to cover myself. "Don't do that, please, there's no need to be embarrassed. We've spent so many nights together, we aren't exactly strangers. You had so many horrible bruises all over you when I saw you in the club. Sometimes, I felt as though I daren't touch you, they looked so painful. I would never ever treat you like that, to see you look as bad as you did then. I love seeing your skin clear of them, and I was just thinking that you looked just as good as when I first saw you, at your introduction. You had lost so much weight by the time you were rescued; hadn't you been eating? Didn't they feed you enough?" I reached up and ran my hand down his cheek. He turned his face into my palm and kissed it tenderly. "I think that I was too stressed to eat much. I couldn't eat anything at first, my appetite wasn't good at all while I was in there. There was nothing wrong with the food, it was beautiful." I looked up into his face, into his eyes. "I fell in love with a man whose face I couldn't see, as if I were blind. I wouldn't have recognised you when we were first introduced. If you hadn't been with Anna, we would never have been able to speak either. So, in some ways, you are a stranger to me; not in all ways, of course.

And are you telling me that I'm fat?" I asked, with mock horror. He chuckled. "You're perfect, not fat at all, just as delicious as you always have been." Delicious, eh? I'd have to think about that one.

*

He lay with her cradled in his arms. At last he was where he wanted to be, had wanted her to be, for so long. He couldn't take his eyes off her. She looked so beautiful and at last he could see her face without the hood. It had surprised him that she gave herself to him freely, when she could have refused, knowing what part he played, unlike previous times when she was with him, when she had no choice.

*

He leaned over me, he was so close, our lips almost meeting. "What would you have done if I hadn't wanted to meet you?" I whispered. He was placing light kisses all over my face and neck and then he looked at me with a smirk on his face. "Oh, my darling, I always had plan B. I never intended to give up on you," he whispered back. "What was plan B?" I asked. He silenced me with a kiss which became more and more passionate, and we ended up making love again but without the urgency of before.

*

Much later he looked at her. She was curled up next to him looking adorable, she had her eyes shut, he knew that she wasn't asleep but there was a smile on her face, and it seemed like a contented one to him. He had never felt so protective towards anyone before, it was a strange feeling.

*

I lay feeling wonderful, a sense of calm and safety surrounding me. I hadn't felt like this in a long time. I moved so that I was even closer and, putting my arm over him, turning my head I kissed his chest and without thinking murmured, "I love you." *Why did you say that you idiot?* I scolded myself. *His feelings might not be as strong for you!* He had stilled instantly, had he heard? Unfortunately, I thought perhaps he had, maybe I had ruined everything. Opening my eyes, I found that he was staring at me, a look on his face I couldn't read. "I'm s—" That was all I managed to say of my apology because he kissed me, preventing me from saying anymore. "Did you mean what you said?" he asked later. I nodded. "Yes."

"Were you going to apologise, for saying that?" I nodded again. "Why?"

"I didn't know whether you felt the same, I didn't want to spoil everything."

"Hearing you say those three wonderful words, well, you have made me an extremely happy man. I loved you from the first time I saw you, and since we have been meeting up and we are getting to know each other, I have grown to love you even more. You are in my thoughts most of the time. I want you with me, I hate it when you leave me to go back home. Will you start coming down every weekend now, please?" I was feeling very embarrassed listening to him, but he hadn't finished. "I realise that we haven't known each other long, and I don't expect you to say anything yet, but I want to marry you. I want you to think if you love me enough. I want you in my future." I was dumbstruck. He laughed at me. "Now that's given you something to think about, hasn't it?"

There was such tenderness on his face when I looked at him. He pulled me into his arms again, and I stretched out so that I was lying against him and sighed. "That's what I was waiting to hear," he whispered in my ear. "I always loved hearing you do that, I waited for it every time. And you were smiling."

"What was?"

"You stretched and gave a sigh. It sounded as though you were contented and happy, at least for a while. Well, I hoped that was what you were feeling. I wanted to make you as happy as I could, even if it was only for the short time that you were with me. How are you feeling? After I was so rough with you?"

"I feel good, more than good. I always thought that this man was someone who cared. I was desperately lonely, with no contact with anyone, apart from the obvious. The problem was that it gave me..." I paused before I carried on. "It gave me hope, but that thought was far too dangerous to contemplate. I had to stifle that completely."

"Dangerous?" he asked, looking serious. "Why dangerous?"

"Because having the most mind-blowing sex that I ever experienced in my life, and the way he treated me, gave me hope, and I didn't dare to do that. I didn't think that I would ever escape the clutches of that place and be set free, so what use was hope? Even if I was released would I ever have any contact with this man again? I didn't think it would be possible. I existed from one day to the next, that's all I could do, enduring all the other men. The nights we spent together seemed as though they were weeks apart. I hoped every day that the night would be spent with you. What really blew me away was the thought that I'd had to be abducted to have nights like that, to find the love that I felt for you. I couldn't believe it had happened that way. It could always have been that you gave me what I desperately needed. I didn't know you, what kind of man you were. Whether you were married and being unfaithful to your wife."

*

He lay listening to what she was telling him. He had never felt so emotional about anything in his life before. Questions were coming thick and fast, the main one being, had he done the right thing for her by booking her so many nights? Whose benefit was it for, his or hers? Especially while it put so many conflicting emotions in her mind, possibly making life even harder for her than she was finding it already. Still, this was with the benefit of hindsight, but why hadn't he considered these facts? He had to be honest and didn't think he could have. Listening to her telling him all that, no dramatics but as a plain statement of fact, made it even harder to listen to, strengthening it immeasurably. He didn't know what to say to her, couldn't find the words. He found there were tears in his eyes. "Mind-blowing sex? That just about sums up how I felt as well, and that was all down to you."

*

I saw the tears and wiped them away, kissing each eye in turn. "I hadn't meant to upset you," I told him softly. His arms tightened around me and I lay listening to his heart's steady beat under me. "Can I ask you something?"

"Should I be worried?" he asked tentatively, but I didn't answer him straightaway. "What's this about? What do you want from me? Is there an ulterior motive or are there strings attached? My main worry before I was rescued was where I would end up when they had no further use for me. I thought that the club would end up killing me in some way. Also, what man would want to have any sort of relationship with me when they found out what I had been involved with? And I have another question, doesn't it bother you, making love to me? You obviously knew what I had to do in that place. Aren't you afraid that you might catch something from me?"

"I had no worries about catching anything from you, because we were all tested, as were you girls. For some reason you were tested far more than the others, I could never figure out why. Also, my darling girl, you obviously have no idea how much I love you. I love you very much. As I told you before, I think maybe I have done from the first time that I saw you, at your introduction. All that time ago, I don't think that I realised it at first, although you were in my mind always, but when I saw you in that little garden after you had been swimming, that was when it hit me hard, that I loved you. I couldn't get you out of my head, I couldn't concentrate on anything, I didn't want any other woman in my life, just you. I hated leaving you, all those men with their hands all over you, who only looked at you as a way of having sex, with no emotional involvement, being shackled as well, no closeness, being so isolated. It was repugnant to me, the thought of you enduring all that. I didn't dare to think about it very closely. It was tempting

165

to carry you out of there from right under their noses. I don't know how I would have got you past the two large security men on duty at the door, but I didn't care about that. I told Anna about feeling that way, and she quite rightly advised me not to do that, they would get you out. As for having an ulterior motive – yes, I had one, and it was to get you out of there to be with me, if you would have me, nobody else, just me. But it would be your choice. I was thrilled when Anna said that you had agreed to meet me, but when she told me you were engaged and would have been getting married if you hadn't been abducted, I was heartbroken. But I'm ashamed to say I was pleased when she mentioned that you had called your engagement off. I felt very selfish. But as soon as I realised how deep my feelings were for you, I called my own engagement off, months before the police raid, and I think we both should have been getting married about the same time. I had to keep a hold on my feelings because I did not know whether you would feel the same and not be interested in me at all. But I did as much as I could to be as close to you as possible, even spending the afternoon with you several times when you weren't well every month. Oh, and talking about spending time with you, I was surprised to see that you had e-readers and music players and a tablet, so many gadgets. How did you manage that?"

I laughed. "Yes, I was extremely lucky. When I was going out with my friends on the day that… well, you know what day, I had decided that I wasn't going to go back to my own house that night, so I had taken all of those with me, because I was going to call off the wedding. So I dragged them around all day, rather than leaving them in the car. If I hadn't taken them I was afraid that Mark, my soon-to-be ex, would have damaged them in retaliation, knowing how much I used them, and if I had left them in my car, I wouldn't have had them with me. I was getting incredibly bored, and had far too much time to think, and miss everybody, making me feel even more upset and lonely. After an incident with a razor that the carers had left in the bathroom and thinking that my plan was to… well, kill myself." Paul tightened his arms around me. "Was that your intention?" I nodded. "Oh, sweetheart."

"Well, I thought about everything that I had with me and decided to ask if I could have them back. I realised the internet would be blocked, of course. I was stunned when they were all there that night, with the proviso that I ate more."

"One of your carers suggested some time before that I book you for the night. I wanted to spend every minute that I could with you and if you had told me you weren't interested in a relationship with me after you had been released, well, that would have been devastating to me, but I had some wonderful memories to look back on, and I hoped that I had left you with some happy memories too. I never dared hope that you would feel the same. As for catching something from you, the test results were posted for anyone to read on your page of the club's website, and as I told you we all had tests done as well."

"So where do we go from here?" I asked. He took a deep breath. "It's far too early for you to get your head round all that's happened, so, if you are willing, if we can keep things as they are for the moment, to give us more time to get to know each other better, does that sound about right?"

"That sounds perfect." His phone chose that moment to ring. He gave me a quick kiss and grinned down at my dumbfounded expression at all he had told me. "I'm sorry but I'll have to answer this." I moved to get out of bed, but he pulled me back. "You don't have to go."

"Oh, but I do, I need the bathroom, you wouldn't like the results."

*

He smothered a laugh but gasped when he got a good view of Chloe's back and the scars. It was Bette, his PA. Paul asked her to wait a minute before he found out what she was ringing him about.

*

I turned at the bathroom door, ready to make a comment, and froze. Paul had seen my back, judging by the expression on his face. He looked shocked.

*

Bette apologised for ringing but told him about a problem that needed his attention. He asked her to send his driver to the hotel in half an hour and started to get dressed. He had just finished when he realised how long Chloe had been in the bathroom. Was something wrong?

*

While I was in the bathroom, I caught sight of my back in the mirrors. The way they were placed I could see them all easily. I would never be free of some of those, they were going to be there for the rest of my life, very unwelcome souvenirs. The tears started again.

*

Paul knocked gently on the door and when he didn't get an answer pushed it open. She was standing looking at herself in the long mirror. The expression on her face worried him, and he went and stood behind her, putting his arms around her shoulders. They stared at each other in the mirror. "What's the matter? Are you all right? Tell me what's bothering you."

*

I covered my face with my hands, and he pulled them gently away. "I feel, used, not clean, all those men! How could you want to marry me? Knowing how I had to live." I paused. "You don't know everything that went on in there, and when you do, you'll leave me, you'll never want to touch me or make love to me again!" He turned me round to face him and put his hands on each side of my face. "I will always want you, that will never change, are you hearing me? Whatever you tell me, it will make no difference."

"Don't make promises like that," I said. "It's something that I can't – won't – talk about."

*

He pulled her into his arms, holding her close to him and, looking in the mirror at the scars, ran his hand over them. She tensed at first. "I will never let you be treated like you were in there, ever again. I want to take care of you, keep you as safe as I can. I'm sorry, but I'm going to have to, very reluctantly, drag myself away from you. There's a problem at the office I will have to sort out. Can I stay with you tonight? To keep you company, if you don't want to be on your own, is that okay?"

*

I finally found my voice. "Oh, I would love that, thank you."

"We could have dinner here; we can order when I get back." I put my arms around him. "I need a hug before you go." He grinned at me and wrapped me in his arms. "I can do that, and I will see you later, and stop looking at me like that or I will never get out of here. Are you sure you will be all right? I don't like to leave you while you are upset."

*

"I'll be fine, go, don't worry." He gave me a kiss and went towards the door. "I'm not expecting an answer yet, just give it some thought. Keep it in mind, that's all I'm asking."

*

As he walked down the stairs, he was smiling happily. He felt as though he was ten feet tall, walking on clouds. He told himself to get a grip, but still couldn't get the stupid grin off his face. Life could just be looking up, but he wasn't about to get too complacent, the situation could change in a heartbeat. What she had just said worried him. He needed to find out more. His phone rang. "Josh, hello, what can I do for you?" His friend had apparently met Maria, Paul's ex, and having more than liked her when she was with Paul, Josh asked him if there would be a problem if he asked her out for a drink. After all, the situation might turn out to be embarrassing at some point in the future. "Look, I don't mind at all, she's a free agent as far as I'm concerned. You didn't need to ask, but thanks for doing so anyway, I appreciate that you did. She's a lovely character, she deserves to be treated better than I did, and I'm positive that you will make her happy, Josh."

When Paul arrived at the office it took him longer to sort out the problem than he had expected. Finally he could get back to Chloe; the very thought made him smile. He called into his apartment to pick up a change of clothes for the next day, and then called a taxi back to the hotel.

TWENTY-ONE

I started to get dressed after Paul had left. I had been intending to put on a pair of loose-fitting trousers and a top, but a memory surfaced of a video I had seen where a woman who had been coerced by somebody she looked on as a friend into prostitution. As soon as I remembered that the warm glow of the past few hours vanished, replaced by fright, and I started with a panic attack, because that woman had gone through all the different stages that she had been taken through, to the point where she complied willingly. Another video talked about a woman needing reconstructive surgery when she was rescued, because of the damage done by the number of men involved every day. Some of the things that Paul had done and said fitted in with what I had heard. Had I been taken in? Dressing quickly and packing my case in a panic, I left the hotel, heading for the train home. All the time there was a voice telling me to get out of there quickly, even though there was another, calmer, voice telling me that I didn't fit the profile of the type of woman who was targeted. My mind seemed as though it was in a fog, and it was difficult to think clearly. I felt as if I were hovering on the brink of hysteria, my heart hammering in my chest. Unfortunately, when I got to the station, I had only just missed a train, and would have to wait an hour for the next one.

*

When Paul arrived back at the hotel, he let himself into the room and called out to tell Chloe he was back but there was no answer. He looked into the bedroom and bathroom, realising that she wasn't there, her case was gone, she had taken everything. His phone rang. "Anna, what's the matter? Have you heard from Chloe? She's gone and I don't know where."

"She has gone back home. She just rang me in the middle of a massive panic attack, and not making much sense, sounding very frightened. She was ringing from the station. She had missed the train with an hour to wait for the next. I wasn't able to leave the office as there was a meeting about a big case we are working on. I couldn't miss that."

"Should I go after her? What should I do?" asked Paul.

"I really don't know what to say, to advise you. I think you will have to go with your instincts. Sorry, I haven't been much help."

"I will ring you when I know more," Paul told her and rang off, already on his way down to get a taxi. The journey seemed to take hours. When he arrived, realising that he didn't know which train to look for, he decided to look at all the people waiting around the platforms. He struck lucky, thankfully, seeing her sooner than he expected. He longed to go and put his arms round her, but he hung back, trying to keep out of her sight, trying to decide what to do for the best. She was looking around, looking very lost and frightened. He walked towards her, and she turned in his direction as he did. The look on her face was of terror when she spotted him and it stopped him in shock; he was afraid that she was going to run away. He stopped a few feet away, trying not to make her feel uncomfortable or trapped. "Chloe, darling, what's wrong? Did something happen after I left you? Did I do something wrong? Tell me! I'm not your enemy, trust me, please." Her answer shocked him to his core.

"But can I trust you? You know the saying about if something seems to be too good to be true, it usually is. This… relationship seems to me to be in that category. The type where a supposed friend says all the right things that you have said to me, and persuades them into trusting them, and they end up in prostitution with no control over their life. I have been in that life. I am terrified of ending up in that situation again." He was speechless. How could he counter this feeling of hers? She heard the announcement about the train she was waiting for, picked up her case, and with tears streaming down her face turned to him. "I'm sorry, I must go." He could only just hear her voice above the noise of the station, she was speaking so softly, and without thinking about what he was doing, moving quickly, took hold of her hand.

*

He held onto my hand, refusing to let go, holding it tightly despite my efforts to pull away from him. "Please don't leave me," he pleaded. "Give me another chance."

*

He put his arms round her, hugging her to him. She resisted him at first but then relaxed. He opened his eyes and looked down at her, his eyes filled with unshed tears, the life of the station flowing around unseen by the two of them. "Don't leave me, please," he begged. "Stay and talk to me, tell me what frightened you so much. Come back to the hotel and we can talk there." Waiting for her to answer was agonising. He let out the breath he had been holding when she gave a small nod of consent.

*

We arrived back at the hotel, with me wondering whether I had made the right decision. I hadn't the energy to say anything on the way back, all I wanted was to sleep, I was exhausted. Paul held me close because I was crying, again, would I ever be able to stop? Why would he want the hassle of somebody who acted like this all the time? I didn't think he would, I would lose him. I didn't want that. Looking up at him I said, "I won't survive without you, but why would you put up with somebody that causes you so much trouble?" He rested his forehead against mine with his eyes shut, and then opening them, said, "When you came into my life, you turned my world upside down, and blew it apart. I didn't know what had hit me, which way was up. I couldn't get you out of my mind. My mind was elsewhere when I was in meetings, my staff thought it was hilarious. They had never seen me like that." I looked up at him. "And they are still working for you?" He laughed. "I can take a bit of teasing, they know that. But I will never give up on you, remember that. It's been wonderful watching you over the time we have known each other, getting better all the time. And I have enjoyed every minute." He looked down at her and grinned; she had fallen asleep.

*

Paul undressed her and pulling the bedclothes over her, bent and gave her a kiss. She never stirred. He left the bedroom, going into the lounge and closing the door quietly behind him. Anna answered straightaway when he rang her. "Did you find her?"

"Yes, I persuaded her to come back to the hotel with me to talk. She fell asleep, she was exhausted." "Probably the best thing for her. Thanks for letting me know. How are you coping?"

"I'm out of my depth if I am honest. I don't know whether I should have let her get on the train. Perhaps her family would have been able to help her better."

"I doubt that," came the reply. "But how can I when she obviously has no trust in me? The look on her face when she saw me was of terror." They finished the call, with Paul promising to keep Anna informed.

*

I awoke sometime during the night to find Paul lying behind me with his arm protectively around my waist. When I finally woke up it was daylight and Paul was in the bathroom. When he came out and saw that I was awake, he came over, and sitting on the bed, leaned down, kissed me tenderly and then pulled me into his arms. "How are you feeling?"

"Okay thanks. I treated you very badly yesterday," I said. "Can you forgive me?"

"Oh, my darling, there is nothing to forgive, believe me. You were doing so well, but there were bound to be some backward steps. Tell me what frightened you so much. It was shocking to see so much terror on your face. What was worse was I seemed to cause it when you saw me." I told him about the videos that I had seen. He was silent after he heard about them. "I don't know what to say. There is nothing that I can say to make you realise that you can trust me. It's up to me to prove it to you. I need to convince you that I had no intention of rescuing you to earn money for me! I rescued you because I love you and you are such a special person and I am very selfish, wanting you all to myself."

*

"What you said before you left." He wondered what was coming. A feeling of dread filled him; was she going to refuse before he had asked her properly? Especially after what had happened the day before. He cursed himself for mentioning it too early. "Were you serious? Do you feel the same after what happened yesterday? Was it a rush of blood to your head, or a spur of the moment rash decision, that you have been thinking about since, thinking why, oh, why did I mention it? One that you will regret bitterly later. You know, the marry in haste, repent at leisure thing?" He let out the breath he had been holding. He could breathe again. It did not sound like a no, not now anyway, what a relief. "That was not a rash decision, or a rush of blood to my head. I am serious about asking you, I just thought that it was much too early, that I shouldn't have mentioned the subject yet. I know what I want the answer to be, but it all depends on you, how you feel. I did not want to put any pressure on you, and if I have, I apologise, that is the last thing that I wanted. I love you, I thought that I had been in love before, but it never felt like this, ever."

*

"What you just told me, about how you thought you had been in love before, but it had never felt the way you feel now, that is just how I feel; you must have been reading my mind. After I had spent the first evening with you, I wrote it off as being a one-off, hoping it wasn't, and then when I realised that it was you who had booked me for the night a while later, and many more after that, I was thrilled. By the time you had spent a few more extraordinary nights with me I was in love with you, I couldn't avoid it anymore. What I was afraid of was, was it because you gave me what I desperately needed that I felt this way? But my feelings were not easy to ignore. It frightened me just how much I longed for you after you left me, how much I loved you. I was always in tears when they took me back to my room. You could have been married; that thought upset me too. I realise that we don't know each other so well yet, but I feel that I know the answer would be yes even though we've been together such a short time. And I do trust you, despite what happened yesterday." We sat grinning at each other like idiots, not saying anything. What was there to say?

Paul cleared his throat; he could hardly speak with emotion at first. "Daft question, but are you saying yes?

And if it is, I don't know if you realise just how happy you have made me. I don't think I ever expected you to feel the same way. The way we met wasn't very conventional, was it? And I thought my connection to that place would be a step too far for you. It could come between us in the future." I was trying awfully hard not to laugh, listening to someone who always seemed so strong and in control, so obviously nervous and rambling. He looked at me. "I'll shut up; I'm not letting you get a word in. Can I say something else first? I just want to make you happy." I ran my hand down his cheek, and leaning over, kissed him, before I answered. "It wasn't a daft question, and no, we haven't known each other long, but despite that, the answer will be most definitely, yes." He pulled me into his arms, and it was only because we were both breathless that we came up for air.

The dinner order that night included an expensive bottle of champagne. I think I might end up with a hangover tomorrow; probably a good thing that the trial had been adjourned. While we were waiting for room service to deliver, I asked him why he had had to leave me that afternoon. "Did you sort out the problem at work? You haven't been spending too much time with me, have you? Is that why the problem happened?" He laughed. "Yes, I have been spending far too much time with you, it's been very enjoyable, and worth it. I can depend on the people who work for me to run the place when I'm not around, and I think they realise that a woman is the reason. It has happened before."

"Oh, did it happen often?" I asked quietly. "Err, yes," he seemed embarrassed. "Well, it wasn't unknown for me to have quite a few girlfriends."

"Really? A philanderer?"

"A recovering one," he added quickly. "I see, and what brought about your recovery?"

"Meeting you." I laughed. "Oh, I hope you don't have a relapse." This was followed by another long and passionate kiss.

"I'm interviewing for a new housekeeper tomorrow," he commented. "Changing the subject?" I asked. "I know what you are doing. So, you need a new housekeeper? Anybody lined up for that?" He grinned at me. "Why, are you going to apply?" It was my turn to laugh. "There is no way that you would want me working for you as your housekeeper. I'm useless when it comes to housework and cooking. I can always find something I would rather be doing, and I try to eat out as much as possible. Housework always seems such a waste of time and effort."

"Believe me, I have a far more interesting position for you in mind." The look on his face made it all too obvious just what the position was, and then he laughed heartily. "There is somebody who is coming for an interview. She worked for me before, and then after she got married she and her husband worked abroad. She has come back, and saw the job advertised, so I think I will take her on again. I don't know whether she is still married or not because her husband wasn't mentioned. Work is a bit hectic because we are in the middle of moving to a new office building, a bigger one, where all the different parts of the business can be in the same place. It's a nightmare, so much to do to keep everything ticking over at the same time. My staff are wonderful, I'm proud of them. There have been many, late nights. I owe them some serious bonuses later. You will have to come and look around. I would love everybody to meet you, and I hope that our meal isn't too long; I'm starving." I looked at him seriously. "Don't tell me you have been shirking, being with me when you have so much to do? Your staff are going to hate me for keeping you from doing your share of the work." He grinned. "As I'm the boss, I can take some time off, it is allowed, and I am sure they won't hate you."

The meal was superb, but anything would have tasted fabulous the way I was feeling. We sat opposite at the small dining table. We couldn't take our eyes or our hands off each other for long, and kept reaching across and touching, not wanting to lose contact. I enjoyed being able to see and talk to him now after having to wear that hood back at the club and not have the ability. We collapsed onto the large comfortable sofa to finish the bottle, and just sat wrapped in each other's arms. I awoke the next morning to find that I was lying with my back to Paul with his arms around me. "Good morning, beautiful, did you sleep well?" he said softly into the back of my neck. "Very well, you?"

"Yes, I did. Are you okay?" I shifted in his arms so that we were facing each other, and just lay looking at him. "What?" he said. "What's the matter, have I got something on the end of my nose?" He crossed his eyes at me, and I collapsed laughing. "Just thinking how lucky I am, and I am more than okay, much, much more, and just admiring the view. I can see you, which makes it even better, and your hair is usually immaculate; it's the first time that I've seen it when it's not been." He grinned at me. "I can see you too, and the view I'm looking at is so special, and there is a very pleasing reason for my hair being in the state it's in." I lay there, wishing that I could spend the day with him, but he had to work, unfortunately.

As the trial hadn't taken place, I had the day to myself. What should I do? I had thought of getting a taxi to the V &

A Museum, but I ended up taking my camera, playing the tourist and trying out a new terribly expensive one that Paul had bought me after finding out that I had damaged mine irrevocably by dropping it. It was going to be quite a while before I got used to this new one; it was top of the range with a load of bells and whistles attached and two lenses, one of which would get me closer to most wildlife and was large. I took the smaller lens, as well as the instruction book; I certainly needed that.

*

The man who Paul had employed to watch over Chloe rang him at the office. "Is everything okay?" asked Paul anxiously, when he answered. "Yes, it is. Miss Winters didn't go to the museum. She has been walking around taking photos instead, she has walked a long way. She is having her lunch at the moment and has stopped many times to look at a small booklet; she seems to be looking through the pictures. I'm just a short distance from her. I'm having to be extremely careful because she is very observant. When she came into this café they gave her a table in the middle, but she asked for one where she had a wall behind her, so she is being very careful, and when she stopped it was always where nobody could creep up on her. I will ring you later unless something happens."

"Thank you for the report, she has just got a new camera so that explains the stops. I'm just going to ring her, so I won't tell her I know anything." He had wondered whether it was a good idea to have somebody following her when she was feeling that she was being followed anyway, but he would see how it worked out.

I was just finishing eating my lunch when my phone rang; it was Paul. "Hello, where are you? It sounds a bit noisy to be the museum." I swallowed the last piece of my sandwich. "I'm just having my lunch. I've been taking photographs around the city instead, giving that new camera you gave me some work and getting used to it. I love it. I seem to have walked miles. I was ready for a sit down and something to eat. I might even do some shopping before I head back to the hotel. What have you been doing?" He told me about a property he had just bought, it sounded as big a wreck as my house had been. "If you don't feel like walking back, I can always send my driver to pick you up." I thought that was a sweet offer. "I'll keep that in mind, but I should be okay. See you back at the hotel."

*

When Paul rang off, he stood thinking and smiled to himself. It was definite progress for Chloe to feel confident enough to set off around London on her own.

*

After I had spoken to Paul, I did some shopping and went back to the hotel in a taxi. I went up in the lift because I had so many bags and was so tired I couldn't face carrying them up the stairs. Once back in my room, I ordered tea and toasted teacake. There was a discreet knock at the door; it was room service. Later I changed and then stretched out on the sofa with my book until Paul arrived. I was tired and started to yawn, my eyelids started to close, and I dozed, only waking when I heard the door closing as Paul came into the room. Gathering me into his arms he kissed me passionately. "I hope that you don't fall asleep on me tonight, because I hadn't planned on allowing you much, keeping you busy, terribly busy. Are you hungry? I was thinking we could go to the Italian restaurant we've been to before." I licked my lips at the thought; the last meal we had eaten there was beautiful. When I looked at the clock it was much later than I thought.

While we were waiting for our order, he asked me about my day, and then he talked about the new office building. Apparently the building work was done, the snagging list had been gone through, checked and approved and handed over officially to the company, and the move into it was nearly completed. The meal was as good as I remembered, and we wandered back to the hotel hand in hand. Paul was as good as his word and neither of us got much sleep.

As I was thrashing wildly a voice started to penetrate my consciousness, a voice I thought I recognised. "Chloe, Chloe, it's Paul, sweetheart, calm down, you're safe." The voice was persistent, trying to calm and soothe. I came out of the nightmare to find that I was lying on my back with Paul sitting astride me holding my arms on both sides of my head, staring down at me with worry written all over his face. When he realised that I had my eyes open and I was awake, he wrapped me in his arms and held me tight because I was still sobbing, and we were like that until I stopped crying and lay exhausted in his arms, and fell asleep, feeling safe. When I awoke later, he was looking at me. "That was some nightmare, you were so violent. How are you feeling? You were going crazy, fighting me as though your life depended on getting away. Do you want to talk? I'm here for you when you do." His lip was bleeding slightly. "Oh, my God, did I do that?" He nodded, and I leaned over and gave it a gentle kiss. "I feel dreadful, I didn't know I was capable of abusing anyone." I ended up sobbing again, but he held me until the tears stopped. "I'll have to watch out for you in future, and as for abuse, nobody could accuse you of that, believe me. You pack one hell of a punch, and I couldn't believe how strong you are." He had a smile on his face, and I couldn't help but laugh when he said that.

TWENTY-TWO

I told him what the dream was about, my introduction, and how sore I was afterwards, but how wonderful the care team were, and how surprised I was that I had any feeling left after what happened on a regular basis. A look of pain crossed Paul's face. "I'm not surprised you dream about that; it was brutal. I'm afraid I was there and saw what they did to you. I don't hurt you, do I? I'm surprised that you want to make love after your experiences."

"I always thought that if I was ever rescued, I wouldn't want a relationship with another man." I didn't tell him about the other nightmares. "Do you have nightmares often?" he asked softly. "Not as much." He kissed me. "Thanks for telling me, I appreciate that you have." I snuggled closer to him; feeling his arms holding me was very comforting and reassuring. "Haven't you been offered more counselling?"

"Yes, I had some after I was rescued, but asked for more help later, and I'm still seeing someone. I was getting very depressed. I didn't want to go there again, it was frightening, even though my family and friends have been wonderful." I paused and admitted to him just how depressed I had become. "I haven't told many people about this, but I wanted to… kill myself. I had planned to try when I was in the club, if there was an opportunity; one of the carers left a razor behind after I had been having a shower. They realised far too quickly and came looking for it." Paul held me close, and then asked, "Why did you change your mind?" I thought about that. "Not so much changed my mind, but I started to realise how much it would hurt my parents and friends. I didn't want to put them through that again, they had suffered enough through something that wasn't my fault. If I had done it then it would be quite different, after I had come back safe to them. It would have been cruel and selfish on my part, but it was just further back in my mind. I don't know how else to describe how I felt about the subject." I think I may have shocked him, saying what I had. He kissed me and then said, "I am here if you need me, anytime. I would love to try to help you in any way I can. Don't forget that, please." I was so touched. "You already have helped me; I don't think you realise how much."

We wandered down for breakfast. We had both finished eating, and I was sitting with my elbows on the table, holding my cup in both hands. Paul was reading his newspaper and I was trying not to stare at him, but it was so difficult not to, he was so amazingly good-looking. And his mouth; remembering last night. I didn't think there was any part of my body that he had missed. The memory was arousing and I suddenly saw that he was looking at me, with his eyebrows raised and his cup poised on its way to his mouth. "What are you thinking about?" I smirked at him. "That would be telling. We're being watched by two men over on the other side. I think they have been taking photos of us." Paul finished his coffee and then leaned over the table to me, with a grin on his face and a mischievous sparkle in his eyes. "And if you keep looking at me like that, we will be giving them something to watch." I giggled and then I stifled a yawn and heard a chuckle from across the table. "What? Tired?" he asked, trying to look innocent. "Yes, I didn't sleep very well last night. I can't think why." He laughed and took my hand. "Neither did I, very pleasurable it was, too and you won't get much sleep tonight either." What was there to say to that statement?

"If we are both ready, we might as well leave, I need to pick up my car from my apartment and then we can go to my parents from there. You are still alright for lunch with them, aren't you?"

"Oh, yes, definitely," I replied, trying to sound confident when I was feeling anything but. After we checked out, we took a taxi to Paul's apartment. When we pulled up outside, I was looking up at an ultramodern building, and if the outside was anything to go by, the inside would be spectacular. We went down into the garage and put my cases in the car before taking the lift to the top of the building. When we stepped into the lounge from the hallway, I gasped; the view was breathtaking. Through the large windows the view of the river was spectacular, and as it was a sunny day the water was sparkling as it caught the sun. I went and drank it all in, noticing a large deck area reached from a door from the lounge. I turned around and Paul was leaning in the doorway, watching me. "That view is amazing; it must be hard to take your eyes off." Paul came to stand next to me. "The view sold the place to me before I had looked at the other areas. I never get tired of that view. It's beautiful at night, too, with all the reflections from the buildings in the water. I am hoping you will see it for yourself soon." I stared around. "The whole of my house would fit into this room alone," thinking how small it would seem to Paul, compared to this. He took me on a tour of the whole apartment, which was huge including the staff quarters, which were spacious as well, ending up in his bedroom, and if we hadn't been expected at his parents, I think we might have spent the rest of the day in there. The place smelled slightly of fresh paint and new carpets. I don't know what it had looked like before, but it was certainly beautifully furnished and felt comfortable, very welcoming, and more of a home. Paul packed some clothes into a case and, holding his hand out to me, we headed down to the garage, and then to his parents. His car was low, silver, powerful, surprisingly quiet, and the leather seats were so comfortable. Not knowing London very well, I had no idea where we were, but the area was full of the most beautiful trees and mostly older houses. It was obvious even to me that it was an affluent area. When we stopped outside one of them, he put a code into the pad on the gatepost, and the gates slid open, revealing one of the older houses that had so much character. I loved it before I had stepped inside, because it hadn't been altered and extended to get as many rooms as possible into the space, unlike some of them in the area, which obviously had been. We stopped outside, and the door opened, and Evelyn, Paul's mother, was standing at the top of the steps, waiting to welcome us. A small dog came rushing out, a Border Terrier I think, running in circles around us and then going to Paul, who picked it up, to its obvious delight, tail wagging madly, and licking his face at the same time. "This is Frodo," he said to me. Putting Frodo down, Paul held his hand out to me, squeezing it in support, and we went up the steps, where Paul's mother hugged him, and then me, and then ushered us inside. "Frodo," I laughed, "what a great name, what an apt name." Inside the house was stunning; with its original features keeping the character, it felt very welcoming and with light flooding into every corner, it seemed, a home with a lot of love. Paul's father appeared from the garden, and I could see where some of Paul's looks had come from; there was no mistaking they were father and son. "Dad, this is Chloe."

"I am so pleased to meet you at last. Evelyn has told me so much about you." Oh, my goodness, what has she said? "It's good to meet you too, Mr Knight."

"Call me Steve, please." Evelyn suddenly looked at Paul closely. "What have you done to your lip? It looks as if it's been bleeding?" I felt that I had to say something. "That's down to me, I'm afraid." All eyes turned to me, the expression on Evelyn's face quite obviously saying that this was what she would expect to happen; after all, I was found in a brothel! Also, she did not like the thought of her son being beaten up, especially by a woman. The fact that he stood head and shoulders taller than me and was a strong man who worked out, could, in different circumstances, be regarded as funny. Paul put his arm comfortingly round my waist, pulling me closer to him, and rescued me from further censure. "Chloe had a very violent nightmare during the night, caused by an incident that happened while she was held captive. Apparently they happen quite often. I couldn't get over how strong she is, and I don't mind admitting that I had to put more strength into calming her down than I would have thought possible. It was quite a shock." He looked down at me, a look of pride on his face. Evelyn's expression had changed to one of concern. "That incident must have been horrific!" she exclaimed. "Maybe you could tell me about what happened, some time when you feel up to it? Lunch shouldn't be long, would either of you like a drink? What do you want, Chloe, wine or non-alcoholic?"

"I would love some wine, please, is there anything I can help you with, Evelyn?" A short time later Evelyn appeared to tell us that lunch was ready, and we made our way into the dining kitchen, which was huge. I put my spoon down after I had eaten my sweet. "That meal was beautiful. I really enjoyed it, thank you." Evelyn looked pleased at the compliment. "I am so glad you enjoyed it, but have you had enough?"

"Oh, I can't manage another mouthful, I'm so full." We all took a handful of plates off the table, so that it was cleared in no time, and the dishwasher filled. Coffee cups in hand Paul and I went out into the garden to drink it and look around. We sat on a bench under a tree in the shade.

*

"Well, what do you think of her, Steve?" asked Evelyn. "She is beautiful, isn't she? But I don't think she's what I was expecting. Mind you, I don't know what I was expecting anyway. But I like her very much, and she seems to be making Paul incredibly happy. She has outlasted all his other girlfriends, except Maria, of course. I liked her, too, but I was surprised that he was going to marry her. I had a strong feeling that he was thinking he should be settling down, and she would do. Am I being unfair in that assessment? Or way off the mark?" Evelyn thought about the question. "No, I think you're right. I must say I hadn't thought about it that way. He seems quite different with Chloe, very protective, and I like that side of him. You don't see it very often, not often enough. He's usually the businessman through and through, a bit on the ruthless side. I feel so sorry for her. She has gone through a very rough time. Paul tried to do as much as he could, didn't he, helping to get her and the other girls out of that awful place? Hopefully, life will improve for her, and maybe Paul will be able to help. And who knows, we might even gain a daughter-in-law, eventually."

*

Paul stretched and looked at his watch. "Maybe we had better be leaving. We should miss the worst of the traffic if we go now." He was driving me home and was going to stay for a couple of nights, so that he and my parents could meet, and he could see where I lived.

I was reflecting on the conversation over lunch. I had been asked a lot of questions about my life, parents, home; I didn't feel as though they were being intrusive about finding out more about me. Paul was obviously loved very much by his parents and was a very wealthy man; it was only natural that there were questions. I could, of course, be after him because I wanted his lifestyle and money. They were bound to be wary until they got to know me better. The place we met was obviously a cause of worry to them about what kind of person I was; they weren't to know how insistent they had been at the club about what kind of life we had led before being abducted. I had, however, found the whole process exhausting.

Unfortunately, we were later leaving than Paul had wanted so that we were caught up in rush hour traffic. With the addition of a bad accident on the motorway, which added to the time, the journey took longer, and what with the large meal, the warmth in the car, soft music playing plus the extremely comfortable seats, I fell asleep. I surfaced and stretched. I looked at the time. Paul looked across at me. "Had a good sleep?" he asked, and reaching over and taking my hand in his, raised it to his lips and kissed it. "Good, thanks, where are we?" The satnav chirped up with a direction, almost as though it was answering my question. I laughed. "About an hour to get there, would you say?" I rang my parents, telling them where we were and when we were likely to arrive, and that we would see them in the morning.

TWENTY-THREE

Again, I dropped off to sleep and was woken this time with a kiss from Paul. It was dark outside. "Wake up sleepyhead, we're there, which way do we go from here?" I was just taking in where we had stopped when a car pulled up behind, and blue flashing lights blinded us for a second or two. A familiar face appeared at the driver's side. He was looking at Paul and hadn't seen me. "Hello Richie." He looked closer and grinned as he recognised me. Coming round to the passenger side, he opened the door and gave me a quick hug. He squatted down beside the car so he could talk to us more easily. "This is Richie, my friend's husband. And this is Paul." They shook hands across me. "I'm sorry to stop, but I wondered if you were all right. As Chloe knows, satnavs don't work very well in this area; there are always people getting lost. Now that I know you are all right, I had better get back to the car. I'll tell Sandra that I have seen you, and it was good to meet you," he said to Paul. As we were near where I lived, we pulled up outside my garage a few minutes later. The old building had been demolished and the new large double garage, with two small bedrooms, a living-dining area and shower room accommodation above, was well on its way to being finished. It was impressive that all that had been fitted into the space. The fact that with a few tweaks to the plans planning permission had been granted was a complete and welcome surprise. The builders had made amazing progress. My car had been parked behind my parents' house out of the way, leaving Paul plenty of room to park and not be in the builders' way. In the light of the headlights we could see what the building looked like, and Paul passed a practised eye over what had been done. "I'm impressed. The workmanship looks excellent, and the design too." With help of the headlights I found the switch for the lights for the garden path and we made our way to the back door. I soon had the door open and the lights on. I made a drink for us while Paul took our cases up to the bedroom. Then he had a look around while he drank it. He sat on the sofa and patted the seat next to him, opening his arms to me. I went and sat down, and with his arm around me we sat close, enjoying the quiet. "I love your house, it's cosy and welcoming, and I see what you mean about it fitting into my lounge." I had wondered if he would be bumping his head on the beams, but the ceiling height didn't seem to be a problem for him. "This place was a complete wreck when I bought it. People thought I was mad; it looked as though it was going to fall down. I did wonder about my sanity at times. I took photos while the work was going on, and after it was finished. I'll find them, then you can see what a state it was in." Paul looked thoughtful. "I hadn't realised how far out the village is. How do you get to London? I could have had one of my drivers pick you up."

"I get the train from the village. We are so lucky to have the station in use; the owners of the abbey led a campaign to have the trains stop here again. It's been unbelievably successful for everyone." We sat finishing our drinks until my eyelids started to close and we decided we needed to get some sleep.

When I awoke the next morning, I lay listening to the birdsong coming through the open window and I turned over gently so that I could look at Paul, who was still asleep, without waking him. My life had been a rollercoaster of emotions since the abduction; my concentration seemed to be almost nil. Despite feeling that I would not want a relationship with any man after my experiences, surprisingly my feelings for this man were too strong to ignore. Somehow with compassion and patience he had broken through most of the defences I had built around myself. I was still amazed at my reaction and the trust that I had in him. He stretched and yawned and, realising that I was already awake, pulled me into his arms. "Morning, gorgeous."

"It's so quiet, just the birdsong, no wonder you love living here." Just then the builders announced their presence when a drill started; we both laughed heartily. "You were saying?" Much later we ended up in the shower. I had always had showers on my own and I did not know why I had not done that before, with Mark, and even though the cubicle was exceedingly small, it was good, incredibly good. Neither of us wanted a big breakfast so it was coffee and toast, and while I drank my coffee I wandered out into the garden and down to speak to the builders. Paul joined me and we wandered about, looking at what was being done, including upstairs to look at the bathroom and kitchen, which the electrician and the plumber, both female I was glad to see, were working on.

We were going to my parents for lunch, and as we had plenty of time, I suggested we could walk there so that he could see the village. As we left the house Paul stopped when we got to the gate to admire the front of the house. "So much character," he exclaimed. "Was there a house next door?"

"Yes, both houses had been empty, for many years; a problem over a will, I think. Unfortunately, vandals broke in next door and set fire to it. The damage was so bad that it was unsafe, so it had to be demolished. I'd been looking for a property for a while, when a relative, who I didn't know very well, died and left me money in her will. The money had just gone into my bank account when the house and land next door were put on the market, I couldn't believe the way it worked out. Anyway, to cut a long story short, although there was a lot of competition to get the sale, mine was cash, and as I knew the people selling, I talked to them and because I could move faster, they agreed to sell to me. They were emigrating to the part of Canada where my older sister lives, in British Columbia near to Vancouver, and needed the money for when they got there. I got an incredibly good deal, the land was being sold without planning permission, they would have had to wait longer than they wanted for the planning to go through."

We strolled through the village arm in arm, which wasn't always easy because there must have been a few coaches in the village and the pavements, not being very wide, made it a little difficult with all the people. It was a stopping-off point for coach parties because an extremely popular television series was filmed there. As we walked down the main street, I saw Sandra and Beth coming towards us. Sandra would have been told by her husband that I was home, and they came and embraced me, and I introduced them to Paul. I told him that Sandra was married to the policeman that we had spoken to the night before. Sandra looked at her watch. "We had better go, or we'll miss the train. I'll ring you later, and it was lovely to meet you," she said to Paul, and they rushed off towards the station. I watched them hurry up the road with a large grin on my face as I saw them both get their phones out and start talking. "I think the bush telegraph has just been activated, it will be working overtime." Paul looked at me. "Why?" I laughed. "Every time any of us start seeing someone new, it's always the same, you know, light shone in the eyes, thumbscrews, wanting information." He laughed, and I really tried to keep a straight face. "You think I'm joking?"

"What kind of information?" he asked with obvious trepidation. "Oh, do they know them? What do they do for a living? Where they met. How long have they known each other? Have they slept with them? How good are they in bed? What they score out of ten? The usual questions, it could get nasty." I daren't look at him, as by this time we had stopped in the middle of the pavement, much to the annoyance of some of the pedestrians, and I was finding it difficult not to laugh. Paul moved us to the side of the pavement and put his arms around me. "And what would the answer be to the last question?" he asked softly. "Which question in particular?" I replied, trying to look clueless, and when I looked up at him, he was grinning at me. "Fishing for compliments? Oh, let me think, triple A star?" He looked pleased. "Really?" There was a comment from a couple of men passing about getting a room, and when I looked at them, they were laughing, giving us the thumbs-up. With our arms firmly around each other we carried on down the street. I stopped and pointed across the road at a shop selling paintings and artists' supplies. "That's my mother's.

She's an artist, and above is one of my father's offices. His main one is in the next town, he's a solicitor. My mother sells paintings for other artists and some equipment and paints, as well as a few things for the tourists. Do you want to have a look?" He led the way across the road between the traffic and into the shop. There was a good number of people wandering around and I stopped to talk to Muriel, who had worked part-time for my mother for years. I went to find Paul; he was standing in front of a portrait of me by my mother that she had finished recently. "That is such a beautiful painting of you. I don't see a price on it; I would love to buy it, if it's for sale. I have just the place in mind. Is it possible to ask how much?" I rang my mother and when I got back to him, he was still in the same place. "She says about negotiating over lunch." As we walked towards my parents' house, I pointed out the coffee shop where my friends and I had ended up on the day that I was abducted. I shivered at the unwelcome thought.

When we arrived at my parents' their two dogs, a golden retriever called Cleo, and Nim, a chocolate Labrador, gave us an enthusiastic welcome, and seemed to take to Paul immediately; the feeling was mutual, it seemed. After making the introductions we wandered through to the living room and the subject of the painting came up. My mother was thrilled because, although she had used me as a model on many occasions, in many ways, she herself considered it her best attempt. She had started it just before I was abducted, and she had been too upset to carry on with it until after I was rescued. "Chloe has spoken of you many times and always told us how much support she has had, especially from you, and how appreciative she is." At that he looked at me and squeezed my hand. "Chloe is a very special person; I would do anything for her." I felt the tears threatening after hearing him. "So, we would like you to have it as a thank-you present from us both, for being so good to her." Paul went over and gave her a hug, shaking hands with my father. "I can't think of a more beautiful present, thank you so much. I have just the place for it in my apartment." My father and Paul were in the garden with the dogs, and I was watching them with amusement. "He seems like a good man," commented my mother. "Yes, he is. Do you remember me telling you about my mystery man from the club?" She turned from what she was doing and nodded. "Have you found him?" I grinned at her. "Yes, I have."

"Who?" she exclaimed. "Paul." She hurried over and hugged me. "Oh, darling I'm so happy for you. Do you feel the same way about him?"

"Oh yes, even more since we have spent so much time together."

Lunch was a very relaxed affair, after which we left them. "I have to call into work briefly to drop off a birthday present, do you want to come with me?" After calling home we drove the short distance to the estate, and as we turned in at the gate Paul said, "I thought the name rang a bell, Philip Drake. Does he own the estate? Because I have met him on a few occasions and got on well with him. What's he like to work for?"

"Very good, everybody likes him, and some have been here for many years, nobody wants to leave." As we had parked in the staff car park, I remembered to put my pass on the dashboard, and we headed to the office. As I was introducing Paul to everyone, Phil Drake came into the office, and seeing Paul, came over to shake hands with obvious pleasure at seeing him. The two of them excused themselves and then left us. As soon as they were out of sight I was surrounded and bombarded with questions by my colleagues. One of them watched the two of them leave with appreciation on her face. "Wow, I certainly wouldn't kick him out of bed. Point him in my direction if you ever get tired of him, please." We all laughed, including me. "Not going to happen I'm afraid," I commented, and handed the present over to the birthday girl. We talked for a while and after Paul came back into the office, we said our goodbyes and walked out into the sunshine. I suggested I give him a short tour.

It was enjoyable walking with his arm around me. We didn't see anybody as we walked; we had the place to ourselves, ending up sitting on my favourite seat by the lake, relaxing in the peace that surrounded us. I got up and went to look down into the water, leaning against a willow; there was usually something to be seen, but not today. As I was watching I saw a movement out of the corner of my eye.

*

Paul watched her and suddenly realised that a squirrel had come down out of a tree nearby. It didn't seem to be worried about their intrusion into its domain, but it must have decided that there weren't any nuts to be had and scampered up a small tree and peered around the trunk at them, and then rushed off up into the higher branches. He managed to take a photo of the two of them. Chloe went and sat down again next to him. "That's a regular. I nearly always have a few nuts; it takes them out of my hands sometimes."

He ran his hands through her hair, he loved doing that.

It always felt so silky and soft. He pulled her into his arms and kissed her. When they came up for air, he got up and held his hand out. "Shall we go? I have plans for the rest of the afternoon." This was said with a wicked grin on his face.

*

That night my parents, Paul and I ate out at one of the pubs and stopped for a drink afterwards. My folks and Paul got on really well. It was as if they had known each other for a long time and it was a lively night. We said goodnight at the end of the road to my house. Paul was quiet. I had no idea if something was worrying him, as he gave nothing away. He didn't say much when we got into bed later, so I decided I had to find out the cause, and I moved so that I was lying with my head on his chest, looking at him. "What's the matter? Has something upset you? Have I done or said something wrong? Tell me." He put his hands on each side of my face, looking serious. "I'll have to go back to London tomorrow. I've an early meeting on Monday, and I don't want to leave you." He paused. "Will you move in with me? I have enjoyed these last few days, being with you all the time. At least give it some thought."

"I feel the same way." He sighed. "I hear a but coming."

"The problem is, what would I do with myself all day? I can't just sit around and do nothing, I am not qualified for anything to get a job." He grinned at last and, knowing what my reaction would be, said, "That sounds good to me."

I heard from Anna the next day that a meeting had been arranged with the other girls from The Harem. They had met up before, but I did not know how I felt about the meeting. I was incredibly nervous. I went back with Paul and stayed with him because the meeting was at a hotel in central London.

I had thought very hard about what to wear and had bought a new dress. I looked at myself in the mirror. I didn't recognise the woman who stared out at me, I looked so different. I wondered what Paul would think. The shoes I had bought were a lot higher than I usually wore, not quite killer heels, but I hoped that I wouldn't disgrace myself and trip over. Paul was going to the office later that morning, and when I entered the lounge, he was having a conversation on his phone. He told them he would ring back later and, never taking his eyes off me, sauntered over. He just gazed at me. "Well, say something, what do you think?"

"I approve, you look ravishing. I am not sure I should let you out looking like that, I should keep you here and ravish you right here and now." He came closer and taking me in his arms, kissed me. Regretfully we went our separate ways.

Anna met me at the hotel. Her boss wanted to talk to us all. She did not know what he wanted to talk about, but all the police personnel who had been helping us were going to be there. Anna and I were the first to arrive, the others coming in gradually, giving me a chance to meet them all without a crowd. When all the initial introductions had been made, Anna's boss got up and told us that, during the course of the investigation, some things had been unearthed. It seemed that the body of Blanche, the missing member of The Harem girls, had been found. An unidentified body had been found, soon after Blanche had disappeared, and on first investigation of where it was found, and how it was positioned, was thought to have been in an accident, but identification could not be determined. There had been many unanswered questions raised by the injuries because they did not fit in with the accident theory. Amazingly a very slight trace of DNA had been found which was causing some consternation; there was something odd about it, and the thought was that it was contaminated. It was upsetting to me to hear this and I felt a bit faint, because I had a strong idea how she had died, and the fact that I could have ended up a victim as well. Anna suggested I go out of the room until I felt better.

TWENTY-FOUR

When I felt stronger, I went back into the room. I asked if they had found out why I had been treated differently from the other girls but they had drawn a blank. My phone rang. It was Paul. When I answered, it must have been obvious that there was something wrong, because he picked up on it immediately. "What's wrong, sweetheart? You sound upset. If meeting up with them has been too much for you, leave now and come to me at my office." He then told me which taxi firm to call. "Yes, I am upset, but it was because of some news that we have been given."

"What? Tell me?" he pressed me for more. "I don't want to say now, when I see you." I could tell he wanted to know more. "All right, but instead of a taxi my driver will pick you up. Ring me when you're ready to leave. The staff have been asking when they can meet you, that would keep them quiet for a while." I could hear the grin on his face as he said it. "Yes, I will," I promised. "Lunch is being served, so I had better go." I went back to the table after convincing Anna that I was feeling fine, and she then went back to work. It was a shame that she could not stay and have lunch with us. We finished our meal and took our coffees over to a seating area where we could talk without having to shout across a large space. One of the girls introduced herself to me as April, or Amber as she had been known. She had been given a very apt name because she had beautiful coffee-coloured skin, and her hair, which was very curly, was almost the same colour. Looking rather uncomfortable she said, "I have a confession to make, I'm afraid. I have asked all the other girls, and it comes down to you." I must have looked baffled. "It was me that beat you up, I am so sorry. I can't apologise enough, but I was blackmailed into doing it." She went a bit pink, obviously feeling ashamed. "You pack one hell of a punch." She looked up at me to see that I was grinning at her. "I figured out that you could have been threatened. I was full of bruises. The same thing happened a few days later, it was one man that time, and he beat me up, and then he had another little present for me. He must have had something on his fingers that was rough when he pushed his fingers inside me. I was in so much pain, bleeding heavily as well. I had to stay in my room for about a week to let me heal enough." I turned to Amber; it seemed easier to refer to each other by our Harem names. "What did they threaten you with?" I asked her. "That they had received a large offer for me, that they were not ready to sell me on then, but if I didn't do what they wanted, they would sell me. The offer, they told me, had come from a man who was known to treat his girls very badly. They didn't last long with him." She did not have to elaborate; we all had a good idea of what would have happened. "I had no way of knowing if they were bluffing or not but I didn't want to take any unnecessary chances."

We decided to meet up again soon and exchanged telephone numbers and email addresses. When we stepped out of the hotel we were besieged by photographers, who had been lying in wait, obviously alerted to the meeting by somebody. I suppose we should have left one at a time. I rang Paul, and when his driver came managed to get to the car without much trouble, sitting back thinking about the afternoon, and much to my surprise decided that I had enjoyed it and wouldn't mind meeting up again with them all.

The car stopped in front of an impressive office block. When I entered the building, I found myself in a very smart reception area. After I had approached the desk, I was shown to the lift. They offered to escort me up to Paul's office, but I declined and I was met by Bette, Paul's PA, when I left the lift. After she had introduced herself to me, she showed me into her office. "I'm so sorry, Miss Winters, but Paul has people with him, so would you mind waiting in here? He won't be long; they were just finishing when I left the room. Can I get you a drink while you wait?" I knew Paul valued her highly, he had told me she was very efficient. "No, thank you, I'm okay, and please call me Chloe." I smiled at her and sat down to wait. Bette was obviously busy, so I looked at some of the magazines. One of them, I noticed, had an article about Paul. In it there was an estimation of his personal wealth. I stared at the page with my mouth open in shock; I knew he must be wealthy but had no idea how much he was worth. It was an astounding amount if the assumption was anywhere near accurate. Since I had received the compensation from the club – the amount had been mind-blowing – I was no longer the part-time worker with no money anymore. I thought back to when I had opened my bank statement, after the money had been paid into my account, and stared at the impressive number of noughts in shock, even though I had known how much I would be getting. It was nowhere near the estimated amount that Paul was supposed to have, but even with the much smaller amount that I now had, I did not need to feel overwhelmed in any way when I was with him. A door opened in the corridor. Bette excused herself and went to show the men who had spilled out of the room to the lift. Paul came into the room and the look on his face made it obvious that he was pleased to see me. He made straight for me, and putting his arms around my waist, kissed me. He then held me at arm's length and looked me up and down critically. "How was it, meeting the others? Come into my office and then you can tell me all about what happened, and why you were upset." The view from his window was as impressive as the one from his apartment. "I don't know how you can concentrate on anything with that view, I would want to look at it all day."

"Chloe? Tell me." He had come over to me and, taking my face between his hands, gazed earnestly into my eyes, no doubt trying to learn what had happened that way. "The reason was because of what the inspector had just told us. The girl called Blanche who vanished, her body had been found, only she could not be identified until after the club had been raided. There was surprising evidence found that linked her to it. She was left where it would look as though she had been involved in an accident, but there were unanswered questions because her injuries did not add up. But when they checked, there was a tiny amount of DNA found."

Paul took me to meet some of his staff and gave me a tour around with obvious pride in both his staff and the building. I was very impressed, he was obviously well thought of by the way that they interacted with him, teasing him as well. I did notice some unfriendly looks towards me. No doubt they had thought that they had a chance of becoming his wife, but they were few, and I enjoyed talking to the rest of them.

*

The painting of Chloe had arrived and been hung in Paul's apartment, just where he thought it would look the best, and it fitted in beautifully. He could not stop looking at it, but although it was a stunning portrait, he would rather have the flesh-and-blood person. When he looked at the signature, he realised that Chloe's mother must be known under her maiden name, so he looked her up on the computer. The more he looked at her website the more he loved her work. An exhibition was advertised at a gallery not far from his office, so he consulted Bette about his diary for the next day; he had time to get there at lunchtime. Looking further there was a mention of her daughter being a talented artist herself. This came as a complete surprise, as it had not been mentioned by her. The exhibition should have been a joint one. He found Chloe's website and stared at the pictures of her paintings; they were incredible. He searched for more on Chloe. She was spoken of as being an up-and-coming artist in her own right with, the article said, an extremely bright future, as she was starting to collect a small but growing following of her own. The next day he walked to the gallery. There was a sign explaining that the gallery was sorry to announce that, owing to circumstances beyond their control, there would be only a small number of Chloe's works on show. He was impressed with Chloe's mother's work but was thrilled to see three of Chloe's paintings. He stood in front of them, drinking them in; they were beautiful. She was obviously extremely talented. He was concentrating so hard that he had not heard somebody speaking to him; it was the gallery owner, no doubt hoping there was a possible sale to be had. Paul excused himself for not hearing what had been said and they exchanged names and shook hands. "Are you looking for something in particular? If you were looking to buy you could not go far wrong with either of them, but it won't be long before Chloe's paintings are as much in demand as her mother's, and then the prices will increase considerably. As you can see many of them are already sold." Paul noticed sold stickers on all three of Chloe's paintings as well as many of her mother's and there were two of her paintings that he bought before he left the gallery. As he walked back to his office Paul was thinking hard. He had been trying to persuade Chloe to live with him, and she was taking a long time to decide what to do. This had led to a few disagreements, making him wonder if she did love him as much as she said she did, but he had the feeling that there was more to her reticence than was being said. One of her reasons was that she would have nothing to do, but he had an idea that might just tempt her. He was thinking about a room in his apartment that was never used which could be turned into a studio. He needed to do some research to find out what would be needed for it to become a good studio space, and who would know better than her mother? As there was a gap between meetings, he decided to ring straightaway. Jean Winters answered. "Hello, Jean, it's Paul, I hope you don't mind my ringing you?" When she answered it was amazing how much alike mother and daughter sounded on the phone. "Paul, how lovely to hear from you," she exclaimed, with delight in her voice at hearing from him. "Is everything all right?"

"I've just been to see your exhibition. The gallery is near my office. I loved your paintings. A lot have been sold, I noticed, and I have bought two of them. That painting of Chloe looks so good in the apartment, thank you so much, I love it. I had no idea that Chloe was an artist as well. She's good, isn't she?"

"Oh yes, she enjoys painting, she always has done." There was pride of her daughter evident in her voice. "There is a room in my apartment that I was thinking of setting up as a studio for Chloe. The room is not big, but the light seems as though it would be good. I was wondering if you would send me a list of all the equipment, paints, storage, everything she would need, and perhaps you wouldn't mind supplying everything as well? I will send you the money when you tell me how much it costs. There is no need to mention this to her, I want it to be a surprise."

"What a lovely idea," she exclaimed. "Yes, I would love to do that, and I won't say a word." She paused and then said, "You're making her incredibly happy; I can't tell you how much she has changed for the better since you two met, and it's all down to you. We have never seen her as contented and at peace with the world as she is now, thank you."

"She has some unbelievably bad nightmares; it really worries me. I have spoken to Anna, and she says that they think that she is holding something back, something she does not want to face. I keep asking her to tell me what's the cause, but it sends her into a panic attack."

"She had some bad ones while she was staying with us, but she wouldn't say anything then either. Just keep trying," said her mother. "I want to spoil her so much, but she won't let me, it's frustrating." Her mother laughed. "That's Chloe, so independent." After he rang off, he sat looking out of the window. Independent was putting it mildly; he was going to have to be careful how he presented anything to her. He was looking forward to showing her the room and suggesting the idea to her, keeping his fingers crossed that she would accept. When he got home, he went straight to the room for a closer look. There was some furniture, an old sofa, a table, and a few other odds and ends that he thought he would leave for the moment, as she might find some of it useful. The thought of her being in there, working, gave him a good feeling. Just coming home to her would turn the apartment into a home, less of a bachelor pad.

TWENTY-FIVE

John rang and told me that the family he had worked for had gone back home early, and he had taken the chance of taking a holiday. He would be able to start working for me on the following Monday, if that was okay with me. I asked Paul to speak to him about car park access. Paul had told me about offering John a job with his company, but that he would still be employed to look after me. It came as a bit of a surprise, but I was more than okay with the arrangement. When John arrived, we showed him to his room, and the rest of the week was spent getting to know each other. I soon became very comfortable in his company, which was important, as I was putting my safety in his hands, a situation I was very happy with.

John had been in the police station where Chloe had been taken, when she was rescued, to give an initial statement. He had been there to pick up some paperwork he needed and knew most of the team involved. Everybody there had been disturbed at her appearance, as she looked so different from the picture of her that had been in the entrance to The Harem. She looked so thin and pale, small, and vulnerable, and extremely nervous. She was swamped against the size and number of the police that filled the corridors. His heart went out to her and he would have loved to put a consoling arm around her shoulders, to give her a bit of support. He was pleased at the change in her when he was introduced to her by Anna. Having put on a bit of weight, she looked a lot better, although to him still a little underweight, and there was a bit more confidence about her. Anna had realised that he was attracted to Chloe and had warned him that she was not free. He and Paul got on very well from the start, making life easier. It was also evident how much they loved each other.

*

We were going to stay at my house for a few days, and when we arrived, we showed John his room above the garage, which had been finished just in time. We decided to eat at the pub that night and we could hear music coming from the room at the back. "There's a group that plays almost every week," I explained. Both Paul and John decided they would like to go through and listen for a while, but before we moved away from the table one of the band members spotted me and came over, giving me a hug. "Can you wait there a minute," he asked, and then rushed back the way he had come. There was an announcement that there would be a short break. Paul wanted to know what was happening, but I didn't have a chance to answer before all the band came hurrying into the room, crowding around me, each one giving me an enthusiastic welcome home hug. I was so touched; the tears weren't far away. Paul, however, did not look happy at the turn of events, and I hastily introduced everybody, hoping to diffuse the situation. It worked, much to my relief, when Jeff, the lead singer, asked me pleadingly if I would sit in for a couple of numbers, telling me they would ask for requests. Reluctantly I agreed. Jeff turned to Paul, asking him if they could borrow me, although not for long. Paul laughed and said that it was fine with him. Taking my hand, Jeff pulled me into the room and onto the small stage, saying into the microphone, "Look who I found lurking outside." This was followed by a standing ovation, with a lot of stamping, clapping, and cheering when the audience recognised me. Oh, how embarrassing, dig me a hole, somebody, please. Paul and John looked at each other in amazement. "I didn't know she could sing; I'm finding out more about her every day." He took his phone out to film what was happening. One of the band shouted for quiet, and asked the audience if they would like to hear me sing. There was another cheer, and they were then asked for requests. There were quite a few, mostly for 'Fairy Tale Of New York'. That always was a big favourite. "Really? But it's not Christmas," I said. "But you weren't here then," came the reply. "I can't remember the words." That was soon remedied when a copy appeared. There was another cheer when I agreed, albeit reluctantly; it was all getting too much. I said into the microphone, "I don't know what I will sound like, I haven't had the chance to sing recently." *Or the inclination*, I thought. I surprised myself, my voice was better than I expected, and I managed to get through it. There were shouts for a repeat, which we did, and the next request was for me to sing 'Love Me Tender', another song that had been a favourite of the audience previously. I couldn't take my eyes off Paul who was at the back of the room, and when I finished the audience were clapping for more, but I left the stage and went to sit with Paul and John and finally finish my drink, I was so thirsty. Paul leaned over and kissed me. We sat and listened to some more of the group and then left to go back home, but not before I had been stopped several times on the way out to speak to people I hadn't seen since I got back home. Eventually we arrived back and left John to go back to the flat. Paul showed me the film he had made.

The next morning, I rang John to see if he wanted to come to the house for breakfast and, after there was a discussion about what to do, Paul suggested that we show John where I work. I got my staff car park pass out of my car and when we stopped at the gates, I lowered my window to speak to Pete, who was on duty, and who waved us in. The general car park was full, and I remembered that there was a clay pigeon shooting competition, the sounds only too evident coming from the ranges. Both Paul and John were interested in looking, so we made our way towards the sound. Before we had gone far the familiar and very unwelcome voice of Mark, my ex, called after me, slurring his words, and as usual, drunk. It would be the first time that I had seen him since I ended our engagement. He repeated what he had said, thinking that I had not heard him. "If it isn't the prick-teasing whore back in town." I turned in his direction, and there he was, standing, swaying, taking another drink from a can, no doubt one of the many he must have consumed already. "I heard you the first time, and you are a motherfucking bastard, so where do we go from here? Keep calling each other names? Was that it? Or is there more of the same? Your vocabulary hasn't improved much, has it?" He stood there looking as if he was about to collapse, looking terrible, so ill, the drinking must be having a seriously detrimental effect; something was on his mind. I decided that I was going to do the talking. "I wasn't coming home to you on the night I was abducted; I was going to stay with my parents. The engagement and relationship were over then as far as I was concerned." That got his attention and seemed to penetrate the drunken haze he was in. I got some satisfaction from the look of comprehension that appeared on his face, looking a little shocked. "Why?" he asked. "He asks why?" I said, loudly enough for the people around to hear. "You were sending some dreadful messages that night when I was late home. Rather like the ones I have been receiving lately; you sent them, didn't you?" Paul had moved to stand next to me with his arm around my waist, giving me support, and also showing Mark that I was not facing him on my own. "You asked me why, well I knew how I would end up if I came back; the way I always ended up after you had been drinking, black and blue with bruises. I got tired of being used as a punchbag, I had had enough."

"I'll kill him," growled Paul, as he started forward towards Mark. I held my hand out. "Back off, I'm first in line for that, I have some extremely unpleasant things in mind." He backed off with a smirk on his face, saying, "He's all yours. Can I watch?"

"You going to shoot me then?" Mark slurred. "Shoot you? Why would I do something so stupid? I have only just got my freedom back. Why would I do something that was going to get me put behind bars again, over a piece of shit like you? You are not even worth the cost of the bullet. No, you're safe. Thought that you would get your revenge because I had called off the engagement, did you?"

"I suppose you're after his money?" he said, indicating Paul. "I could be after hers," came from Paul. "She is a wealthy woman in her own right." Mark had obviously not heard about the obscenely large sum of compensation money that I and the other girls had been awarded. Mark was thinking that out and then came back with, "Earned it on your back, didn't you?" There were gasps from the people around us. It made me laugh out loud, however, when I considered his question. "Yes, I suppose I did, but do not get any ideas, because I am far too expensive for you. Then again you couldn't touch me the last time we met, could you? You obviously thought that I would contaminate you. What was it that you said in your latest message? That I was contaminated and diseased, and that if an animal was as diseased as I, in your opinion, am, it should be put down, and that is what you intend doing. Was that an empty threat? Or a promise? Come on, I want to know." He stood, very unsteadily on his feet, then he seemed to make his mind up and, throwing down his half-empty can, produced a gun from one of his pockets. At this I saw John moving around behind him, ready to grab the gun. "So, what is it to be? What are you going to do?" I asked, hoping to keep his attention on me and not on what John was doing. "I'm going to put you down, just as I promised I would," he shouted, and then aimed unsteadily at me. At that point John moved in and easily took the gun out of his hand and put him down onto the floor, just as the police arrived on the scene, no doubt having been called by somebody in the crowd. At that I held up my mobile for him to see it. "Gotcha!" I had been holding my phone where it was not obvious, filming what was happening. I had tried unsuccessfully to record his other attempts at threatening me; this time I hoped that I had something that would help. Paul wrapped his arms around me and held me close and I rested my forehead against his chest. I was shaking. The police took Mark away and asked me for a copy of the film that I had taken. We watched the competition for a while and one of my friends came up to ask if I was shooting that day. Paul looked at me in surprise. "You can shoot?" he exclaimed. "Yes, just a bit, but I haven't touched a gun in a long time, for obvious reasons."

"Do you have one of your own?" asked John. "I do. I'm a member of the estate gun club. Members can keep their guns in the gun room here, it makes it easier, and security is particularly good, better than it would be at home. I do not think that I would like them at home anyway. We can go and have a look at them, they need cleaning. Do you want to see them?"

"You've got more than one?"

"Yes, a handgun and two rifles." When I had opened my locker, I lifted them out. "Good makes, all three. I was armed when I was in the police," commented John, and the way he handled them made it obvious he was used to handling firearms. "Any tips and help you can give me would be most welcome, not that I'm aiming for the Olympics or anything. I will never be as good as that. I am in one of the teams, but not the one competing today. I am not all that consistent, sometimes I do all right but not always. There is an indoor range here, it's extremely popular."

"I used to shoot a bit when I was younger, but I didn't have time when I was starting the business," Paul said. "Do you still have guns?"

"Yes, they're locked away in my apartment. How about you?" Paul asked John. "I do, and they are still at the club in London. I'll have to find somewhere different to keep them. I have kept the paperwork up to date." We had a walk around some more of the estate, and John brought up the subject of the messages, wanting to know why I had not said anything to the police about my suspicions. "If I had been absolutely sure that it was him, I would have said so, but I couldn't be a hundred percent certain, and I didn't want to say anything while I wasn't."

"Did he knock you about a lot?" Paul asked. "Whenever he got drunk, which was getting more frequent. He had sold his flat quite quickly and my house was up for sale, with a good offer on it. Mark was having to move out, and the nearer it got to him living with me, well, it filled me with horror, I could not face it. My house didn't feel like a home anymore, I was afraid of going back home. So I took it off the market, deciding that I was not prepared to marry him. I had been having second thoughts for a while. I couldn't understand why I had said yes."

After we had eaten and John had gone back to the flat, I caught Paul gazing at me. "What? Why are you looking at me like that?"

"Like what?" he asked, trying to look serious. "You're staring at me."

"I like staring at you, you're worth staring at. I'll never get bored staring at you." By this time, we were grinning at each other. "I was thinking that I have learned so much about you." I looked surprised. "Like what? There's not much to know." He came over and sat next to me, pulling me close to him. "That you are an artist, a good one, becoming increasingly popular. You can shoot, and you have a beautiful singing voice as well. You are an incredibly talented and beautiful woman, and I won't list the other talents you have, not ones I want you sharing with anybody else, ever." How embarrassing was it listening to him. Later in the evening my friend Sandra rang, asking if she could come to see me. There was something I needed to know. It would not take long, she assured me. When she arrived, she seemed surprised that Paul was with me, at which he offered to leave us to talk alone. "I haven't any secrets from Paul, it's all right for him to stay." When we were settled with coffee Sandra took a minute before she said anything. She told me that Mark was sleeping off the drink in the cells, but that he would not be given bail. There was obviously more she had to tell me. "When Mark was drunk and beating you up…" she paused, seeming to struggle with how to put what she had to say next. "Did he do anything else, abuse you in any other way?" They were both looking at me. Paul took my hand in his and squeezed it reassuringly. "Yes, he did. He raped me. Why, what's he said?" Sandra and Paul both gasped. "How many times?" asked Paul quietly. "Just the once, but I managed to get away from him twice." He put his arms around me, pulling me close. "Why didn't you report him?" Sandra asked me, a horrified look on her face.

"Strangely it was only when I was taken to the police station after I had been rescued, and they were talking about the other girls and me having been raped, that it dawned on me. That was exactly what Mark had done, but I thought it too late to do anything about it by then. What's he been saying?" I asked again. "He hasn't said anything, but when they looked, he had a record; there have been complaints made about him before. But you did not hear that last bit from me. I had better go, will it be okay if someone comes to take a statement?" She gave me a hug, and then left, leaving me reeling.

TWENTY-SIX

Moving in with Paul was in my thoughts a lot and I had discussed it with my sister to get her opinion. What she said was that I needed to actually be living there to make any friends, which was a fair point and one I had come to myself. Living the lifestyle that Paul did, and in such opulent surroundings would take some getting used to. My family wasn't exactly poor, but the difference would still be great. I would miss my family and friends so much. I would have to find a way of making friends. My friends and I met up at least once a week, sometimes more, and most of them were settled in the area, not showing any signs of moving away. But still, situations change, don't they?

Paul was thrilled when I told him that I would move in with him and had a large grin on his face. On the day I was moving in Paul came to pick me up. It's good that his car was a big one because it would have needed two trips otherwise. When we arrived and had unloaded, the lift was kept busy. Paul showed me the walk-in wardrobe in his bedroom. I stared, it was massive. No worries about my small amount of clothing fitting in. Paul appeared with cups of tea. I was thirsty, and they were welcome. We sat down to drink them, and he handed me the keys, showing me where they were for, also the alarm code and the code for the lift. He took me around to show me where everything was, also in the kitchen. I wasn't sure I needed that but still it might be useful sometime. When I thought we had seen the whole apartment he told me there was somewhere else I needed to see along the corridor. When he opened the door, I couldn't believe the amazing studio that had been set up for me and flung my arms round his neck and kissed him for being so thoughtful. The studio was wonderful, and I spent a lot of time in there. Of course I realised that he had done it to give me another incentive to live with him, a crafty move on his part, I thought. Well, it worked for me. I love Paul dearly, and could not imagine being without him, but I did miss my parents and friends and often went back for a few days, to keep up with what was happening. Paul had surprised me by buying an old garage with quite a large field on the fringes of the village. It had a large industrial building behind it, as well as a house on the same site. After discussions with the owners of the only two houses nearby, he put in for permission to land helicopters on the site. There was woodland which would help to muffle the sound, but there were many things to be done to make the enterprise possible. The house was undergoing refurbishment and would be used for the pilot to stay in if necessary; there would also be room in the hangar for a car to be kept, and the tanks that had been for the garage, after a bit of work, would be used for the fuel for the helicopter. This would make getting to and from London so much easier, and Philip from the estate was showing interest in using the helicopter for estate business.

I was so glad Paul had persuaded me not to sell my house. I had organised for a local firm to keep the garden tidy, as I thought that my parents had enough to look after with their own, and them both working. I had consulted an architect about plans to build an extension to my house, the outside being built to blend in with the original part. The plans he had shown me so far were stunning. I loved them, he had such wonderful ideas, and they were to be submitted for planning permission very soon.

The time seemed to fly by when I was in my studio, and not having to work I could spend more time on my paintings. Paul came in one night when he got back from the office, trying to creep in and not disturb me. I was trying a cityscape. It was a different subject for me, and I was using the view from the window. He came and stood behind me, looking at what I was working on. "That has an otherworldly appearance, almost like an illustration for a sci-fi magazine. Is that for your next exhibition?"

"Yes, but not for sale, to see what people think. The colour of the sky was just like that one night, I took a photo and printed it off to copy from." I showed him the picture.

*

Paul often worked on his computer while Chloe was painting. He loved to watch the concentration on her face. He loved just being with her.

*

We had been to visit some friends of Paul's. They were a lovely couple who we had met before, their two little boys were so entertaining and were enthralled with their litter of kittens. They were nearly ready to go to new homes, so they were very playful and beautiful. The breed, I was told, was Maine Coon, a large breed. One of the kittens came and sat on my knee, settling down for a sleep. She was brown but had streaks of lighter shades in her fur, big green eyes and large tufts on her ears. Paul had some business to discuss about the club with his friend, but after that we spent a relaxing afternoon sitting in their garden.

I had yet another nightmare. Paul just held me until I calmed down. He did not say anything for a while. "Chloe, I am so worried about you. Something is very wrong. The way these nightmares affect you they must be caused by something that frightened you badly, and I can only think that it is what happened at the club. Please, please tell me what causes them, what they are about. I'm sure that keeping quiet isn't helping you." I did not say anything at first, thinking what to do, and yes, I think that it was more than time that I said something, starting with Paul.

*

Chloe was quiet for so long that Paul thought she was not going to talk, but he felt that to keep quiet and let her take her own time was the best policy. Then, much to his surprise and relief, she started to talk.

*

I told him about the punishments, how bad they were, and about the experiment, the part that I had blanked out as much as I could. I was totally honest, leaving nothing out.

*

He listened to what she was telling him with horror and increasing anger on her behalf, the more that he heard. He was getting very emotional as well. When she had finished and lay in his arms, looking exhausted, he did not know what to say to her. He was speechless and horrified in equal measure. He finally managed to find his voice. "Chloe, what can I say? That is a horrific situation for you to go through. Have you told anyone about that?" She shook her head. "Not even Anna?" She shook her head again. "I think you ought to tell her." He stopped talking, waiting to see what her reaction was before he said more, and much to his surprise she nodded. "I think you're right; I should have had the courage to tell her, shouldn't I?" He pulled her into his arms, holding her tightly. She pulled away from him so that she could look up into his face, asking, obviously dreading the answer. "I don't suppose you will want to make love to me anymore, will you, after what I've just told you?" He smiled down at her. "You suppose wrong. I will always want you, that is never going to change. Do you hear what I'm saying? That explains why you had far more tests done on you than any of the other girls. I think, as it is time for us to get up, that we ought to have some breakfast and then contact Anna. What do you think?"

"I don't know whether I can eat anything yet. My appetite seems to have vanished."

*

After we had finished, I realised that the time had come to ring Anna but, taking pity on me, Paul offered to ring her. I accepted with gratitude.

His phone was charging in his office, about which he was glad because he could talk to Anna without Chloe hearing. Anna answered immediately. "Paul, is everything all right?"

"Yes, it is. I've had a breakthrough with Chloe, she wants to talk to you, and she didn't tell you everything before. She has just told me all of what happened. It isn't very pretty I can tell you." There was a sigh of relief from Anna. "Thank God. Can she come in and talk to me today?"

*

When we arrived at the front office of the police station, a call was made to Anna telling her that I had arrived. Anna had made a call to Tara, the prosecution barrister, asking her if she wanted to sit in and watch the interview with the team members who were able to get there. Anna came through and hugged me. "You're doing the right thing. Come through, I know Paul has been very worried about you." She took us into the interview room. Paul sat on the sofa close to me with my hand very firmly in his. When I had been interviewed after I was rescued, I had not talked about being punished, or the experiment. I could not mention them as it upset me too much. It was time I did; I was finished with acting the victim. I told Anna everything, leaving nothing out.

While I had been talking the inspector had joined us. "When you were taken to the apes, did you get a look at what the rooms were like that you were taken through?" I must have looked puzzled at the question. "What was in the rooms? Was there any equipment of any kind? How many people were there around?" I thought hard and closed my eyes, envisaging the route in my mind, picturing what I had seen every day. I did not think what I could remember would amount to much help. "There was one that seemed to have at least one laptop, the people with me had paperwork."

"How many people?"

"I can't say for certain; I could hear other people in that room that were out of sight, but there were at least four that were always around me. I don't know how many others. How did they get away with all that happened? Surely somebody must have known?" He looked at me and then said, "It was a very slick operation, both setting it up and getting out. Apparently work started in an area that wasn't used, a lot of very noisy building work that was upsetting the apes. At the same time the keepers were introduced to another team and the two were paired off, so the new ones could learn the routines and get to know the apes. The original keepers were worried about their jobs but were assured that all of them were safe. There were comments that the new people did not appear to know very much about keeping any animals and had a lot to learn. When the building work was finished, they split into two teams, the original keepers in one and the new ones in the other. The rotas had changed; the original keepers would only start work in the afternoon, with no loss of pay. Nobody, apart from the new keepers, was allowed into the new part of the building; then one day they were informed that the rotas had changed, the rotas had been reversed, no reasons were given. One day the morning shift waited for the changeover, no one arrived. The door through to the other part was found to be unlocked and when they investigated there was nothing left, everything had been removed. When that area was tested nothing showed up, the whole area had been deep cleaned. All the cameras both inside and outside had been disabled so no activity could be seen. The gates at the end of the drive were always closed at midnight and there was a password needed to get in after that. A gatekeeper was on duty all night, but he had been drugged. As for sounds of vehicles, they were electric, so no sound. So that is where the investigation is now, at a full stop, and unless we are lucky, that is where we are going to have to leave it, probably on hold; it is not going to be closed." We were all silent. "Thank you for telling me," I said. "And I don't suppose the men in charge are going to come clean, are they?" I commented. The inspector shrugged his shoulders. "Not a word, all no comment answers."

I was exhausted and sat with my head in my hands, resting my elbows on my knees. Paul pulled me closer to him and wrapped his arms around me, holding me tightly. It was quiet in the room. Anna was looking stunned. I heard later that all who had been listening in to my interview were equally affected. Tara, who had been making many notes, got up and called a taxi back to her office with a grim look on her face.

TWENTY-SEVEN

Afew weeks later Anna rang me to tell me the trial was on again and when. I had been staying with my parents, because Paul was abroad on business and John was on leave; there had been an emergency in his family. I sent a text telling Paul about Anna's call.

I awoke on the morning I would be giving evidence at the trial, a feeling of dread filling me. I was lying on my side with my back to Paul, his arms wrapped around me. I was so glad he was here. "Good morning, beautiful." I lay there wishing I could spend the day with him, but he had work, and I had court to attend, unfortunately.

"I am dreading today. I'm so nervous, I feel like hiding. You would think it was me in the dock, the way I'm feeling. But I suppose I had better try and drag myself away from you." After I had had a shower, had breakfast, and finished getting prepared for the day, I went through into the living room when I was ready. Paul was standing looking out at the river. He turned when I entered the room and came and took me into his arms, bending down to kiss me, although not as far as usual because I was wearing a pair of shoes with much higher heels than I usually wore. I hoped that

I wouldn't fall out of them and make a fool of myself. "Do you think this outfit is suitable?" He held me at arm's length. "You'll knock them dead; you look fabulous."

"Not quite the image I was going for."

"You look very smart, and I think just right, but you still look fabulous." There was a knock at the door. Anna had arrived to take me to the court. She smiled at me and said hello to Paul. "You're looking very businesslike and smart, isn't she, Paul?"

"Just what I have been telling her," came the reply. There was a knock at the living room door; it was his driver, Louis. "I'll go to work, now that Anna's here, and I'll see you tonight." After he had kissed me, he walked towards the door. Before he left, he turned and said, "I know you're nervous, but this is your chance to make sure they pay for what they did to you. It isn't you in the wrong. Don't forget that." He left the room, giving me a dazzling smile as he did so. "I. Am. So. Nervous," I admitted to Anna. "I'm shaking badly already."

"What Paul told you is true; this is your chance to help put them away. They are facing many serious charges. With a bit of luck, they will be going to prison for a long time. The case doesn't depend on your evidence alone, I hope that helps, a little."

"Yes, it does, and I am being silly."

"I didn't say that you were being silly at all, standing up in court is an ordeal, whichever side you are on. I'll feel just as bad when it's my turn to give evidence, I always do, despite the number of times that I have had to do it. It never gets any easier, I always find the experience daunting."

The journey to court was uneventful, thank goodness. When we arrived, I was shown to the room for the prosecution witnesses. Anna told me she hoped that the defence barristers would not be too bad, and then left me with the court official. She was so kind and told me it could be some time before I am called. I scrutinised the people waiting, for anybody I recognised, so I picked out a chair which looked comfortable and not near to anyone and sent a message to Paul.

"Hi, just arrived at court, with no problems. I am told it might be a while before I am called. Miss you. Chloe xxx." His reply came back almost instantaneously. "Missing you too, cannot wait until tonight, I ordered a sandwich and orange juice for lunchtime for you. Is that okay? Or is there anything else you would rather have? I can change the order. Paul xxx."

"That sounds wonderful, I think there is a café somewhere, but thank you, that was very thoughtful, I am looking forward to my lunch. Love you. Chloe xxx."

Paul had offered to come and sit in court to give me support, but I knew he had an important meeting that day, so I told him no, that I would be okay. I settled down to read my book, changing over to listening to music; my concentration was nil and was not allowing me to do anything for long. I could not look out of the window because there was a film over it. The court usher took me by surprise, coming into the room and calling my name. So, after turning my phone off, I followed the usher, with much trepidation, into the courtroom.

For weeks before the trial there had been speculation in many of the papers and on social media, rumours of a mystery witness who was going to give evidence. There were many theories put forward as to who it was, and what this evidence could be. They were all way off the mark with their ideas of what would be said. All this made the trial already sensational, because of the high-profile people involved, even more so. Our Harem names had already been discovered, and with Scarlet not being mentioned the media had correctly identified her as the mystery witness. When it was announced that Scarlet was going to give evidence in person, on the day I was going to be in court, the place was besieged with people wanting to be in the room to see and hear what I had to say. "Packed like sardines they are," the usher told me. She had a kind smile, light curly hair, large glasses and, it seemed, an impish sense of humour. It was standing room only in court.

When I was shown into court, I found the place very intimidating, as Anna had told me it probably would be. I managed to look around enough to know where everybody was and I was glad to find that I was not going to have to look at the public gallery, which was at the side, and I was looking straight across at the jury. Tara was sitting at a desk nearest me, with the defence barristers at the other end, one on the same row as Tara, the two others on the second row. A court usher came across and asked me to swear the oath. I had already been asked if I wanted to swear on the Bible or make an affirmation. After I had done that the judge asked me when I was giving my evidence not to talk too quickly as he was making notes on his computer, and then indicated to Tara that he was ready. Tara got up and gave me an encouraging smile and asked me to state my name, and then said, "You were known by the name of Scarlet, weren't you?"

"Yes, I was."

"You mentioned in your statement about being punished, twice, can you tell the court what happened the first time? You were in a threesome, you said?" I swallowed. "Yes, it was with another female and a man." I went through what had happened. "And how were you punished?" Again, I went through what they had done to me; talking about what had happened brought tears to my eyes. "What happened the second time, which was soon after, wasn't it?"

"The bruising hadn't faded from before. This man, who was on his own, beat me up as well. I think that he had something on his finger, because when he put his finger inside me, it was rough and made me bleed. I was kept in my room to let me heal; it must have been for about a week. I had no way of telling the time or what day or date it was either, every day was like the one before. But I was in a lot of pain."

"And he got you punished as well?"

"Yes."

"How?" It was so painful to bring it up again, to remember. "The same as before; the pain was excruciating, and the same kind of shock, but stronger that time. I had to be carried back to my room because I lost the use of my legs and could not walk for quite a while afterwards. It did cross my mind that he had done it on purpose, like the one before, so that they could watch me suffer." There was a reaction from the public gallery. One of the defence barristers got up and objected to what I had said.

There was a break for lunch then, and as I walked back to the room I had been in before I was looking forward to my lunch. The usher handed it to me as I entered. I did wonder whether I had any appetite, but the sandwich looked tempting, and tasted amazing, and I ate it all. The orange juice was beautiful, sweet, and refreshing. I sent a text to Paul.

"We are on lunch break, and thank you for ordering lunch for me, I have enjoyed it so much. I am waiting to be called back in, this next bit is going to be rough, I can tell. The court room was packed this morning. Think of me this afternoon, I miss you. Chloe xxx."

"Thinking of you, as always, baby, you can do this. Stay strong. Paul xxx."

I spent time prowling up and down the room, to try to stop myself from getting stiff. There was a toilet attached, which was good; I would not have to put my hand up and ask to leave the room, like at school, and giggled to myself at the thought. I was just coming out when the court usher came to call me back into court. It was a different one from the morning, and I thought that this one had no sense of humour. And, trying to calm my fruit-bat-sized butterflies, I followed her out to the court room, and I found it just as intimidating as I had earlier. One of the defence barristers got up to question me. "Miss Winters, why did you not make any attempt to escape your... prison? Surely there must have been someone who would have helped. Got together with the other girls, who were also... prisoners, for example. Are you sure that you are not fabricating the whole tale? To make you sound like a victim, no doubt looking for a large pay-out?" I glared at him. How dare he insinuate that all of us had been making it up? He did, I thought, look a little uncomfortable, but not enough as far as I was concerned. Trying to make my voice as glacial as possible, and staring fixedly, I spoke to him as if to a child, with words of one syllable. I answered, "No, I have made nothing up, and as for escaping, I looked for ways to do just that, and the only place that there was the slightest possibility was when I was allowed out into the garden, and there were absolutely no areas where there was a chance of climbing out. Other than developing superhuman powers and being able to jump about fifteen feet straight up, from a standing start." There was a ripple of laughter at that. I was on a roll, and he tried to get another question in, but I carried on. "It was also electrified; I could hear the clicking from the current. Even when I was only being taken down the corridor, I had a collar round my neck with a chain attached and my hands were handcuffed behind my back. There was simply no chance of seeing who was with me because the people all had suits and visors so that I couldn't identify anybody." I think that the barrister tried to object but was overruled; I am surprised that I got away with it. "There were always two people with me at all times. I was also naked all day. The other girls and I had no contact with each other, that was all in my statement. If you have read it." I had run out of steam at that point, and he had no more questions, although where that got him, who could say. Stupid man. Looking at Tara I got the impression that she was trying not to smile.

TWENTY-EIGHT

Then came the part I was dreading most, questions about the experiment with the apes. Tara smiled at me and asked, "Was it true you were included in an experiment where apes were involved?" The noise from the public gallery when that was mentioned was quite loud. I did not answer straightaway. The judge asked for silence, which was followed by a deathly hush, with all eyes on me, waiting for my answer. "Yes," I said. More noise erupted from the gallery; the judge again demanded silence. The next question followed: "How were you involved in that experiment?" There was complete silence, it was unnerving. I was shaking, it must have been obvious. I took a deep steadying breath. "I was told that the apes were going to mate with me." It took some time to quieten the court down and I closed my eyes. When I opened them again the judge asked me if I wanted a break. I thanked him and said I would rather get it over with. "Did you go willingly?"

"No, not at all."

"What happened?"

"That time I was screaming hysterically. I fought with them all the way, kicking, biting where I could; I threw my head back and it connected with the minder's nose. They gasped, they brought in more people to help them, there were four of them. I was tiring by then; I stood no chance of stopping it happening. They hit me across the face and then used what I think was a cane on my back several times, hard enough for it to bleed, they were very rough with me. They eventually got me tied down. I have had violent nightmares ever since."

"So, you were shackled in place?"

"Yes."

"How?"

"Face down, on some kind of bed."

"What happened next?"

"He did what they wanted him to do." I paused. "He mated with me." At that the noise in the court was deafening. The judge was getting annoyed, and threatened to clear the court if there was any more disturbance. "How did they get him to do that?"

"They rubbed some foul-smelling stuff on me, I thought it was maybe to mimic a female that was ready to mate."

"What happened then?"

"I think he was encouraged out of the area, and people came back in. They cleaned me up and then injected me with what I thought was tranquilliser, because there were three other apes that did the same and I went along with it far too easily. I was scared to death, mostly of the second ape, because he regularly beat me up and bit me, as did the other two, but neither of them was as violent. I still have scars on my back from when they bit me, some are still visible. One was so violent he wasn't always put in with me." Tara turned to the usher and asked for the photos that had been taken of my back to be shown to the jury and let them have a good long look at them, pointing out the scars. I took the chance to look across at the three men on trial, and I was surprised to find that one of them was watching me, it seemed with a troubled look on his face. As well he should. The other two just looked ahead, stony-faced. "As you can see, the bites are obvious; they were at first thought to have been made by a human. And what look to be scars left from when the cane was used, hard enough to have raised open wounds that would have left visible scars like those. Those photos were taken on the day when Chloe was rescued by the police. This young woman will probably carry some of those for the rest of her life." She turned back to me. "Were you scared of the apes?"

"Yes, terrified. I realised they could tear me apart at any time. I did not think that I would get out of there alive; any one of them could have killed me. It's no wonder that they were pissed off at being in captivity, rather than in the wild, where they had been taken from, and pushed into living a life that was unnatural to them. I could relate entirely to how they must have felt; I was, after all, in the same position." Tara smiled at me and turning to the judge said she had no more questions. The defence surprisingly said they had no questions either. Tara got up again and asked, "Is it true that you contemplated suicide?" I paused. "Yes, frequently." I looked across at the three men. They did not look at me and stared straight ahead. I hoped that they felt some shame about what they had put us all through, but I doubted they would feel anything at all. I was then told I was free to go.

I stood in the witness box, not able to move at first, until the court usher came and put her hand on my arm and asked if I was all right. Tara was looking in my direction with a look of concern on her face and when I started to move gave me a smile of encouragement. Finally, the ordeal was over. I was exhausted by the whole experience. I thought I had been released. My mind was confused, and I hoped that I hadn't made any mistakes and said the wrong thing, but as I was being escorted out, I went over what I said. No doubt that I would hear from Anna later. I sent Paul a message.

"They have finished with me, thank heavens. Chloe xxx." His answer came back quickly.

"Hi sweetheart, fantastic, glad to hear you have finished, I will be with you soon. Cannot wait to see you. Paul xxx."

Anna came to find me, and beamed at me after she gave me a hug. "That's it, I don't think you will be needed after today, and you did really well." Which answered my unspoken question. "We are all very proud of you, especially the way you stood up to the defence. I think Tara was going to step in on a couple of occasions, but the way you answered she didn't need to." She paused. "The questions about the apes must have been upsetting." I could not speak, I was so emotional, and the tears were pouring down my face. Anna said nothing and took me in her arms and just held me until the tears stopped. "What will happen about my impact statement? Will I have to go back into court to read it?" I asked her, wiping my eyes. "Tara is going to read it for you unless you want to read it yourself."

"No, that's fine, I don't think that I want to be back in court again, although part of me would like to."

When the car stopped outside the apartment block, I asked Anna if she wanted to come in, but she had to get back to work. She still had more work to do on this case before being called to give her evidence, but before she left me, she told me I could ring her anytime for anything, that she wasn't going to cut me adrift, which was very comforting.

I stepped out my shoes; I was so glad to get those off. I made myself a cup of tea, taking it into the bedroom with me, and changed into a pair of comfortable loose trousers and a top, my normal way of dressing around the house, and tried to relax with my tea and my book, but I had been so stressed that I couldn't settle. I curled up on the bed and the tears started.

When he got back home Paul came into the room, took one look at me and, after he had taken his jacket and shoes off, gathered me into his arms, holding me close, letting me cry. We stayed like that for some time until I fell into an exhausted doze. When I awoke, I was still lying with his arms around me, and I looked up into his face. "There you are, feel better for your nap?" I stretched, feeling comfortable, I did not want to move. It seemed Paul was in no hurry either. 'You give me so much, you're always there for me with all your support; all I do is cry, I don't do anything but take. You get nothing out of this relationship except trouble, that you end up sorting out for me." There was a look of astonishment on his face; he leaned down and gave me a long passionate kiss. "Not give me anything but trouble? Just take from me, and I get nothing out of this relationship? Have I got that right, is that what you think?" He smirked. "Well yes, you are trouble, I didn't realise how much you would cause." He was laughing when he said that, but he became serious. "But I hadn't reckoned how much I would benefit from the relationship we have; it's astounding to me how much. You turned my life upside down when you came into it, I couldn't think about anything but you. My staff found it hilarious, because when I was in meetings,

I wasn't concentrating on what was being discussed; my mind was very firmly on you." I must have looked sceptical. "Don't ever think that way because it isn't true. I always felt there was something missing in my life. I told you before that I got a bad reputation because of the number of girlfriends that I went through. When I saw you, I couldn't think of anything or anyone else." He laughed at himself. "I even went on flights of fancy about how the future would be with you. Which was not me, ask anyone. You have brought me contentment; I see the world differently after seeing how you see it. I love just sitting watching the world go by when I am with you. Something I would never have dreamed of previously. I am so happy just being with you. Unless you have not realised it yet, you give me plenty. I seemed to spend much of my free time at work, or on things work-related. That is changing; the time I spend there will be reduced so that I can spend more time with you. So, you can get those thoughts out of your head, are you hearing me? I would be lost without you in my life, completely and utterly."

Later he asked me about the day and what had happened, I would rather have forgotten all about it, but I told him everything. I was thinking about what had gone on, when I heard Paul saying, "Earth to Chloe, come back to me." He ran his finger down my cheek tenderly. "Not good thoughts?" I shook my head and squeezed his hand.

*

We had just finished breakfast one morning and Eva, the housekeeper, had just cleared away. I liked her immediately, she was very down to earth, efficient and discreet. Her attitude surprised me because her CV was impressive; with some of the people she had worked for, I fully expected her to be a bit starchy and formal but she was neither of those things.

Paul put his arm around me. We walked over to the window and he drew me down onto one of the large sofas. "There is a meeting at the club tomorrow; the new management team are to be voted on and I need to be there. We have to talk about the future of The Harem, what we are going to do with it. It should not take long, and I want you to come with me. Before you refuse, I have asked your parents and mine, as well as some of your friends, to come for lunch and a tour of the place. You will have them all with you while I am in the meeting so you will have plenty of people you trust not to let anything happen to you, including John. I've been told everything has been removed that would remind you of what went on." I sat and looked at him, a cold feeling forming in the pit of my stomach, a feeling of fear. Paul took me in his arms and held me close. I tried not to think about the next day, but it was difficult.

Paul held my hand all the way. The car stopped in the car park, and when John opened my door for me there was a concerned look on his face; he asked if I was okay. Paul came to see what was happening. "Are you all right? You've gone so pale." I looked at him. "Yes, I am, let us get this over with, shall we?" I finally left the car to join the others, who were studying the front of the lovely old building. Holding Paul's hand very tightly we walked up the steps into reception. Paul turned to me. "I'll have to go, the meeting starts soon. Shall we meet back here at one o'clock? The gardens are beautiful and worth seeing while it's such a beautiful day. If I'm not finished, order drinks at the bar, put them on my bill, and I'll see you later." He bent down and kissed me and said softly, "Don't worry, I won't be long."

The gardens were as beautiful as Paul had told me and we all enjoyed looking around them immensely, but I did keep looking towards the buildings with trepidation. John kept very close. I felt comforted by that even though I had so many people looking out for me who wouldn't let anything happen. Paul came looking for us when the meeting had finished, so we wandered back to reception and then through to the dining room, although not before I had looked nervously towards the discreet door that had been the entrance to The Harem. All it had on it was a sign saying members only, nothing to say what lay behind. There were quite a few diners in there already, and we were shown to a long table that had been set up for us all. I did not think I would be able to eat anything, but surprisingly I found that I ate most of what was put on my plate; the food was just as marvellous as I remembered. When we had eaten the main course, the waitress came to me and gave me a small tube. Everybody at the table looked mystified when she told me that the chef had said that I would know what to do with it. I suddenly laughed, much to everybody's surprise; Paul had not been told about this. I drew on the plate two smiley faces and five stars and then held my plate up for everybody to see, and answered the unasked question, what was I going to do with it, and why? "I used to send the chef messages this way to thank him for his wonderful meals. It started off with me drawing in any sauce that was left, and then he started to put one of these tubes on my plate." Just then the man himself appeared at my side, although I would not have known who it was if Paul had not introduced me. "I had to come and speak to you, because I never got

244

the chance to do so before." He put his arms around me, giving me a hug; there were tears in my eyes. "Thank you, you made life so much more bearable for me." After giving me a kiss, he shook hands with Paul, excused himself and made his way back to the kitchen. We were causing a bit of interest amongst the other diners; I think that some of them had recognised me, and most of them knew Paul. As we were leaving the dining room a man came to speak to us. Paul introduced him to me as Ken. He seemed familiar, but from where? Ken, but Ken who? I thought maybe an actor, but what was his last name? I would remember eventually. Paul seemed to know him well and they were having a long conversation. We were in the entrance hall again and I kept looking at the door that had been the entrance to The Harem. I realised that I had been asked a question. Paul was asking me if I had any objection to Ken coming with us, because he had not been a member of that side of the club, and he would love to have a look, he had always wondered what it was like. I smiled at him and told him he was welcome; he was such a lovely person. Where did I know him from? Paul put his arm around me protectively. "Shall we go?" I could only nod, and we went through the door, to be faced with life-sized photos of all the girls. I gasped, feeling dread as we went along the row, ending up with my picture. I could have died with embarrassment, everybody looking at it, like the other girls, completely naked. I turned to Paul and leaned my forehead against his chest. I could not look at anyone. "I thought they had moved everything out?" Just then Ken came and wanted to speak to me. I forced myself to look at him. Taking my hand in his he took me to sit in a seat facing my photo. Paul had often sat in that same one when Chloe was put on show in front of her picture, taking in every precious part of her, committing it to memory, wanting her in his arms rather than there. Everybody gathered around, wondering what was going on, Ken looked at the picture and then at me. "That's a beautiful picture of a beautiful woman. But remind me, what's your name?"

"Chloe?"

"What's the name under that picture?"

"Scarlet," I answered; where was he going with this? "That is Scarlet in that picture, not you. Just think of that as being a publicity shot for a play, or film, a character from either of them. But look at the expression on the face of that character, and the pose that she has. That says, excuse the language, fuck off, leave me alone and do not mess with me. There is something else about that picture. Look closely at the eyes. Those eyes are dead, there is no hope in them, whatever the pose or the expression on the face, those eyes say something different. That is a sad picture, it breaks your heart when you look at it closely." The tears start rolling down my cheeks; I get up and put my arms around him. "Thank you, so much," is all I manage. Paul mouths his thanks over my head, and we move on to the meeting room, where I was taken to the men who I was booked with; the place makes me shudder. After looking at some of the other girls' rooms, we arrive in the beautiful room with the four-poster bed, where I spent some bad times, but also some very memorable ones with Paul. "Not all bad memories, are they?" he murmured to me so that nobody else could hear him. "Amazing ones, as I recall, from my memory anyway," I responded, smirking at him. "But the nights I have spent with you since have been even better." We finally found the room that had been mine, and there were exclamations about what a beautiful room, which undoubtedly it was. How strange it was to have my family and friends in what had been my prison for all that time, and it seemed to help break some of the fear that had followed me. We went past the window that looked out over the small garden. It was beautiful, but even better viewed from this side of the glass. We then went to see the apes, and the first one seemed to have grown larger. As I got closer, he sniffed the air, looking at me closely, and then he started to make welcoming noises, obviously recognising me. He put his hand out to me, and I took it. One of the keepers came into the room. She had a young gorilla on her hip. She greeted us all and told us that this was one of his babies, a male; unfortunately, his mother had rejected him, and he had been raised by the keepers. He was adorable, and I told his father what a clever boy he was, and as if he knew what was being said, he put both his arms out to me and gave me a hug. It was then time to move on to see the others, so I had to extricate myself from him; a few titbits helped. The breeding centre was fantastic, they were having so much success, and all the apes looked healthy and seemed content. Paul told me that the man who had funded the centre would like to meet me the next day, if I was willing. Paul had booked us into an hotel nearby; not into the club, for obvious reasons. Later we said goodbye to everybody and went to our hotel. I sank down thankfully onto the bed, I had the found the day exhausting. Paul came and sat on the bed next to me, he was preoccupied. "What's on your mind?" I asked. "There are other people who want to meet you, if you feel strong enough."

"Who?" I asked.

TWENTY-NINE

Paul put his arms around my shoulders, pulling me closer. "If you have any doubts, you can always say no."

"Paul, you're worrying me, who?"

"Two men who booked you for a threesome." We stared at each other. I said nothing, thinking it through; I think I surprised him with my reaction. "How do you feel about my meeting them? Is it going to be a problem for you?" I asked. "Why would it be a problem for me?"

"Oh, let me think, because you get possessive when any man touches me." I looked at him, my eyebrows raised, smiling, challenging him to disagree with me. "I am never going to want any other man but you, that will never happen. It's you I love; I might flirt with other men, but they mean nothing to me. Okay? As for these men, they were good to me, treated me well, so yes, I would like to meet them. Have you known them long?" He grinned. "I will try to keep from punching them when they touch you. It will be difficult, but you're right, I do feel like that. I think I always will, especially because of where we met, so many men having had sex with you. I don't want any man to think you are still living that life. Our friendship goes back many years; they were both concerned over your welfare, they were in love with you as well. You had quite a large fan club, who were all upset about the way you were treated. Maia, one of your carers, kept us informed about what was going on; she told us that you were the only one who was punished out of all the girls. She told me and I relayed the information back to the other men. We were all determined to make life easier for you. I didn't tell them about my plans to go to the police, I thought it better not to. We often talked about you, and we got the club to keep some of the men away from you and lower the numbers." I was stunned by this revelation, that others were concerned about me; I was so touched and so emotional. "So, I was not as alone as I had thought, was I?" I whispered, the tears starting to fall, and Paul tightened his arms around me in support.

Later, after a delicious dinner, we sat in the lounge while we finished our drinks. "How was the meeting? What was decided?" I asked. "The new management team have been voted in, and I think they will be good for the club. They have some ideas that will work very successfully. All the previous team's money-making schemes have been stopped. The breeding centre is going to be moved, and an excellent new home has been found; it really did not fit in with what was already here. It was set up under the previous management team. The trust that had been formed to set up and run the centre advertised for anybody with a few acres that they were not using to think about renting it to them. One of the members of the club saw the advertisement and suggested to the members that the club should offer some of its land. It was a unanimous vote in favour as it would help conservation. The last management team were offered a large sum of money from an organisation to allow them to carry out the experiment, the payment going into the management team's pockets. The man who funded the project was here for the meeting." I remembered he had said that he would like to meet me. "I would love to meet him."

"What about The Harem? What conclusion did they come to?"

"There was an overwhelming vote for it to go back to how it was." I looked at him in surprise. "But won't it be closed down by the police?"

"There is always that chance, yes."

"What will happen to the breeding centre area?"

"The area will be cleared and grassed over until a decision is made, but there are a few ideas already: extending the health spa for one, building a bigger pool and extending the building to provide more bedrooms and making part of it an hotel, that non-members can stay in. There are more excellent ideas; these people have been busy."

The next morning, we arrived back at the club and before we entered the bar, Paul took my hand. "Ready?" I nodded. There were very few in the bar at that time and as we walked in two men got up from their table ready to meet us. Paul introduced them to me as Gerry and Mick. I felt suddenly nervous, and held Paul's hand tightly. They came forward, and kissed me on both cheeks, not seeming to be able to take their eyes off me; it was more than a little disconcerting if I am honest. I think it was Mick who exclaimed, "You're looking so well! Paul is doing a fabulous job of looking after you." We sat and talked for most of the morning, and the longer I spent with them the easier I found the meeting, but I never let go of Paul's hand, holding on tightly, using it as a lifeline. When it was lunchtime the four of us went into the restaurant and had lunch, and later, when Gerry and Mick were leaving us, they asked if I would consider meeting up again. No, this situation was not at all weird, I thought to myself. I found it very odd, but I was quite happy to meet them again, with Paul of course.

As we were early, and it was a beautiful day, we walked around the grounds of the club; it was a place that I would love to visit again. I enjoyed the fresh air as well. We entered the club and sat in the lounge to wait, and it was not long before the receptionist came to tell us our visitor had arrived. Holding Paul's hand, I really should not have been nervous, but I felt more confident with my hand in his. When we left the lounge, the man standing waiting for us, who was quite tall, dark-haired and had a kindly look about him, was introduced to me as Philip. He took my hand when we were introduced and kissed me. "I am so pleased to meet you at last." He did not let go of my hand and studied me closely. He had penetrating, bright blue eyes that seemed to see right through me. I started to feel uncomfortable under his scrutiny. "Shall we sit down?" suggested Paul, and we went back into the lounge, where we could talk without being interrupted. "I think it's amazing that you made this centre possible; they are beautiful animals, and from what I have heard, it has been successful. I believe that the care and standards have been praised." He appeared pleased to hear that. "It's worked far beyond my expectations. I am more than happy with the set-up." His face clouded. "One aspect that angered me was the way the whole concept was highjacked and made into something sordid, which was not what I intended. It made me incredibly angry to hear what was happening, and how you and the poor girl before you had been dragged into this bogus research project. I nearly withdrew the funding, it was sickening. I believe that you were attacked on many occasions; you must have been terrified of them." I shuddered. "I was, I thought I was going to have a heart attack or be killed. There was one that was the most violent, he scared me the most and wasn't always put in with me. I was more than grateful when he wasn't, they must have thought it was better to keep him out than have another death on their hands." He looked serious. "So, he killed the previous girl?" Paul took up the story. "I was told by one of the staff that she suddenly vanished and there was complete silence about what happened. I asked to have a tour of the place because there had been so many changes; I wanted to have a clearer understanding of what was going on, especially behind the scenes. My guide told me that any questions about Blanche were actively discouraged, threateningly, by what he said." Philip sat thinking, looking troubled, and then he turned to me. "What do you think should happen to the centre? There has been a suggestion that it should be closed down." I could not believe what I was hearing. "Why would anyone want to close something down that's doing such a marvellous job? If you are willing to carry on with the funding it should carry on." He looked extremely surprised. "You don't feel bitter about what was done to you?"

"Why would I? Nothing that went on in that place was anything to do with them; they were just as much victims as Blanche and I were."

"That is very forgiving of you." I reached out and took his hand. "You didn't fund the project intending it to be used in that way, did you? What you did was to help the population of gorillas, which you have done, very successfully it seems." He appeared a little happier. "Thank you, it puts my mind at rest, hearing you say that. I have to say that I was nervous about meeting you as I didn't know how you felt about the subject. Did Paul tell you that the centre is moving? I think that although it was successful here, the new home will be even better and very much larger."

"Yes, he did, I'm so glad that it's not being closed down. It is the people who were in charge who are the ones I feel bitter about but, having said that, bitterness is a negative feeling and does nobody any good."

"I hope that you haven't been left with too many issues after all that happened to you?" Paul answered for me. "She had many but has had a lot of support from her family, and her friends and I have done as much as possible as well." I glanced up at him. "Paul has been amazing. I can't tell you how much he has done for me. It can't have been easy, putting up with me. He has been unbelievably patient, has had to be on many occasions."

"I am so glad you have had so much support. Changing the subject, I understand you have a good relationship with one of the apes?"

"He is so laid-back and gentle; he makes a greeting noise when he sees me. I have been in with him on a few occasions. Whenever I had been bitten or beaten up, when he saw me the next day, he would stroke where the bites were, and then lick them, as if he was trying to heal them for me or apologise. I found it sweet of him, and entirely unexpected." It seemed as if Philip was trying to find how to put the next question. It was not what I was expecting, however. "When you go in with him now, does he try to mate with you? I'm sorry to ask, and if it makes you uncomfortable talking about the subject, I will totally understand if you would rather not."

"No, he never has. I am fully clothed, so I look different, and I don't have the foul-smelling stuff that they coated on me. I had a theory that was to mimic a female that was ready to mate."

"You could be right," he said thoughtfully. "Would you be willing to go in with him now?" Philip seemed pleased when I agreed, and we headed out to the apes. He was sitting in a small area where, if he did attack me, help would be close, and as soon as he saw me, he came rushing over, making noises of greeting. I went to the gate, where one of the keepers was waiting for me, and as soon as I went into the small paddock, he greeted me enthusiastically. I was under no illusion; it was the treats that were the main attraction. I sat on the trunk of a tree, and he came and sat down next to me. He was so much bigger now, he dwarfed me, and he started to groom me. I didn't think that he would find anything, but he looked anyway. I tickled him in a spot behind his ear. He had always seemed to enjoy that, as he did this time. When I left, he was sitting by the fence, staring after me, making the same noise he made when I had left him before. Philip was quiet as we walked back to the club. When we arrived back in reception he took my hands in his. "I want to thank you for this meeting. It's been an eye-opener for me. You have such a bond with that ape, and I can't believe that you can still go in with him. He didn't show any aggression towards you." I laughed. "That could have had something to do with the treats I had for him, but he was always very gentle with me. I was quite shocked when I found out he hadn't been brought up in captivity as I had thought but captured from the wild." We left Philip, after we had eaten dinner and had drinks in the bar, to go back to the hotel for the night. The next morning we drove back to London.

It was my birthday, and we were going out to a restaurant later. Paul had been out and when he came back, he told me to close my eyes. When I was allowed to open them, he was holding the most beautiful kitten. It was the one that had taken to me from his friend's litter which we had seen previously. I took her from him and hugged her to me. She started to purr loudly. I went and kissed Paul, thanking him for this special little bundle of fur. "Of course, you do realise that she will rip everything to shreds with her claws? This place will never be the same again." He did not seem too worried, but he had not seen the damage that one small kitten could do. Yet. I would have to think of a name for her. Eva and I went shopping. The kitten had come with a blanket, that smelled of her mother, so I decided to buy a heating mat for under the blanket, which hopefully would give her a little comfort and warmth, and a soft cuddly toy that she could snuggle up to. It would be her first night away from her mother; she was going to be upset and would need something to settle her down for the night, but she surprised me by sleeping very well. She must have been exhausted because she had done a lot of exploring before she slept. Both Paul and John had said that they preferred dogs, but she had them on her side and complete fans in no time. I even found John playing with her one day. He did look a little embarrassed at first, but she had him exactly where she wanted him, under her paw, as she did everybody else. I think there is a saying, that dogs have slaves, but cats have staff. How true that is.

A few days later Anna rang to say that if it was convenient, she would call the next morning, as she had a copy of my medical records from the club. I did not know how I felt about having them; they would probably end up unread in the same drawer that my client list resided in, also unread. I thought that it was probably good to have them as they could then go onto my medical records. Anna came not long after Paul had gone to work. She stopped long enough for a coffee, to admire the view and catch up on what had been happening, and of course to meet the kitten, who had been called Tigger, because she had markings that looked a little like tiger stripes. Anna became yet another member of the admirers' club.

Much later in the day I decided to have quick look at the records. They started with the tests that had been done when I first arrived. I found that I wanted to know everything that was in them. I had assumed that one of the shots I had been given on a regular basis would have been a contraceptive but apparently not; how odd. I read one piece several times, getting more upset each time I read it. I had been reading it sitting on the bed; I ended up curled up, crying hard. Eva, the housekeeper, came and knocked on the door with my phone, as there was a call. She was shocked to find me distraught.

THIRTY

Paul was in the middle of a meeting when Bette, his PA, opened the door and, apologising for the interruption, asked to speak to him. He knew she would not interrupt unless it was something important. "I'm sorry about this, but I thought you ought to know. I had a phone call from Eva to say that Anna had been and given Chloe the paperwork, she said that you would know what that was. But apparently something in it has upset Chloe; she is in tears, nothing will calm her, and Eva is worried."

"Thank you, Bette, you did absolutely the right thing. Will you tell Eva that I am on my way home, but not to tell Chloe." He went back into the room, apologised for having to leave the meeting, and asked Rebecca to carry on in his place. He then rang his driver, telling him he needed to be driven home.

When he got home, John was pacing, looking worried, and there was relief on his face when he saw Paul. "We couldn't get a word out of her." Paul went into the bedroom, and then the bathroom; she was not in either. When he went back into the living room, John and Eva were talking quietly. "She isn't there." They searched the apartment, and

John went to check the cameras. "She went out, and didn't take her bag with her, probably not her phone either." When they called her phone, it was charging. Paul paced the room, thinking of the places where she could have gone, but did not come up with anywhere; not having lived in the city long, she would not have had time to know the area well. He came to a decision. "I know it's too early, but I'm going to ring the police. She was upset about something and not necessarily thinking logically."

Well at least he had done something, he told himself after coming off the phone, and it will be on record, even if they are not taking any action yet; and hoped that it would become unnecessary for them to have to. "I'm going out to search around. Probably useless, but I've got to do something."

"I'll come with you. Paul. Eva, ring if she comes back before we do," John said, before leaving.

*

I do not remember getting there, everything had been hazy, but I suddenly realised that I was standing on a bridge looking over at the water flowing beneath; there was somebody talking. To me. I think. I started to walk again. I had been walking for hours. Sometime in the evening I looked at my watch. I couldn't read it because it was dark, and very quiet. Normally this would have worried me, darkness in a strange area, which I realised wasn't exactly the most salubrious part of the capital. I did not feel as if this was real somehow, that I was in a dream that I would wake up from. How far had I walked? It was a long way; my feet ached, I was tired, cold, and ravenous. Where was I?

Lost, unfortunately. More by good luck I must have walked in a circle, and ended up in an area that I recognised, not too far from the apartment. I walked into the lounge. It was quiet, and I went straight to the bedroom, closed the door and collapsed on the bed, curled up and closed my eyes.

*

Eva rang Paul to tell him that Chloe had just walked back into the apartment. She had walked as if sleepwalking, had gone straight into the bedroom and when Eva had looked in the room she could see that Chloe was asleep. Paul suddenly found that relief had turned into anger at Chloe. She had some explaining to do. Why had she put herself in so much danger? There was still a threat hanging over her. John could see the anger on Paul's face, and when they arrived back, he made straight for the bedroom. "Paul," John called after him. Paul either ignored him or did not hear because he was so angry. Eva met him in the hall, and they looked at each other in trepidation. "He wouldn't hurt her, would he, John?" asked Eva. "No, but I will stay around, don't worry."

Paul entered the bedroom and slammed the door shut behind him. Striding over to the bed he leaned over her. His anger left him instantly and the words he was going to say died on his lips when he saw the look on Chloe's face. Anger was replaced with a feeling of love, the intensity of it shocking him. Sitting on the bed he drew her into his arms, hugging her close. Without saying a word, she clung to him, burying her head against his chest, tightening her arms round him. That is how they stayed.

There was a gentle knock at the door. "I'm sorry but the police are here," Eva called through the door.

Paul took my face between his hands and wiped tears off my cheeks. "I called the police earlier. You don't have to talk to them now, we can ask them to come back another time."

"I want to get this over with." I straightened myself up and, taking Paul's hand, dragged myself into the living room, where there were two policemen with John and Eva. All eyes turned my way. Eva gave me a sympathetic smile. One of the officers came forward and introduced himself and his colleague. "We were told that you went missing this evening, that you were upset about something?" I nodded; did we have to do this now? All I wanted to do was go to bed and sleep for a week. "We got a report of you going missing earlier this evening, and then a man reported seeing somebody on a bridge. He was worried about you and rang us. Afterwards he followed you. He rang us back then and told us he had seen you entering this apartment block. We then saw the report of you having been reported missing earlier and you fitted the description we had of you. We thought we had better follow the report up." There was a gasp from Paul. "What were you thinking? Were you going to jump? What?" I ignored him, and finally managed to collect enough energy to talk. "That was so kind of him. I was aware of somebody talking to me at some point. Will you thank him for his concern, please?" My voice sounded slow and flat, with no life to it, even to my ears. "Is it possible to talk to you on your own?" asked one of the officers. I nodded. Paul must have gone into his office, and John and Eva into the kitchen. We went and sat down near the window. One of the two policemen looked out. "What a superb view," he commented, and then took pity on me.

It must have been obvious that I was exhausted. "We won't keep you long. The worry is that you were considering suicide. Was that on your mind?" I shook my head. "No, never." They looked at each other and seemed relieved. "Good, where did you go?"

"I couldn't tell you, I don't know, I just walked. I haven't lived in London long, so I don't know the area, and I got myself lost. I hadn't got my phone. Fortunately, I found myself in an area that I recognised, not far away. I couldn't have walked much further, I was exhausted."

"We won't be much longer, and then you can get some rest. You were described by the man who reported seeing you on the bridge as being in a trance, as if you were sleepwalking."

"It felt like that." One of the officers asked, "What made you act like that, do you think?"

"I was abducted some time ago, and my support officer brought the medical records they had found. It was an item in there that upset me so much." One of the officers exclaimed, "I thought I recognised you from somewhere. There was a big trial, and you gave evidence." I nodded. "I have got to ask, but are you all right? You're not under pressure in any way? Being treated well by," he consulted his notebook, "Paul Knight?"

"Oh yes, but he's angry with me for leaving the building with nobody knowing. I have had threats made against me. I shouldn't have gone out on my own without John with me. He has been employed to keep me safe." The two men had been watching me when I answered, and it must have been evident that I did not have a problem with Paul. "I am so sorry to have taken up your time, there are more serious problems for you to deal with."

"That's quite all right, but if there's anything that you

need help with, here's my card for you to call." After I had seen them to the door, I stood unable to move, with my back resting against the wall, and I felt myself sliding down, ending up sitting with my forehead resting on my knees. A pair of strong arms picked me up and carried me into the bedroom, undressed me and then brushed my hair. It was so soothing, and then he slid into bed behind me, holding me tightly until I fell asleep.

*

John and Eva watched as Paul carried Chloe to the bedroom. "Thanks for tonight," he said, as he passed them. They looked at each other, breathed a collective sigh of relief, and made their way to their rooms.

*

When I awoke the next morning Paul was behind me with his arms round my waist, pulling me against him.

"I was going out of my mind with worry about you last night. It didn't do my blood pressure any good. My world is centred around you. I have never ever loved any other woman the way I love you. I don't know how I would exist without you in my life." I turned round so that I was facing him. "I'm so sorry, my mind wasn't working properly, and I feel the same about you." He needed to know what the problem had been. I sat up and leaned over to where the medical records were, found the page and pointed to the relevant section that I had ringed. "Read that." He read in silence and reread it. "You were pregnant? And had a miscarriage?" he whispered slowly. "Yes."

"Did you know?" he asked. "How could I? I was told nothing; I did not know that I had had an operation. I don't think it could have been yours." He looked at the dates and a memory came back to him. "No, when I wanted to book you at first that must have just happened, as you had been off for about a week."

"The bastard who beat me up, tore my insides up, who knows what other damage he did, caused a miscarriage. What really upset me was that I had been told that I could never have children. It wasn't so much the loss of the baby, it was the fact that I had fallen pregnant, against all the odds, and I might never have another chance because of the damage he might have done." He did not know what to say; he just held her close. "How do you feel about some breakfast? You need to eat; we'll talk more later." I nodded, and after a shower we arrived in the kitchen, where Eva waited for us, a smile on her face when she saw me. After we had eaten, Paul led me onto the deck and sat me down, running his fingers down my cheek. "You look so sad. I would do anything to make you happy, I think you know that."

"Right now, I'm so confused." He paused before he said anything. "Did you find out more, when you were told about not being able to have children?" he asked me gently. "No, Mark was totally opposed to the idea of any children, so there didn't seem much point in following it up with any further enquiries." He found that he felt anger at the man who had not considered Chloe's feelings in the matter of having children or not, but he pushed that to one side. "Can I suggest something? If you do not like the idea, I will drop the subject, it is entirely up to you. You could always investigate further, see if any permanent damage has been done, and if it is possible for us to have children. Look, I would love to have children with you, but if it is not possible, I am okay with that, we will have each other, and there may be other ways. What do you think?"

"I'll go with that." I felt him relax and I put my arms around his neck, and we ended up with a passionate kiss that went on a long time.

THIRTY-ONE

I was busy for the next few days, finishing paintings off that I had been working on before I was abducted. My mother had come to stay while another, smaller exhibition was set up. It had been requested by the gallery owner; the last one had been so successful, helped by the publicity of my reappearance, and it was hoped that this one, although much smaller, would be just as good. My father was taking a few days off, as he had no commitments for a while, and he came a few days later. The opening had created a lot of interest and was busy all the first day, which was for invited guests only. I was thrilled when my cityscape was well received, with many positive comments in the book I had left for people to leave their opinions, and with many requests for me to paint more of the same. I was so glad to get my shoes off at the end of the day as my feet were numb. It was good to have time with my mother. We talked a lot about the revelations in the medical records from the club, and I felt better having heard her views. My parents had gone to stay with Paul's folks, so that we were alone in the apartment, apart from Eva and John. Paul had called into the gallery during the day with one of his clients, who was very complimentary, and I think bought one of my pieces. When he came home, he confirmed that, saying that he thought I was selling them too cheaply, that I should raise my prices. The gallery owner had said the same thing; of course, it would have nothing to do with the fact that he would get increased commission. We went and sat on the deck, staring at the view. Paul seemed to have something on his mind. "Do you remember me asking you to consider what I said to you after that first night we spent together?"

"Everything is a little hazy, let me think, oh yes, it's coming back to me, I think I do, something about you were going to ask me to marry you?" He was watching me with narrowed eyes. "And?"

"And what?" I said, trying to look innocent. "And shouldn't you be on your knees? Isn't that how it's supposed to be done?" He laughed, and taking me by surprise, got down on one knee in front of me. Taking a small box out of his pocket, he took my hand in his, and looking very solemn, asked me, "My darling Chloe, I love you so much, and you would make me the happiest man in the world if you loved me enough to marry me and be my wife." I swallowed. "I love you too, so much, and yes, I will marry you." He took the most exquisite ring out of the box and slipped it on my finger; it fitted perfectly. The kiss that followed lasted ages and left us both panting for breath. "We can tell both sets of parents tomorrow, and we will have to start planning the wedding. I want you married to me as soon as possible, I don't want to wait." I thought that it would be impossible to organise a wedding in the time he wanted, and I thought he was joking, but he was not. Both sets of parents were overjoyed at the news and they too were incredulous when he said how long we had in which to plan. They looked at me, and I just shrugged, what could I say? He was overruled on the time limit by everyone, but it was decided it would be at the hotel I had stayed at previously, a small celebration. They could not do enough for us and had some wonderful ideas. The arrangements went very smoothly, far more so than when planning the previous one with Mark. It was not going to be a large affair, thank goodness. When we sent the invitations, we specified no presents, but donations could be given to the two charities we had named.

A group of my friends were coming, and we had arranged transport and accommodation for them. I could not wait to see them all and catch up on all the news. I had not seen them because of all the work to be done. We met up the night before to have a get-together; it got very lively, and I enjoyed that so much.

I lay in bed on the morning of the wedding, trying to come to terms with how my life had evolved in such a short time, and how different my feelings were towards Paul compared to Mark. The only part that made me sad was that my sister could not come over, but Paul had suggested that we could go and see her and her family, and I was looking forward to that. The morning just flew by, with the hairdresser, and make-up. My mother and my friend Beth had arrived to help me get dressed. I had the strange feeling that the people around me were keeping something from me, and I demanded to know what. Paul had not arrived or been heard from; I had been trying to contact him since I woke up. Every time I rang it had gone to voicemail, but nobody else had heard anything either. Where was he? I was in the room next to where the wedding was going to be held, with all the guests milling around. As I ended yet another call that had gone again to voicemail, the doors were flung open, and two men entered the room. I didn't recognise them; the second to enter made straight for John, holding a gun to his head, and taking his from him. My feet seemed to be rooted to the floor. I could not move. I was frozen in horrified silence, realising that my worst fears were possibly coming true. I had been sure that there would be another attempt to kidnap me, convinced that I was being followed; this feeling had made me paranoid. All the previous attempts had been foiled by John; I just hoped that this would end up the same. All the guests had gone deathly quiet. Fright permeated the room. The taller of the two men was brandishing a large knife. Was that blood on the blade? It looked like it, from where I was standing, and if so, whose? He was making everybody move out of his way, making a path straight to me. He grabbed one of the female guests. She screamed, and as he held onto her, he put the knife against her throat. He prowled in my direction. It felt as though I was being stalked by a predator. He pulled his victim with him. By this time there was a clear area all around the centre of the room and he used that to try and stalk around me, but as he moved so did I, keeping him in front of me. I was surprised that my legs were still supporting me, the way they were shaking. "Put your gun on the floor," he ordered. "Now," he shouted. The woman whimpered again. He swore at her, shouting at her to shut up, and turned his attention back to me. "I know that you are armed." I had been watching for him to take his eyes off me, but he did not. I hesitated. "Put the gun down, or she has her throat cut." I took the gun out of its holster, making sure that he could see what I was doing. I held it up. "Unload it," he shouted. I took all but one of the bullets out and held them up. "And the last one. Do you think I'm stupid?" he shouted

268

again. I held it up and let the last one fall into my hand. He signalled to me to put the gun on the floor, but instead I threw it, hard and fast at his head. It took him by surprise, but he reacted quickly and managed to move so that it just missed. I managed to put the bullets into the holster. He released his victim and pushed her away roughly, so that he could concentrate all his attention on me. "Well, well, well, did you think you could escape so easily, Scarlet? I paid a lot of money to the club for you, and you were stolen from me. I have come to claim my property." I had had nightmares about what would happen when the club had no more use for me, and this situation had been a distinct possibility; it had been a frightening thought. "You don't own me, no one owns me, and I don't answer to that name," I shouted at him in defiance. "Keep telling yourself that," he sneered. "Of course, after I have had enough of you myself, I will hand you over to my men to have fun with you." I looked at him and shrugged, trying to act nonchalant. "Gang rape? Been there, done that, got the full set of T-shirts. What is one more, bring it on." Taking me by surprise he stepped forward, took hold of my hand, and twisting my arm, pushed me to the floor, making me kneel. "Just where you should be, bitch, on your knees. You should know that position by now, and if you have forgotten, when I get you out of here, I shall chain you like that just to remind you who you are and where you belong. And with a few strokes of the lash, you will remember, and learn." At that point John took the chance to get the gun from his captor; unfortunately, he ended up being punched hard in the stomach, followed by a vicious kick to the head. I managed to get a quick look at him. It was not reassuring; he was obviously unconscious and a ghastly colour. He had fallen with his face towards the room so I could see a deep gash to his head, which was bleeding profusely. My attacker dragged me up by the hair and threw a punch at my jaw that sent me staggering across the floor, landing near John. He followed me and dragged me to my feet by my hair again, and this time punched me in the stomach, knocking the breath out of my lungs. I said slowly, again through clenched teeth, as it was painful to use my jaw, "You. Do not. Own me." He shouted into my face; I had to control myself not to flinch. "Do not speak! You will not be rescued where I am taking you. And when I'm finished nobody will recognise you." He dragged me over to a mirror. "Take a good look and remember that image." The underlying threat was only too evident. I could see the guests behind us through the glass; they were so quiet, it was unnerving. In a low menacing voice, he said, "Now, are you coming quietly, Scarlet?" If I did what he wanted I would be playing into his hands. Once out of the hotel, I would vanish completely, to who knew what hell awaited me there. Going quietly didn't seem like an option to me, whatever the consequences. I had to take what was coming and hope I did not die in the process, which seemed to be a possibility, the way he was acting. I did hope, vainly, as it turned out, that a room full of witnesses would make him ease up on the inevitable violence. Drawing as deep a breath as I could because of the pain after his last punch I said, "I'm not going anywhere with you," trying to sound a whole lot braver than I felt, having, in my opinion, a large yellow streak running through me. "It's no good trying to stall for time on purpose," he told me conversationally. "Because, you see, Scarlet, the last time I saw Paul, he was lying in a pool of his own blood. I made sure that his injuries would kill him, and I'm sure that he wasn't breathing when I left.

He won't get help in time to save him." I gasped and tears started to stream down my face, looking at the blood on his clothes and the knife. His blood. I could not stop sobbing, but glaring at him through my tears, I shouted at him, "How many times have I got to tell you. I am not going with you, anywhere."

"I am going to enjoy breaking you and bringing you into line," he said, as he aimed another punch at my stomach, and by some miracle I dodged just out of the way in time to stop it landing. "You will learn to obey me; I will beat you into submission." His face took on a crafty look. "The club paid a lot of money for you and the other girls, and when it wants to sell the girls on, they make good profit, did you know this?" I answered him back, "Why are you telling me this? Why would I have any interest in hearing that? It won't affect me." All the time this exchange was happening I kept moving, and I could tell that it was getting him angry. Hmm, pulling the tiger's tail, is that a good idea? "Oh, but it does affect you. I have a buyer for you, and you will make me a lot of money." I looked at him with a sceptical look on my face. "How much?" I asked. I was shocked to hear the enormous sum he quoted, because for that amount he was not going to give up. He grinned at me, knowing that I had come to the right conclusion. "The client's jet is waiting at a small airfield for you, so within an hour of leaving here, you will be out of the country, and nobody will ever find you."

THIRTY-TWO

This information came as a shock, and my legs were in danger of collapsing under me. I didn't want to show any weakness, but unfortunately, he must have seen me stagger slightly and he took the opportunity of catching hold of my arm and pulling me to him with a vice-like grip. "You told me earlier that by the time you had finished with me I wouldn't look as I do now; wouldn't that reduce the price you get for me? I am sure that any buyer would want whatever he bought unmarked, in good condition? Maybe I have that wrong. You don't seem to be making much sense." There were still no noises in the room; no doubt listening to me bargaining with this man for my freedom, or my life. I had thought earlier that his eyes were dark, but being close to him, closer than I wanted to be, I could see that the pupils were dilated. With drugs? This could explain why he did not appear to care how he treated me, as if we were alone with no witnesses. He had to be taken seriously. "I fucked you several times, and one time I brought a little something to give you pleasure." I had a horrible feeling I knew what was coming. "How thoughtful," I said, with as much sarcasm as I could put into two words, and any of the guests who could see my face would have seen my expression harden with hate. "I enjoyed you very much that day."

"Did you?" I said through gritted teeth. "It's so good to get customer feedback, and I am so pleased you got satisfaction. You got me punished as well. Thanks for that."

"I enjoyed seeing you lying bleeding and writhing in pain on the floor. You had to be carried back to your room, because you couldn't walk, as I remember. They took you out far too early for me, I wanted to see more. I believe nobody could fuck you for over a week." I think I surprised him with what I said next. "I feel sorry for your wife if you can't keep her satisfied in bed. You must be a disappointment as a husband, from your performance that day." All the guests could hear the exchange, with a look of horror on the faces of the ones I could see. I managed to move my head a little to watch where he put his feet, having to move my dress out of the way, and when he was in the position I wanted, ground the heel of my shoe into the middle of his foot, making sure that I put all my weight onto that one. I was wearing shoes with very thin heels that could cause a lot of damage. It had the desired effect, and he let me go, briefly, with a satisfying howl of pain, and cursing loudly, limped a few feet away. Unfortunately, although I never thought it would have much effect on him, he recovered far faster than I had anticipated, and came after me, aiming another punch at my stomach, finishing off with a backhand to my face which sent me sprawling, banging my head on the floor as I fell. I had fallen facing John, who was still lying unconscious. My attacker had followed me, and I braced myself for more. "Didn't do much for you, did he?" he sneered, and as he leaned down towards me, I saw him take a syringe out of his pocket. I was hovering on the edge of passing out; if he got whatever was in it into me, and put me out, I was lost. I needed to get that away from me, any way I could. My timing was spot on. As he made to push the needle into me, I had just enough strength to knock it out of his hand, and it flew under the sofa that was partially hiding John, thankfully out of my attacker's reach. He swore violently and aimed a kick at my side and then to my head. This momentarily stunned me, the pain and difficulty in breathing increasing in intensity. When I came to, he was on the phone, apparently to the rest of his gang who, it appeared, were just entering the hotel. I was just about to move when I felt a touch on my right hand. Opening my eyes I saw with relief that it was John. His eyes were open, but he hadn't moved, and he had a large gash on the side of his head which had been bleeding, heavily. He winked, and then signalled to stay as I was and pretend that I was still unconscious, otherwise I would have been beaten again, and I did not think I could have survived another round. It was getting more difficult to breathe; the attacks had done some damage, unsurprisingly. He signalled to me to look at my right hand. When I did, there was the syringe; he had pushed it to where I could reach it. I managed to take hold and looked at John. He indicated where I should look. When I did, moving my eyes, not my head, the attacker was standing near me, and one of his legs was in a very convenient position. I realised what John wanted me to do, but on his signal, and after he moved into a better position, without giving away that he was conscious, he gave me the signal, and with much difficulty, and my last bit of strength, I rose up slowly, before he realised what was happening, and sank the needle into his leg, emptying the contents into him. It was getting increasingly painful and difficult to breathe. The effort increased the pain level so much that I passed out; if I had had the strength, the knife was just where I could have reached it and got it out of his way. It was not to be, however.

I learned later what happened after that. While the other attacker was distracted with what had happened to his colleague, John knocked him out, took his gun, and called for something to tie him up with. Tie backs from the curtains worked well. As soon as the two attackers were secured, John rushed over to see what state I was in. There was a crowd around me. He put his ear to my back, listening to my breathing. Not liking what he heard, he made a comment to nobody in particular, "He'll kill me for letting her get into this state. Better not to move her until the ambulance arrives," he said to my mother, who was kneeling next to me and just about to turn me over and put her arms around me. The police arrived quickly. One of the staff had been passing along the corridor and looked through the open door, and seeing the attacker brandishing a knife, he went back the way he had come and rang the hotel manager, telling him what he had seen, so they had already been called. As they entered the hotel, the police were made aware of a group of three men who had pushed their way into the back entrance. They were suspected of being with the two people upstairs. The police split up, and the three men were caught before they could join up with the others. John suggested that the two attackers were moved out of the room before Paul arrived, so they were dragged into the next room, out of sight. At that point John had not heard what my attacker had told me. The paramedics arrived just as I was beginning to regain consciousness, and I was aware of a face above me smiling kindly. "Hello, my love, my name's Dave and I'm a paramedic, where do you hurt?"

All over," I gasped. "Where's Paul? Is he here? I want to see him." It took all I had to ask but I had to know; I did not want to accept that he might be dead. "I don't know, I haven't heard anything," said Dave. "I am so sorry, but I am going to have to cut this beautiful dress off you, and just check where you hurt. I'm sorry that it will hurt, but I'll try to be as quick and as gentle as possible." When the extent of the bruising and injuries were revealed, there were exclamations; the bruised area was massive, and a dark purple already. They did a quick assessment, had a muttered discussion, and then got on the radio to ask for a doctor to be sent as it was thought I needed treatment before being taken to the hospital. It was then that Paul arrived, insisting that he saw me. There was a large bandage soaked in blood around his chest. He was followed by a couple of paramedics, they explained that he wanted to see me before agreeing to be taken to hospital. He paused, looking devastated at what he was seeing, and with difficulty he dropped on his knees beside me. Looking at the damage with horror, he took my hand in his.

I was just losing consciousness again, but unbelievably I thought I could hear Paul's voice, as though from a long way off. I struggled to open my eyes and heard him ask, "Who did this?" followed by John telling him to concentrate on me and himself, that we were the priority, not them, that the police had the attackers. "Can I hold her?" he asked what I assumed were the paramedics. "Best not until we know what we're dealing with." I managed to open my eyes, and turned so I could see him, and saw with horror the large dressing that was soaked with blood. I tried to move, but he stopped me. "Get that treated," I managed to say. "I'm going with you in the same ambulance, I'm not letting you out of my sight," he said stubbornly. "How's John? He was unconscious for a time. He needs help too." I heard the paramedic who was attending to me ask one of his colleagues to have a look at him. My mother had been holding my hand, she hugged Paul carefully. "They will look after her, she's in good hands." His mother had just realised he was there and rushing up to him, threw her arms around him, sobbing. "He told Chloe that he had killed you, that he had injured you very badly, and you weren't breathing when he last saw you," she told him between sobs. He winced when she hugged him and then she noticed the dressing. "What did he do to you? Are you all right?"

"Yes, I'll live. They got to me in time, and it isn't as serious as it looks, apart from losing a lot of blood. I'll need stitches, I'm told." Just then the doctor arrived, gave me a quick examination, and said to my mother and Paul, "We need to treat her here, and then take her to hospital. She has taken a hell of a beating. We will know better what we're dealing with when she has had a scan." He turned to the guests, saying, "I would like the room cleared, please, and you as well. I am sorry, you will be better out of here, leave her with us," he said to Paul as he was obviously getting ready to object, insisting on staying with me. With difficulty, leaning down, Paul gave me a kiss before he left the room. When we got to the hospital and Paul's wound had been stitched up, the police asked him if he would give them a statement about what had happened to him.

After being anaesthetised, I got the treatment I needed, and was then taken to hospital. Unfortunately, I did not come out of the anaesthetic as soon as expected. This caused concern, I was told later, because there was no obvious reason. I was aware sometimes, of hearing people talking in the background, and tried to wake up. The cause was thought to be a head injury that had not shown up on the first scan, until they scanned me again later, and it was just visible, but not thought to be serious.

I was aware of noises at first, and people talking, regular beeping coming from somewhere, also bright lights and something over my mouth. I panicked, thinking I was back at the club, that I hadn't escaped my attacker after all, that he had got me away from the hotel, I was back there. I was reliving the first day I had been abducted, all over again. I was not staying in that situation if I could help it. Pulling whatever it was off my face, and the wires that I was hooked up to, I started to get off the bed. There were alarms going off all around me. I heard shouting for someone to help, please, coming from close by, and hands gently holding and supporting me. Everything was hazy, caused no doubt by the drugs they must have given me, and nothing was working properly. Suddenly two familiar voices started to penetrate the haze, and as the mist cleared a little, there was the welcome sight of my parents, looking very worried, in front of me. I started to cry with relief. I was safe if they were there. I looked around; I was in a hospital room. I could see all the faces around me. Two nurses came and carefully helped me back into bed. I felt such an idiot. I apologised to them for making more work. They were brilliant and got me settled and comfortable in no time. They asked if the troublemakers outside could come into the room again, as they were making a nuisance of themselves. I could see worried faces outside and gave as good a smile as I could manage, but the doctor arrived to check me over, so they had to curb their impatience a bit longer. The doctor told me that there was no reason why I should not be able to go home soon, probably the next day, and to take life easy for a while. I did not think I would be able to do anything else with all the bruising. She also told me how lucky I had been. Amazingly no lasting damage had been done. It was just a matter of time, and rest, for me to heal. They had been certain serious damage had been done when I was taken to hospital, and amazed that the results of the scans were so positive. Some of the pain had been from broken ribs, that would heal on their own, and a collapsed lung which had been caused by one of the broken ribs penetrating it, and despite having made the site bleed again when I panicked coming round, that was healing well. The head injury was also improving, so I would be better off at home where I would improve more quickly.

THIRTY-THREE

"Can we come in yet?" said a voice from the doorway; his patience was wearing thin. I could not believe what I was seeing. "Paul? I thought, I thought, he told me you were dead!" I was crying again, this time in relief. He came over and sat on the side of the bed, taking me in his arms, holding me tight. We both winced. He relaxed his embrace, both of us trying not to laugh. "Sorry, I think we're in the same state, thanks to that madman." He held me at arm's length. "Don't you remember, darling? At the hotel? You saw me then?"

"I don't remember. My memory is sketchy, most of it lost, it must have been the head injury, or the drugs that I was given. How were you found? He said that you wouldn't be found in time." He laughed. "He didn't ask for my phone, so that I still had it in my pocket, and it didn't make a noise and alert him, so I could ring the police and ambulance." Suddenly the door opened, and it was evident there were a few people wanting to come in. The doctor looked up from the notes she was making on my chart. "It's up to you, I've finished. We could throw them out if they are bothering you," she said, laughing. The room filled up immediately when they were told they could come in. "Well, what did she say?"

"That I can leave here tomorrow." There were so many questions about what happened at the hotel, so I filled them in from my point of view, telling them about how John had been teaching me what to do in a situation like that, and the hand signals by which he communicated what he wanted me to do. I also told them that had he not done that, I would probably have been beaten up even more, because for some reason, when consciousness returned to me, I was starting to get up, and he had told me to stay where I was. John, who had joined us by that time, took up the story, and said that he had regained consciousness just as I had used my shoe heel to good effect, and saw me knocked across the floor, and fortunately land near him. He was still feeling groggy from the punch he had received and would not have been very steady on his feet if he had got up straightaway, so would not have been much help. Apparently, he kept his eyes open a crack, watching me, until I had started to move; by then he had managed to move the syringe close to my hand, hoping that an opportunity would present itself to use it. "Just as a matter of interest, where did using your heels as a weapon come from? I did not show you that one. It would hurt like hell." I laughed. "Oh, what a shame, I couldn't care less how much it hurt him. I had used that once on a man who was being a nuisance. He limped away from me, helped by his friend. I suddenly remembered it, surprisingly, and thought I might try it again. It didn't slow him down as much as I hoped, I thought I might get a bit of a breather."

"Ouch! Nice one," he said with an approving grin. The room cleared after we had both received hugs and kisses and handshakes from everyone as they left, leaving Paul and John behind. Paul was sitting on the bed behind me, and I was leaning against him, his arms protectively around me, when my phone rang. It was the police, to ask if I would be willing to give a statement. After I told them I would be home the next day, it was arranged they would talk to me there.

We had not been home long, and there was a sizable welcoming committee waiting for us, including both sets of parents, when the police arrived. They introduced themselves as Detective Inspector Dave Fleming and Sergeant Pete Marcos. The inspector looked at John and his face broke into a smile of recognition. Stepping forward, he held his hand out, and they shook hands with every sign that they were on friendly terms. "John, good to see you again. I heard that you had left the force; what are you doing here?"

"Chloe employed me to look after her. I wasn't fast enough to stop her getting beaten up, I'm afraid." The inspector turned to me, commenting sympathetically, "That looks so painful."

"But very colourful, it looks like warpaint," the sergeant put in, which made me laugh, making the bruises hurt, and earned him a glare from the inspector. "I haven't looked yet; they wouldn't let me have a mirror, but I don't think it's a look that I will be copying anytime soon." The inspector returned to the reason for the visit. "We have many statements from your guests, about what happened. If you are willing, we would like to hear your side. We can wait until later, but the sooner the information is collected, the better. Hopefully we won't need to bother you again. Is it all right now, or would you rather wait?" I think Paul was going to ask them to come back later, but I told him that I had no objection to doing it now, although I did add that my memory was not clear about all of what went on. "Do you want to speak to Chloe alone? Shall we leave?" asked Paul. "No, that's all right, stay where you are. Now, starting from when the two men came into the room, can you tell us what happened?" I told them everything that I could remember, when the sergeant stopped me, and said, "Many of the statements made comments about your attacker telling you to come quietly; he would go easy on you, and then he lowered his voice, so that nobody heard anything else. Is it possible to remember what he said? Because from the statements it was obvious that he was threatening you. They also said that you paused and seemed to be working something out." I took a deep breath. "He told me that I had to go with him. I was trying to think if I had any options, and I decided there weren't any. If I had agreed to go with him, not that I would have had a choice, and left the hotel, I would have vanished without a trace. He told me that he had a buyer for me and that he would make a fortune from the sale; the amount he mentioned was mind-blowing. He told me that the client's jet was waiting at an airfield. I would be out of the country in an hour." I shuddered at the thought, and there was a gasp from the other people in the room after hearing that. I carried on telling them what happened, and when I got to the part where I mentioned his dilated pupils, the inspector and the sergeant looked at each other, and the sergeant wrote a comment in his notebook. When I had finished, the inspector asked, "When you had the syringe in your hand, you obviously intended using it on him, with whatever was in it, am I right?" I nodded. "Did you give any thought to the fact that he might have taken drugs already?" I answered him honestly. "He had every intention of putting me out, why not do the same to him, and keep him there until the police arrived." The inspector paused. "We had to get him to hospital because he didn't regain consciousness, and he died of an overdose later that night." There was a gasp from everybody in the room, including me. The inspector watched me closely. I looked at him, my mouth open with shock. I was speechless; what had I done? Then I got my voice back. "So, where does that leave me? Can I be charged with anything?"

"As far as we are concerned, we're thinking of it as self-defence. We will decide soon, but there is nothing to charge you with. As to what he told you regarding the private jet waiting at an airfield, he was telling you the truth." I gasped again and Paul held me even tighter, if that was possible. "We had a report from a small airfield telling us that the people working there were getting suspicious about a small jet, and what was happening around it. We went to investigate and found two of the girls from The Harem on board already; we think they couldn't find the others. Nobody else appeared, so we think there had been a message aborting the operation. We are still investigating where the plane was registered and who owns it."

I sighed with relief when they left. It had been quite a day, and it was only lunchtime; whatever would the rest of the day bring?

THIRTY-FOUR

I needed to talk to my sister, so I sent a message to her about a video call. It did not take long to connect with her, and I had a lump in my throat when she and her husband appeared on screen. It was so good to see her. I introduced Paul to them, after all the exclamations about the bruises on my face. "Those must hurt like hell, what does the other guy look like?" commented Tim, my brother-in-law; trust him to inject a little humour into the situation. "They aren't comfortable," I admitted. Val had been scrutinising me closely while we were talking. "Are you sure that you're okay? You have had a lot to deal with." Paul answered for me, "I'm so proud of her. She has some way to go yet, but she is getting there, with a lot of help from your parents, and she has some wonderful friends, as well, and I do as much as I can too." I could not let him get away with that. "Paul has been fantastic, and yes, I have had help from our parents and my friends, but he's been, how can I put it? As the saying goes, he's been my rock. I depend on him so much. He has had to be so patient with me and had a lot to put up with himself." He swallowed and squeezed my hand. "We are going to come over to see you. I'm looking forward to meeting you both so much, that's if it's okay with you," said Paul. At that Val gave a most un-Val-like squeal of pleasure. "Of course it will be all right. I cannot wait to see you both, but we won't be able to have you stay here, I'm afraid. The house is bursting at the seams as it is without the new baby to take into consideration. We could really do with a new house; there is no way to extend this one anymore. What we need is a builder," she said, with a pointed look at Tim. "They are so hard to pin down." This was said with another sharp look. I laughed loudly and explained to Paul about Tim being a builder. "Well, I am very busy," he replied, rather defensively. Grinning, I jumped in with, "All right we don't want a domestic about it please." Turning to Paul, I told him, "Tim builds some beautiful houses, he's in demand." Tim told Paul, "I teamed up with an architect a few years ago, he designs them, and I build them. We aren't in partnership, but it works well."

"I have some pictures of some of the houses, they look wonderful, and seem very practical. I saw some when I was there. I'll find the photos for you," I promised Paul. "I also do some work for film companies. As you probably know, there are many films made in this area, so work is increasing," Tim added. Paul looked interested. "Really, what kind of work, hands-on, or advisory? That sounds fascinating. And how did you get into that kind of work? Did you apply?"

"I do a bit of both. I built a house for the CEO of a film company, and somebody left, leaving them short-handed. It was nearing the end of the filming, but a bit of work still to do. Since then I get called every time they are starting on another film. Don't leave it long before you come over here, I'm looking forward to seeing you both so much."

"Where are the terrible two?" I asked; this was the way they were always described when the talk was about my sister's two boys. She laughed. "Tim took them up on the ski slopes for the day, they are fast asleep, absolutely worn out."

"So, what did you do?" I asked. "I sat with my feet up, in peace, this little one is getting rather large," she said, referring to her bump. "I get tired easily. Still, not long now." We said our goodbyes. Paul and John were going to the gym for a short workout. I did not think I could face going, as my bruising was still painful.

*

When they had finished Paul and John met up for a long cold drink. John had been quiet since the attack at the hotel, so Paul decided that it was time for him to try to find out what the problem was. John said nothing straightaway, and then said, "I'm thinking of handing in my notice." Paul looked shocked. "Why?" he asked. "Because I feel I let Chloe and you down. I didn't protect her like I should have. The whole thing could have ended badly."

"But it didn't," Paul replied. "Chloe is here and recovering, she wasn't kidnapped. And you have saved her on several occasions, remember that." Paul remembered one of the cars that was fit only for the scrapyard after one attempted kidnapping, and shuddered, thinking about seeing the wreck before it was taken away. The replacement was bulletproof, and handled like a small tank. "Those could have ended up even worse, because where they happened was always isolated, no help anywhere." John looked unconvinced. "She trusts you, I trust you; you wouldn't still be working for her if we didn't. And you know very well that I would not trust just anyone with her safety, she is too important to me. And if you do not believe me, ask her." When they got back to the apartment Paul went into his office to make a call, and to give John some space.

*

John came into the lounge where I was sitting on the sofa, watching what was happening on the river. I looked up and smiled at him. "The police were chasing somebody just then, it looked like a scene out of a film."

"I nearly applied to work in that section," he commented. "Can I have a word, if it's convenient?"

"Of course, sit down." Just then Eva knocked to ask us if we would like a drink. "Thanks, that would be lovely." I looked at John, waiting for him to say something, noticing that he looked uncomfortable, no doubt about what he was going to say. "I feel I should stop working for you." I stared at him, totally stunned. "But why?" I asked. "What's wrong?"

"I feel that I let you down when you were attacked, that I should have been able to do more, to prevent you from getting beaten up." I did not know what to say. "I certainly don't think that way, that you let me down, please don't think that. I trust you, I always will. Please don't leave," I begged him. Eva came into the room with drinks and some of the beautiful cake she makes, followed by Paul. I had a feeling he knew what John had said. I hoped that after we had talked to him, he would change his mind and stay.

We had been planning wedding number two, intending it to be smaller than the first, but it seemed to have increased in size by a lot, and finding somewhere to take a larger one, including accommodation for everyone, was proving difficult. We ended up booking a historic castle. It was a stunning place, and I fell in love with it. The organisers had dealt with many large weddings of celebrities, and the hotels in that area could accommodate everybody. This time everything went without a hitch; it was a day I shall treasure. But the cost! Well, it was an eye-watering amount. Paul was not in the least concerned. He was only doing this once, he told me, so the cost was not an issue. None of the jets were available, so the honeymoon we had planned was put on hold. We had time in the Lake District instead. It was an area we both loved. The weather was kind to us, and we arrived back in London ready to face the world again.

Mrs Paul Knight, I kept having to remind myself, and kept repeating it, checking that my wedding ring was still on my finger. I thought I should pinch myself, make sure I was not dreaming. I had taken a great many photographs, and I could not wait to get to work on the paintings from them.

Maia, who had been one of my carers in the club, had become a good friend, and she often came to see me. She was so thrilled that she had sorted all her paperwork out, with Paul's help, and was officially allowed to stay in the country. Paul had given her a job in his company and was more than happy with the way that had turned out, as she had become a very valued hard-working member of his staff; she could also act as an interpreter, when one was needed.

One day she came to the apartment unexpectedly, and we sat on the deck, enjoying some of Eva's excellent cake and coffee. "I have been watching you for a while now." I looked at her in surprise. "Why?" She had a very knowing look on her face. "I wasn't sure before, but I am now."

"You're being very mysterious, sure about what?"

"You're pregnant." I almost choked on the piece of cake I was eating, nearly spraying it all over the sofa I was sitting on. After I had stopped coughing, I looked at her as if she was completely mad. "What? But how?" She laughed at me, wiping her eyes because she was laughing so hard, fixing me with a 'are you that stupid' look. "I would have thought you would have figured that out by now."

"But I was told that it wasn't possible for me to get pregnant." But I suddenly remembered the medical records from the club. I had been pregnant, even if it might not have been viable. "Are you sure?" She produced a box from her bag, handing it to me; it was a pregnancy test kit. "Go on, see what it says." And she pushed me out of the room. When I came back to her, we sat close together. She was holding my hand tightly, we hardly dared to look. I was shaking as I saw what it said, hardly believing the result. "OMG!" I exclaimed, looking at her with wide eyes, and grabbed my phone. "I'm going to try for an appointment to see the doctor, will you come with me?" We jumped in a taxi and arrived just in time. Much to my amazement and the doctor's amusement at my reaction, the test proved correct.

I could not wait for Paul to get home to tell him the brilliant news, well, I hoped it would be brilliant for him. When he arrived home, he told me that his parents wanted us to go for lunch the next day, and as my parents were staying with them, I thought that I would tell him in the morning before we left home. I had decided to leave the news until the next morning, because there was a part of me that wanted to keep this knowledge to myself and get used to the idea before I told him, I couldn't figure out why.

Was it because of Mark's reaction to having children? Who knew? Before we left the next morning Paul said that he needed to call at a house he had bought. It wasn't far from his parents. He was planning on refurbishing it and would probably rent it out. He had met up with the architect the day before and had left the plans for the alterations behind. He wanted to pick them up so he could have a closer look. We drove through a pair of gates that must have been beautiful once, but badly needed work doing on them. We pulled up in front of a beautiful old house that was desperately in need of work. "How has this got into such a state?" I asked. "Well, it has some serious structural problems; they will be expensive to put right. I think the problems have put buyers off; it had been on sale for a long time. It surprised me that it was not demolished and sold as a building plot. Properties are not on the market long in this area. I did get it for a ridiculously low amount. Do you want to look around?" I could not wait. "Yes please." He took my hand and opened the door. It was fantastic; it would be a sin to knock it down. It had a lovely welcoming feel to it, as did many old houses. We started from the top floor and worked our way down, even into the basement, where, wonders of wonders, there was a swimming pool, a large one. Paul saw my look of obvious delight at seeing this. "This, I'm afraid is the reason why there is such a big structural problem. There were far too many supporting walls removed when this was installed, so the whole building could end up as a pile of rubble in the pool." It was then that I saw all the metalwork supporting the structure; I had been so intrigued with the pool that I had not noticed them. We then went out into the garden, which was big considering where we were, with some beautiful mature trees. There were so many in the neighbourhood. Paul had a phone call to answer, so while he was talking, I went back upstairs and looked at the master bedroom, which I was pleased to see was at the back with a view of the garden, instead of at the front. The room next door took my attention; a plan forming in my mind. My train of thought was interrupted when Paul came looking for me. He came up behind me and put his arms around my waist, pulling me back against him, kissing the back of my neck. "I was looking for you, are you ready to go?"

"Have you decided definitely what you're going to do with the house, when you have put it back together again?"

"The cost might be prohibitive, so demolition might be an option, but as I said, if it can be repaired, either rented out or sold – why? What are you thinking?"

"You did say once about buying something for us to live in."

"Yes," he said tentatively, wondering what was coming. "This is so beautiful, isn't it?" I commented. "Would you consider having it as a home for us?" I left him to absorb that idea for a few moments. He looked around the room, and then down at the garden. "Would you like to? I thought it had a lovely feel to it when I looked around before I bought it. I must say I hadn't thought of it as our home, but I could see us living here quite easily."

"I would miss the view of the river," I said. "I would feel at home anywhere as long as I was with you," he murmured into my neck. "So, what would this room be?"

"Well, I thought of this as the master and this," I said, taking his hand and pulling him into the next room, "could be the nursery." He looked at me as though I had gone mad. "What brought this idea into your head?" *Oh, well, here goes,* I thought. "Because I'm pregnant." He had the same look on his face that I must have had when Maia had dropped the bombshell the day before. "But? How?"

"That, is exactly what I said to Maia." I nearly laughed at him, but the hurt on his face stopped me. "You told Maia, before me?" he said quietly. He obviously thought I had told Maia before I had told him, I had to put him right. "No, of course not, she told me that I was." He looked confused. "How did she know?"

"I have no idea, but some women can do that, there are signs that they pick up on. How do you feel about the news?" He was almost near to tears, I hoped of joy. I held my breath. "I am speechless, you have made me so happy yet again. You will need to make an appointment with the doctor, won't you?"

"I went yesterday as soon as I had done the test at home."
"And?"

"The answer is a definite yes." He held me close for a long time, not saying anything, both absorbing the news. "We can tell the parents today," he said, sounding excited. "Better to leave it for a few weeks, anything can happen. Let's just keep it to ourselves for a while; our secret."

THIRTY-FIVE

I was kept busy for the next few weeks. The other girls from The Harem and I had met up on several occasions; we got on very well and we were quickly becoming good friends. We had all received job offers and we had a very entertaining time discussing them because, coming from The Harem, all of them were in porn movies. We often ended up laughing at the flimsy plots until the tears were running down our faces. I told Paul that I was seriously considering two of the offers; I was not sure which, though, because the money was seriously good, and after all, I had to take advantage now, before people lost interest after the publicity had died down. This was not a good move on my part and I regretted teasing him, because he became very possessive and told me in no uncertain terms that he didn't want me to be in the position that I had been in the club, for other men to see. Oh, dear, why did I say that! I was stupid, and had to work hard to convince him that I had been joking. Life was very tense for a while. John and I were members of the gym that Paul was a member of, which was within walking distance of the apartment. We were taking a break one day and John asked me if everything was all right between Paul and me, commenting about us being quite distant and not all over each other like we usually were. I put my head in my hands and sighed. "Yes, things between us are very tense, to put it mildly. I'm afraid that it's my fault, I didn't put my brain in gear before I opened my mouth." I told him what had got me into so much trouble. He looked at me and roared with laughter and I ended up laughing too. "I am sure you will work it out between you."

"Why would I want to do something like that anyway? The other girls and I have probably featured in many hours of film, because apparently there were cameras everywhere filming all the time, so the footage must be lengthy. I would like to know what happened to the recordings; I can quite imagine it ending up on the internet. I would hate that. At least Paul knows that it's possible for that to happen, it isn't as if I need to hide the fact."

The other girls and I had been asked to play a part in a fundraising show, for charities involved with helping people who had been trafficked, either within this country or from abroad. We all decided that we were very keen to get involved, but we needed to decide how and what we wanted to do. We were invited to appear on many chat shows together, to get publicity for the show, which turned out to be great fun. The rehearsals were a laugh, and the time went by quickly, which was a good thing because my pregnancy was just beginning to show, and the outfits that we were going to wear were skimpy.

Amber had been found to be pregnant when she had tests done after we were rescued so she was not able to be in some of the show. Her partner was thrilled at that, and she was really looking forward to having the baby. They had planned on having children anyway through IVF or a surrogate, although the circumstances were not ideal. The father had been identified through a DNA profile and was approached with the news. He wasn't married or in a relationship at the time, and he was quite happy not to have any further connection with the child and signed a document, putting that in writing. He put a large amount of money into a trust fund for when it got older, which could be used for university fees, although that wasn't a stipulation; the child would only be eligible to have the money when it was eighteen.

I had been persuaded to sing; I enjoyed that. We also appeared in many parts of the show. It was a great success and raised a staggering amount of money for the two charities. I was so star-struck; we were introduced to many of the big names who had given their time. I also got an offer to make a record, any money raised going to the charities. I asked the group from home that I sang with occasionally to back me. The recordings brought in an enormous amount of money; it was very gratifying. The group gained a big following of fans and got a lot of work. I was sometimes asked to sing with them, and featured on one of the tracks on the album they released. This led to them signing a recording contract. Their music sold well, and they had a tour organised. I was so proud of them. I was also offered a recording contract; I could not believe how lucky I was, but whether I wanted to go in that direction, I was not sure. Ken and his wife had got all of us work; they were turning into close friends, I loved both of them. Most of us had ended up with partners or husbands, all of whom had been members of the Newford Club. Amber already had a partner when she was abducted; she was called Julia, and was a complete opposite to Amber in looks, having a pale skin tone and natural blonde hair that was almost white, and she was short in stature, whereas Amber was tall. We all met up a few times and, as the men knew each other, it made for some lively meetings.

The house had been almost taken apart and was now well on the way to being put back together again. I had been taking photographs of the progress, it was looking stunning, and little of the original features had been lost. The builders had done a wonderful job. We had tried to get the builders who had worked on my house but unfortunately, they were so busy that they had to decline, so the architect recommended a firm that took it on. The work was just about going to be finished so that we could move in by the time the baby was born. The structural work hadn't taken as long as scheduled; I had been there when some of the steel joists had been lifted into place. There would be no chance of the place falling around our ears when all that steel was propping the house up. The cost of the structural work was astronomical; it was a good thing that it was going to be our home.

I wandered around, having a look at the apartment. It wouldn't be long before we moved out. None of the furniture was moving, as we would still stay on occasion, but I would miss looking out over the river. The sunsets and sunrises were beautiful, but I would have the garden to look at instead. I was excited about getting the garden into shape, it would be a challenge.

I hadn't been able to do much as I was so near to giving birth. I was more than ready. I had grown huge; it seemed as though I could explode at any minute. All I could do was supervise the move. I felt guilty about that, but I had to keep calm and let everything happen around me. I tried not to get in the way, I really did, but I did not succeed very well.

Anna came to see me. I think everybody was glad, because it kept me from getting under their feet, for a while at least. We sat chatting on the deck as it was a beautiful day. She stayed longer than I expected, telling me about a case that she had been working on that had just been in court, and had finished early, which was why there was time for her to relax a little, sitting in the sunshine with me, and of course with Tigger, who took over pestering for attention. From what she said it had been an upsetting case to work on, and the whole team had been glad that hopefully this was the end of it and there would not be an appeal.

We had so much help from both Paul's family and mine. They all tried to keep me away from the house, insisting that I stay at the apartment until everything was ready for me to walk into. I had been very bored, so it was great to see Anna. She had some news, she had said on the phone before she came, and I was itching to hear what she had to tell me. What she told me came as a complete surprise. One of the team which had worked on the case from the club had discovered, quite by chance, an article about some research carried out in Russia by Ilya Ivanov, encouraged by Stalin, involving apes. It appeared that these experiments had been carried out very differently then, but with no success; these people obviously thought they would try the experiment another way. The experiment had this time ended in a resounding failure, just as in Stalin's time. I was finding it hard to get my head around what I had been told; a copy had been sent for me to read. The people who had been involved had vanished without a trace, leaving nothing behind. The area looked as if nothing had been there, not even a speck of dust had been left behind, everywhere had been deep cleaned, no finger prints, nothing. Anna had another surprise for me; not necessarily a happy one. "Do you remember asking me about how you were chosen, how they found you?" she asked. "Oh yes! I had completely forgotten."

"One of the men who abducted you was in charge and organised the surveillance and the pickup. Apparently one of his contacts had sent him pictures of you, which ended up at the club, for them to decide whether you were what they wanted." I looked at her, my eyes wide. "Did I know his contact? Had I met them?"

"You had a lot of work done on your house, didn't you? Well, it was one of the builders." It was horrifying to hear this, as that firm was going to start work on the extension to my house soon. I was going to speak to the boss about what I had heard. I was not having the man involved working on my property. Anna had another surprise for me, again, not a good one. "After the three men had been sentenced and sent to prison, one of them contacted the officer who had done the interviews with him, asking if he could speak to him. He said it was about you. He was asked if it would be all right to take me with him and he had no objections. He told us that he was kept in the dark about what was happening, the other two did not tell him anything. He did not really get suspicious even when so much money started coming into his bank account, even though it did seem an extraordinarily large amount. Apparently when the pictures of you were sent to them, there were two other girls' photos sent at the same time. He backed off and told the other two it was up to them to decide. He was there when they were discussing the choice, and one of them was pushing for you very strongly. The other one went along with him, with you as his choice as well. Our informer told us that the one who had pushed so strongly for you admitted to him, after having drunk quite a lot one night, that he had encouraged some of the men to be very rough with you, telling them it's what you liked. They seemed to be given permission to treat you as badly as possible. Also, your feeling that they stayed and watched, when you were punished, was correct; it is just what they did, and the hope was that you would suffer the same fate as Blanche and be killed by one of the apes. Why he had done this became evident when he appeared quite proud of the fact that it was in retaliation." I must have looked more than a bit puzzled. "But what had I done to him? I didn't recognise him when I was giving evidence."

"It wasn't you he was getting at but your father." I was speechless. "His son had been accused of raping two young women. There was, for a change, good solid evidence against him, but his father didn't believe it, saying they were false allegations, and he also gave his son an alibi, which was soon discounted, as the tests they did confirmed that it was his son. Your father worked extremely hard to put him in prison."

"Has anyone told my father this?" I asked. Anna shook her head. "Good, because I'm not going to tell him, not even my mother. I think it's best that they don't know." Anna had some other welcome news. "We have come to the conclusion that there is no threat to you now because, as far as we can tell, it was only the one man who maintained he had a claim on you, so you can relax now." I was so grateful and told Paul as soon as I saw him. He held me close, giving a sigh of relief.

We finally moved into the house. It felt lovely to walk in with everything finished, looking comfortable and loved at last. It was not obvious how much structural work had been done, as it was all hidden very well. The pool had had to be rebuilt, because when it was examined there were big cracks so the water would have leaked out very quickly. It would be filled later. There was no rush; if I had got into it, I would have either sunk to the bottom or floated on top. I was so big the water displacement would have been considerable.

We had been living in the house for about a week. Paul had gone to work, and I was relaxing in the conservatory with my breakfast when the pains started; was this it? Much later I sent a message to Paul. "Don't panic, but I think, ONLY THINK, that the baby is on the way, A LONG WAY TO GO YET. Chloe xxx." I checked that I had everything in my case so that I was, hopefully, ready. John had brought the car to the front of the house in readiness for a quick getaway. Paul's car pulled up outside in a shower of gravel not long after. He raced into the house and was, I think, taken by surprise when we were sitting around with nothing happening. He sat down next to me, taking my hand just when another contraction started. I looked at Maia, who had called unexpectedly, and had been tasked with timing the space between. "I think we had better go to the hospital," she pronounced. There was a move to the cars, and we set off. I was holding onto Paul's hand as if my life depended on it, as I was suddenly very scared. "I'm here, and I'll be right by your side all the time," he said as he kissed me.

It felt as though labour had been going on for weeks, I was so tired; it surely could not go on for much longer. Could it? One final effort, and our baby, our miracle baby, had arrived. Paul could see better what was going on and turned, beaming at me after there was a healthy-sounding wail of protest. "We have a daughter you clever girl," he said, leaning down and kissing me tenderly. I could not take my eyes off her when she was put into my arms. Finally, our baby was born, and was found to be healthy after all the checks had been done. I could tell Paul was wanting to hold her as well, so reluctantly I allowed him to take her out of my arms. He looked at me with so much love on his face, it made me want to cry, and then he leaned down and kissed me again. I had just been taken to my room when John came to the door, asking if it was all right for him to come in; he had a large bunch of flowers from him and Eva. I exclaimed with delight; they were gorgeous, I was so touched. "Thank you, they are beautiful. You do realise that you have two of us to look after now, don't you?" He rolled his eyes at me. "Oh no, double trouble." Paul roared with laughter. "You're not wrong there."

"I am here, listening," I commented. There had been an excited call made by Paul to his parents, so they, and my parents who were staying with them, had all set off for the hospital to see the new grandchild. She would be the first on Paul's side, and I do not know how many speed limits they must have broken on the way, but it did not seem to take them long to arrive. A hard drive full of pictures must have been taken, some of which would be sent to Canada to my sister. Her new baby had arrived some weeks previously.

Finally, the staff came into the room and made it obvious that they wanted everybody out so that I could settle for the night and get some rest. I would probably be home the next day, so that we would be able to spend more time with them then. Paul was the last to leave; he took me in his arms and kissed me before he left. "I love you, and thank you for our beautiful daughter, sleep well darling," blowing me a kiss as he left the room.

The nurses moved in then to settle me for the night,

bringing me a cup of very welcome tea. I had been feeling a bit strange, and as the tea was put on the table next to the bed, the voices seemed to be getting further away and everything was getting darker, I thought that I heard my name being called but before I could answer, all went black.

*

Back at Paul's parents' the champagne was being opened and pictures were being compared when Paul's phone rang; it was the hospital. All attention turned his way, his face had gone pale as he listened. "I'm on my way." He looked shocked; everybody had stopped talking. "Chloe collapsed, just after we left, she is in the operating theatre now."

The house emptied immediately; nobody spoke on the way. On arrival, they were shown into the relatives' room. One of the nurses went to enquire about what was happening. When she got back to them nothing was known because they were still operating, but she assured them that they would be told as soon as there was any news. Paul could not just sit and wait, so he went to spend time with the baby, sitting with her in his arms, talking to her.

John found him some time later. The operation had finished, and the surgeon was going to speak to them. The surgeon looked tired when he and some of his team entered the room. He shook hands with them all and sat down, pausing before he said anything. "I noticed from Chloe's records that she had been beaten up and suffered a miscarriage because of it. We think that what happened after the birth was caused by that; we assume that damage was done then that did not show up at the time. The damage was probably getting worse as the baby grew larger and was hiding what was happening, the strain of giving birth finally making it rupture. We have repaired the damage, but only time will tell whether it will hold. She is going to be kept sedated for a while, just to give some time for some healing to start. I do not mind telling you it was touch and go at times if she made it through the operation as she had lost so much blood. As soon as she is settled you will be able to see her. I cannot tell you much more; now, it's up to her." Paul shook hands with the surgeon. He was too emotional to say anything, and as soon as they were told they could see her, everyone moved towards her room.

It was a quiet group of people that arrived back at the house.

THIRTY-SIX

Paul left Bette, his PA, a message to tell her what had happened, and to ask her to organise everything at the office. He knew he could rely on her and his staff. John had stayed at the hospital, not only to make sure that Chloe was kept safe, but to be there if he could help in any way. He had become close to the couple; he hated to see this happen to them and was prepared to do what he could, despite it not being in his job description. He sent a message to Anna; he was sure that she and the rest of the team would want to know. He found Paul sitting beside her bed, looking devastated. "Go home and get some rest, she's in good hands, she won't be waking yet. I'll stay here, and we can change over later." Paul looked as though he was going to object, but he agreed. "That is good of you, thanks. I'll be back in later and then you can get some rest yourself."

When he got back home, the house was quiet. Eva appeared and insisted that she made him a sandwich and a drink; he was surprised when he ate all of it. He went up to bed, not expecting to sleep, but woke up having slept well, considering what had gone on the night before. The space beside him looked very empty, and he fervently hoped she would be waking up next to him again soon; he missed her. When he had eaten breakfast, he called a taxi to take him back to the hospital, and when he arrived at Chloe's room sent John back home to get some sleep. He sat by her bed, holding her hand and talking to her. Whether or not she could hear him he did not know but he hoped she could. He kissed her on her forehead and pushed some of her hair off her face. He could not understand it; how such a kind and beautiful person, with so much empathy for other people, had attracted so much violence in her life, was beyond him. He watched as the nursing staff got on with looking after Chloe and they looked after him too, which he appreciated. He went to see how the baby was. She didn't have a name yet, something they must decide on. While he was there it was time for her to be fed, and he volunteered to feed her. She would be able to go home soon, he was told. That was a situation he hadn't thought about. He spoke to one of the nurses about the problem, and after he had talked to Chloe's surgeon decided that he would employ a nurse instead of a nanny. She could look after both of them when Chloe was ready to leave hospital, and Chloe might be able to go home earlier if there was somebody to care for her. Paul made a call to John, asking him to bring the buggy and the baby's clothes with him when he came back. Eva could show him what was needed; she had been a great help getting it all together. He could then put the baby in the buggy and take her to spend time with Chloe. When John came back, Eva came with him, and when Paul told them what he had arranged, both thought it was a good plan. All the parents took it in turns to sit with Chloe, which gave Paul a chance to put his plans in place. The day finally came when Chloe was going to be woken up, but again she did not wake as soon as they expected. By now the baby had been taken home and was settling in well with the nurse.

*

I thought that I could hear voices and then they faded. I was sure that I had heard my name called and I tried to open my eyes, but as soon as I thought I could open them, I drifted off again, how frustrating. What was wrong with me? I did not usually have this much trouble waking up! Gradually I became more aware of noises, and a voice that I recognised; Paul. I sighed when I heard him speaking. Finally, I managed to get my eyes open and look around the room; the hospital, still? But why? What had happened? My parents and his were there, and Paul was next to the bed, holding my hand. He was looking away from me, listening to what was being said. Nobody had noticed I was awake, until I squeezed his hand, and when he looked at me, a huge grin spread over his face. "Hello sweetheart, you had us all worried." He leaned over and, trying not to disturb me too much, gave me a very welcome kiss. I was surrounded by our families, it got very emotional.

When I had been checked over, and phone calls had been made to give people the good news that I was awake, I wanted to know why I was still in hospital. I was shocked when I was told what had happened. "Where's the baby? Is she all right?" I felt so weak it took all my strength to lift my arm off the bed. I was disappointed when I was told she was at home. Paul was sitting on the bed as close to me as possible and, holding my hand tightly, told me about the nurse, so there was a possibility I might be able to go home sooner. The surgeon came to see me and told me he would like to keep me in for another night, and if all the checks were normal the next day, and as there was somebody to look after me, I could go home early.

The next day I was taken home. I could not wait to see the baby, it seemed like weeks since I had seen her. Paul told me he had taken her in to see me every day. He carried me into the house and upstairs. I did protest that I could manage on my own two feet, but not too loudly, because thinking about it, I really would not have been able to cope with the stairs. I insisted on going into the baby's room first, and we just stood with our arms around each other, looking at her. "We'll have to decide on which name, won't we?" Paul commented. "Didn't we decide on Hannah Louise? One name from your family and one from mine?"

"Welcome to the family, Hannah Louise," said Paul. I reached down and ran my hand over Hannah's head, feeling the softness of her hair. Julie, the nurse Paul had engaged to look after both of us, came into the room, and Paul introduced her to me, and told her what the baby's name was. I thought that she had a lovely attitude and took to her at once. She sat me down and did all the checks on me, and then I was packed off to bed. I felt like a child again.

THIRTY-SEVEN

I woke up early the next morning, needing the bathroom, like now! But how to manage this? Paul was asleep with one arm wrapped around me and his leg across one of mine, effectively pinning me down. The problem was going to be getting out from under him; I did not want to wake him or disturb my stitches and make the area ache. Paul was in a deep sleep but I managed it, amazingly. When I came out of the bathroom, I stood looking at Paul lying fast asleep, thinking how lucky I was to have this beautiful man by my side supporting me. I quietly let myself out of the room and made my way slowly and very shakily to Hannah's room next door. Julie looked up when I entered and smiled at me. "How did you sleep?"

"I woke once, and apart from that, well, thanks."

"I was going to feed her; do you want to do it?"

"Yes please." Before I fed her Julie wanted to do all my checks; they were all normal, much to my relief. While her feed was being prepared, I stood and looked down at my daughter, and I was going to bend down and pick her up when Julie stopped me. "You go and sit down. Let me take her out of the cot to start with, and then you won't pull your stitches and make yourself uncomfortable." It felt wonderful when Hannah was put into my arms, and I was feeding her. Finally, I was holding my, no, our, baby, our little miracle, the baby I had been told I could never have. I felt tears welling up. When she had finished the bottle, Julie gathered everything together to take downstairs to wash, and have a well-earned breakfast while she was down there. I decided to take Hannah into the bedroom and, still feeling very weak, thankfully sank down onto the window seat, looking down at the garden. It looked dreadful, all the scars from the building work only too evident. As soon as I was mobile again, I would have to do something about that.

The door was pushed open, and Tigger strolled in, licking her lips with gusto, obviously having thoroughly enjoyed what she had been given for breakfast. She paused and looked first towards the bed, no doubt wondering whether to get onto the bed and settle down for a sleep, then, as she surveyed the room, to the window seat. The window seat won, and she set off with great purpose towards her goal. She jumped up next to me and made as if to sit on my knee, looking surprised that it was already occupied, so instead sniffed at Hannah's head, rubbed up against her and then looked at me. I bent down to her, and we touched foreheads. I tickled her under her chin, she closed her eyes and started purring, loudly. After that she settled next to me, leaning against my leg for support, and gave herself a good wash. It was always fascinating to watch her wash her paws, separating and stretching them, making sure that all was clean between her pads; the way she closed her eyes while she did was lovely to watch. There was something very peaceful and relaxing about watching her. I always loved brushing her and she seemed to get enjoyment out of it as well. A movement at the corner of my eye made me look over towards the bed. Paul was awake and watching me; he had his camera in his hands. He put it down and, getting out of bed, stretched and then came over, leanng down, kissing me and then Hannah. "Good morning, beautiful, sleep well? Shouldn't you be still in bed, resting?"

"I slept very well, it's lovely to be back home again. I've had all my checks done, everything is good." He bent down and kissed me again, rubbing his nose against mine. "You're looking so well, considering what happened to you. Do not do too much too soon, you heard what the surgeon said. Can I?" he asked, obviously wanting to hold Hannah. I handed her over and he moved to sit on the bed, propped up on the pillows, and patted the bed beside him. Tigger appeared to be a bit disgruntled about losing her support when I moved. I climbed onto the bed and snuggled up to Paul and, settling her between us, we both sat looking down at Hannah. Tigger decided that she was getting left out and came to jump onto the bed and after having a scratch behind the ear from us both, curled up for a sleep.

Here were two of the people that I loved most in the world, but strangely, if I hadn't been abducted, what would my life have turned out like? Certainly, it would not have been with Mark, but Paul and I would never have met. Fate works in very convoluted ways, and oddly, it made what I had gone through worth it. Really? That was some revelation. I felt as though I had won all the lotteries in the world having met Paul, my soul mate, and the love of my life.

It did not look as though the reason for the experiment with the apes would ever be explained; the trail had gone cold, nowhere for the investigation to go. Another question that I had asked was what had happened to the recordings from the cameras; they had vanished without trace. I wondered whether they would turn up on the internet; it seemed a distinct possibility. I was dreading that day, the other girls had the same worries.

Over the last few weeks, I had been coming to a few conclusions and now, since Hannah had arrived in our lives, I was sure that the ones I had reached had been confirmed. I had begun to realise, gradually, that the ominous black cloud that had been keeping me imprisoned had been lifting, a little bit at a time, and finally, after Hannah's birth, had been blown away completely. A quote came into my mind that summed up my life in The Harem. 'It was the best of times; it was the worst of times' from the beginning of *A Tale of Two Cities*. To me it seemed to fit the situation completely.

I concluded that with the threat to me completely gone, with all the help and support of both my family and Paul's, but mostly of this amazing man who I loved deeply, who had been so kind, supportive and understanding, with plenty of much-needed patience, and finally the arrival of Hannah, the future looked bright and welcoming.

I had escaped at last.

ACKNOWLEDGMENTS

I am extremely grateful to everyone at Matador who worked on this book, you have done a wonderful job of improving it which I much appreciate.

To Bernie, Ann, Jackie, Lynn, Margaret, Sue, Val and Vicki I cannot thank you all enough for your unwavering support and encouragement, I hope that I didn't bore you too much about the subject.